'First novelist W... werewolf story from... ... he does a fine jo... ...s canine hero ... Smith spices the narrative with some sex and violence ... readers will enjoy this exciting tale and its unconventional point of view' *Publishers Weekly*

'A dog lover's page turner. Definitely recommended'
Library Journal

About the author

Wayne Smith, a former disc jockey, bike messenger, bookstore clerk and cab driver, lives in San Francisco. *Thor* is his first published novel.

Thor

Wayne Smith

NEW ENGLISH LIBRARY
Hodder and Stoughton

Copyright © 1992 by Wayne Smith
First published in Great Britain in 1994
by Hodder and Stoughton
A division of Hodder Headline PLC

A New English Library paperback

First published in 1992 by St Martin's Press Inc. New York, USA

The right of Wayne Smith to be identified as the author of
the Work has been asserted by him in accordance with the
Copyright, Designs and Patents Act 1988.

10 9 8 7 6 5 4 3 2 1

All rights reserved. No part of this publication may be
reproduced, stored in a retrieval system, or transmitted,
in any form or by any means without the prior written
permission of the publisher, nor be otherwise circulated
in any form of binding or cover other than that in which
it is published and without a similar condition being
imposed on the subsequent purchaser.

All characters in this publication are fictitious
and any resemblance to real persons, living or dead,
is purely coincidental.

British Library C.I.P.
A CIP catalogue record for this book is
available from the British Library

ISBN 0 450 61747 5

Printed and bound in Great Britain by
Cox & Wyman Ltd, Reading, Berkshire

Hodder and Stoughton Ltd
A Division of Hodder Headline PLC
338 Euston Road
London NW1 3BH

To Keiko,
my absentee muse

ACKNOWLEDGMENTS

My deepest thanks to Jane Cushman, whose invaluable guidance and suggestions went above and beyond the call of a literary agent's duties; to Jim Waide, who graciously volunteered (under duress) to proofread the manuscript; and to L. Jim Khennedy, for background on both the historical and Hollywood versions of lycanthropic lore.

THOR

PROLOGUE

THE smell of blood changed everything.

The bear had been wandering the woods aimlessly for hours, driven by a hunger that seemed to have gained a life of its own and was now trying to claw its way out of his gut.

Something had gone wrong the previous autumn; his favorite fishing stream was thin and shallow and the salmon didn't swim past his waiting paw in thick schools as they had in years past. He'd spent whole days staring at the water, when he should have been gorging himself on fish.

And when the days grew short and his instincts told him to crawl into his cave, the meager layer of fat he'd built up wasn't nearly enough to carry him through the winter. His stored calories were gone before it was time to open his eyes, and hunger tormented him as he slept. He woke early, ornery and angry at the world, only to discover that the forest hadn't restocked itself yet.

There were no leaves on the trees, and it was much too early to find berries or honey or salmon. His nose, the best in the forest, found only the sterile smells of green wood and moist soil, smells that ordinarily wouldn't have bothered him but now mocked him with their emptiness.

His mood grew darker and darker as each step he took seemed to add to the strident demands of his stomach. His tongue felt thick and bloated in his dry mouth. Tension tightened the muscles in his neck, giving him a dull headache that enveloped his skull.

The forest was ugly and hostile, and life was cruel.

Suddenly, sharp pains stabbed the corners of his jaw as the rich smell of blood jolted his long-dormant salivary glands into action.

And just as suddenly the forest became home again; a good place, a friendly place—a place that would soon provide him with food.

He turned toward the breeze that carried the blood scent and set off after it, plunging through the woods at high speed, unconcerned by the noise he made. He was not a fearful animal; as the biggest and most dangerous predator in the forest, only another bear could take him on one-to-one. And on the few occasions when he found himself forced to retreat from another bear, his emotions were a jumble of anger, frustration, and confusion—but not fear.

But as he neared the source of the blood scent, a vague, unfamiliar sense of foreboding came over him.

He stopped and listened to the forest.

Nothing.

Hunger quickly pushed his newfound caution from his mind. He pressed ahead and spotted the carcass, strangely alone in a clearing. He charged forward, eager to taste his first meal in months.

The prey had been badly mauled yet appeared to be whole. The torso was open; splayed ribs displayed uneaten organs within. He poked his snout into the carcass and was surprised to find the liver still intact. The liver was the best part, the first thing eaten by any predator. He consumed it in two bites without chewing. His stomach lurched, then settled, and he sat down to enjoy himself.

But halfway through his meal, as his hunger faded, an odd feeling of unease came over him. He lifted his nose from the carcass and looked up, half expecting trouble. He saw nothing, but couldn't shake the sensation that a threat hung in the air. The forest around him was utterly still, which was normal considering the noise he'd made on his arrival, but for some reason it bothered him. He began to feel irritated, ornery. He scanned the horizon for anything moving, and saw nothing. He wasn't reassured.

He *felt* something out there, something in the distance that he shouldn't let catch him unaware. He snarled and let out a low growl of warning. Nothing moved. He dipped his nose back into the carcass, but the feeling nagged at him, and he looked up as soon as he had a mouthful, and watched the horizon while he chewed.

His wariness was robbing him of the enjoyment of his meal. Each time he lowered his head for another bite he felt more uneasy about taking his eyes off the horizon.

Finally he could stand it no more. Snarling his displeasure, he gripped one limb of the cadaver with his teeth and dragged it backwards in the direction he'd come from, watching the woods in front of him the whole way, troubled by the knowledge that it wasn't the kill he was removing from the area. It was himself.

He dragged the carcass more than a mile before the feeling faded.

Then he promptly forgot everything but the tasty meal that had been interrupted.

He was about to dip back into the bountiful torso when a powerfully sweet smell caught his nose. He poked his snout into a pocket of the open down jacket the cadaver still wore, and pulled out a Baby Ruth. He ate the candy bar with the wrapper still on.

CHAPTER 1

THOR got a bad feeling about the Stranger from the moment he saw him, while the man was still almost a block away—just a tiny figure striding up the sidewalk past the neighbors' neatly groomed lawns, apparently coming straight to the Pack's front yard—where the kids were killing time.

It was the Stranger's walk that bothered Thor. Every walk is unique, a signature that even humans can recognize from a distance, often by the sound alone. But a walk tells more than just the identity of the walker. Walks are triumphant or defeated, genuinely proud or artificially boastful, innocent or guilty—all of which seemed to escape most humans. None of it escaped Thor.

The Stranger's walk made Thor's gut tighten. The muscles in his legs and jaw tensed slightly, and a tingling sensation at the base of his neck told him the thick black fur between his shoulders was rising. He willed it down (which he could do in the early stages of an alert) and tried to hide his unease from the kids. But he didn't take his eyes from the Stranger.

There was something arrogant and secretive . . . almost *malicious* in the Stranger's gait, and it didn't look better as the man came closer. Thor instinctively sniffed the air in the Stranger's direction, knowing it was a futile gesture. The Stranger was downwind. There would be no scent until he was much closer.

Too bad. A good snoutful could tell so much.

He hoped the Stranger wasn't a troublemaker. It was Saturday, the day the Pack spent together, and the Pack had big plans—it didn't need any trouble from Strangers.

Thor looked over his shoulder at the house. Mom and Dad were still inside, banging things around, getting ready for the trip. He considered barking to bring them out, but rejected the idea. Nothing had happened yet, and he knew from bitter experience that his barks would be taken as a false alarm. And then *he* would be in trouble, not the Stranger.

For now at least, he was on his own.

There was nothing to do but wait and play it cool. And why not? Thor was in full view of the Stranger, and he was well aware that his appearance tended to put Strangers on their guard—and on their best behavior.

Just the same, he wouldn't take chances. To take chances with the Pack's safety was unthinkable.

Nothing in the world was more important than the Pack.

The Pack's plans had begun over dinner the previous night. Thor didn't know the days of the week, or exactly how many there were, but he always knew on Friday night that the Pack would spend the next two days together. And it was always a big relief. During the week, when Dad went to work and the kids went to school (which, thankfully, they hadn't done since summer started), they were beyond Thor's protection, and he waited anxiously for their return. He always slept best on Friday nights, secure in the knowledge that the Pack had survived another week of day-long separations.

And now another Friday night had arrived, and Thor lay

contented on the kitchen floor with his eyes closed, apparently oblivious to the Pack's dinner-table talk. He generally ignored conversations between Mom and the kids or Dad and the kids, but any conversation between Mom and Dad held his undivided attention, whether he showed it or not. And in fact, he was listening intently, not to the Pack's words so much as to the emotional currents in which their words swam like schools of fish.

The emotions were warm and positive and flowed like music. There was a note of mischief in Dad's voice—a certain teasing tone that Thor had heard many times in the past. Only Thor noticed it, and only Thor understood what it meant: Dad was sitting on a secret, getting ready to spring a surprise on the Pack. Curious about Dad's secret, Thor shifted his attention slightly to listen for familiar words and phrases. He didn't have to; Dad's secret was revealed in a single word so charged with meaning, it would have wakened Thor from a deep sleep.

" . . . maybe the BEACH tomorrow . . . " Dad said.

Thor's head snapped up, eyes wide and ears erect. Brett and Teddy, the Pack's male pups, yelled "All right!" in unison, and Debbie, their little sister, squealed with delight and banged her spoon on the table. Thor almost got up to nuzzle Dad's hand excitedly, but caught himself—it was dinnertime, and when the Pack went out after dinner, Thor usually stayed home. So he lay on the floor and listened.

It quickly became obvious that the Pack wasn't going anywhere right away. The BEACH was for tomorrow, which was good news. Thor would almost certainly go along.

While the kids made grandiose plans and compared notes on previous BEACH outings, Mom and Dad withdrew from the discussion and turned to more mundane topics. Mom listened with moderate interest as Dad mentioned people Thor had never met, but whose names came up almost every night. Thor's attention shifted back to the emotional currents as the kids calmed down and the Pack settled into its usual routine.

After dinner, the Pack retired to the living room to watch TV. Thor waited until they left the kitchen, then lazily hauled himself off the floor and ambled into the living room. He tried to make it look like he'd decided to change his location on his own, independent of the Pack's move. Sometimes he felt self-conscious about following them around all the time.

The Pack watched the tube for a few hours, while the world darkened outside. Then Dad lifted himself out of his easy chair, the signal that the Pack's bedtime had arrived. As usual, Teddy, the oldest pup at twelve, whined to stay up later. Brett, his eight-year-old brother, halfheartedly supported the protest, but they both knew it was no use. Mom and Dad kept early hours, and there was no way the boys could get permission to stay up later than their parents. Four-year-old Debbie was already asleep in Dad's arms.

Thor followed the Pack upstairs, first into Debbie's room, then into the bedroom shared by Brett and Teddy. He watched Mom and Dad tuck the kids in, turn out the lights, and close the bedroom doors. Then he followed the Mating Pair to their bedroom door, watched it close, and waited for the light underneath to go out. His nightly security check was almost done.

He went back to the kids' bedroom doors and poked them with his nose to see that they were latched. As he pushed Brett and Teddy's door, he heard them whispering about the BEACH and felt a physical thrill of anticipation. He had completely forgotten about the BEACH since dinner.

He listened for a moment, lost interest, and climbed downstairs to finish his rounds.

He took a last walk through the ground floor, briefly stopping at each window to look and listen for intruders. Finally, his rounds complete, he hopped onto his favorite easy chair, the one strategically placed at the base of the stairs, where any unusual noise from upstairs or down would wake him.

He curled up on the soft cushion and fell asleep in less than a minute. His paws, ears, and nose twitched lightly as he drifted into dreams filled with the smell of brine, the roar of surf, and the strangely fluid yet solid feel of sand beneath his feet.

Mom's footsteps on the stairs woke him instantly. She was up an hour before the rest of the Pack, as always, for her morning jog.

Thor leaped out of the chair and met her halfway down the stairs, wagging his tail and nuzzling her hand to hurry. He poked the palm of her hand with his wet nose, licked it, then ran to the back door, then back to Mom, then back to the door, then back to Mom. He didn't want Mom to get distracted and forget why she came downstairs.

"Okay, okay!" Mom said, as she did every morning. She followed him to the kitchen door and opened it. Thor shot through the door, across the backyard, and over the little creek that separated the Pack's territory from the woods behind. Then he turned around and gave Mom a friendly bark.

Come on, Mom!

Mom did a brief loosening-up routine in the backyard, ran in place for a few steps, and followed Thor into the woods. Thor nuzzled her hand, trotted alongside as she started down her favorite jogging path, then ran ahead and left the path for the real forest.

Wisps of steam rose from the ground as the morning sun warmed the air, lifting and magnifying the fecund odors of the outdoors.

Thor plodded happily through the underbrush, savoring the lush aromas of foliage and mulch, intrigued by the telltale traces of fur and feathers—especially fur. He found a squirrel scent that was strong enough to track but too old to produce results. He decided to follow it anyway, just out of curiosity. He was snuffling along aimlessly, taking in the smells of the forest, when his nose crossed a trail that stopped him in his tracks. The scent hung in the air a few inches off the ground, as fresh scent trails do.

A rabbit had passed this way only minutes before, possibly seconds. Thor meticulously examined the scent, forcing himself to take quiet, shallow breaths despite his excitement. The scent told him the rabbit was young, male, and hadn't defecated recently, which meant it hadn't eaten recently. There was no scent of fear, so the rabbit was probably foraging, which, along with the sheer strength of the trail, meant the rabbit wasn't moving fast. If it hadn't already heard Thor, it was probably very near. Thor moved forward with remarkable delicacy, one paw at a time like a cat, carefully stepping over leaves and twigs.

The trail was leading toward some large bushes with a clearing behind. Thor walked with his eyes on the ground, intent on the trail, which got stronger with every inch. He inched his way along, and was halfway into the clearing when something moved in his peripheral vision. He looked up and froze. His toes curled, digging his claws into the ground. A surge of adrenalin coursed through his body and made him tremble slightly.

Less than ten feet away the rabbit stood staring at him, also frozen, also trembling.

Their eyes met for one infinitely long second, then the rabbit broke eye contact and glanced at the bushes to its right. Thor's hind legs kicked off at the same moment the rabbit's did. He surged forward, not at the rabbit, but at the point in the bushes where the rabbit had looked—the same point the rabbit was headed for. But the rabbit got there first and disappeared into the foliage before Thor was even up to speed.

He squinted and flattened his ears against his head as he plunged into the bush after the rabbit. The bushes in this part of the woods weren't very dense (or he wouldn't have tried barging through). He broke through easily and spotted the rabbit on open ground, a good thirty feet away and widening the gap.

But not for long.

Pure ecstasy engulfed Thor as he charged through the forest, the physical pleasure of running immeasurably magnified by the thrill of the chase. He felt like he was flying, and in a way, he was. Each thrust of his hind legs hurled his body forward, a living cruise missile just clearing the ground, his front legs mostly guiding and stabilizing his flight. A fresh surge of adrenalin goaded him on as he watched the gap between him and the rabbit begin to narrow.

But the rabbit was blindingly fast, and it knew enough to run under bushes to slow Thor down. The bushes weren't thick enough to offer a hiding place, so it ran through them, into a thicket, and out the other side, frantically looking for a better escape. Thor caught on immediately and ran around the bushes or jumped over them, and each time the rabbit emerged from the bushes—surprise! surprise!—there was Thor, still on his heels. The rabbit desperately tried to shake him off by changing direction as suddenly as a tennis ball bouncing off a wall, but Thor had had plenty of practice chasing bouncing balls. He skidded to a stop, turned, spun around, and hit the ground running before he really knew where the rabbit had gone. He scanned the landscape as he lunged forward and saw that he'd guessed right. The rabbit was dead ahead, a few yards farther away than before, but not out of sight.

And not getting away.

The rabbit tried every evasive maneuver it knew, but soon it was acting out of pure panic, and once it actually turned in Thor's direction. For a shocking instant, the two were heading straight toward each other. Thor was so startled he almost stopped, but before he could react, the rabbit pulled another hairpin turn, darted into a particularly large bush, and disappeared.

Thor crashed through the branches and into a small gully completely enclosed by steep hillsides. He stopped short about three feet from the frightened animal.

The rabbit stood with its back against the natural wall of earth, panting uncontrollably.

It was cornered.

Total silence descended on the forest; all other small animals in the area had scattered at the sound of the chase.

Without taking a step, Thor leaned toward the rabbit, delicately sniffing the smell of fear that poured off its body. His attention was riveted on the animal.

Except for his left ear, which swiveled backward and pointed directly behind him. The ear scanned the forest in rapid, twitching movements until it found the familiar beat of Mom's footsteps in the distance. On some unconscious level, his brain noted the position and distance of the sound, that the footsteps were steady, and the pace was normal. Everything was fine on Mom's end. If Mom needed Thor, she had a dog whistle that could be heard over much greater distances than what separated them now, but it was not in Thor's nature to wait for trouble before checking on the Pack.

His ear snapped forward and joined its twin in focusing on the rabbit, but every few seconds it flipped back to check on Mom.

He was no more aware of his ear's actions than he was of blinking.

Thor and the rabbit stood transfixed, hearts racing, staring at each other, unsure what would happen next. Thor began to feel embarrassed. This was his big moment of triumph, and he was supposed to *do* something, he could *feel* it, but he didn't know what he was supposed to do. And worse, he was sure the rabbit knew what it was, but the rabbit was so terrified that Thor couldn't begin to figure out what it was thinking.

The rabbit was scared right out of its tiny mind.

Scared of Thor.

Why?

Despite having worked up a ravenous appetite, the thought of eating the rabbit had never entered Thor's mind. Practically every morsel of food he'd ever eaten in his life had come directly from the Pack, and none of it smelled like an animal. At least not like the outside of an animal. Some of his food—

the very best, in fact—smelled like the *inside* of an animal, but Thor hadn't discovered that yet, and dogs are not instinctual killers. If he had grown up in the wild, in a wolf pack, he would have learned to hunt by watching others. But he'd grown up in a human pack. He didn't hunt; he chased. No one in his Pack hunted.

He watched the rabbit in open bewilderment, feeling more uncomfortable with each passing second. Finally he decided it was time to get back to Mom.

He barked once at the rabbit, startling it horribly, but he'd only meant to say something like, "I won!" He grinned at it open-mouthed, with his tongue hanging out and his back teeth showing, but his fangs barely visible—a friendly, non-threatening grin. Then he barked a good-bye, turned, and dashed away, glad to run off some of the excess adrenalin and leave his confusion behind.

Mom was plodding along in his direction, but instead of meeting her head-on, Thor circled around and joined the jogging path from behind her. As he entered the path and saw Mom, he poured on the steam and shot past her in a second. It was his way of showing off.

He slowed to a loping canter to let her catch up, but Mom still fell behind, so he slowed to a trot, and then slowed down some more. By the time Mom caught up with him he was barely doing more than a fast walk. As she finally came abreast of him, he looked up at her with the same wide, human-looking grin he'd shown the rabbit. Whenever Mom saw it, she wondered if dogs might actually have a sense of humor. Thor didn't know what a sense of humor was. He only knew that what passed for running among humans would be completely pathetic if it weren't so funny.

He understood that Mom was jogging, not running, but he'd seen her run too, and it wasn't much better. Even Dad, the Pack Leader, could barely move by Thor's standards. It was amusing, but also a little embarrassing.

He looked up at Mom again with that silly grin, then

abruptly grabbed the ground with all four feet and took off, leaving her behind as if she were standing still.

Watch this, Mom! This *is running!*

By the time they got back to the house, he'd completely forgotten about the beach—again. But the Pack hadn't. The Pack never forgot anything. As he and Mom entered the kitchen, Brett and Teddy were barreling down the stairs in high excitement, babbling about the BEACH. Thor didn't need to hear the magic word to be reminded of the Pack's big plan. The powerful scents of the nylon bathing suits under their clothes and the vinyl and rubber toys they carried told the whole story.

The kids were running around like maniacs, yelling and whining and urging Mom and Dad to hurry. They made no attempt to hide their excitement—not like Mom and Dad. Mom and Dad almost never expressed their feelings as openly as the kids. It was part of being adult, as Thor understood. He was an adult too, and he didn't always show his feelings, either.

Of course, no matter how well Mom and Dad might hide their feelings from others, they could never fool Thor. He knew they were almost as excited as the kids. He felt what they felt.

As usual, everyone but Thor had some responsibility. As much as he wanted to be part of the project, there was nothing for him to do but sit back and watch.

Mom kept looking at a piece of paper in her hand (didn't she always?) and so did Dad (for a change). Teddy, Brett, and Debbie piled up towels, rubber swim fins, snorkels, face masks, and most important, Thor's Frisbee and his tennis ball—solid proof that he was going with them.

Thor had no idea what things like snorkels and swim fins were, nor did he care. About ninety percent of the Pack's possessions were a total mystery to him, and for that matter, so was about ninety percent of the Pack's behavior. But it didn't bother him. He'd long ago learned that if he didn't understand something, it was a safe bet that it didn't concern him.

But whether he understood something or not, he never forgot its scent, and he never forgot what was happening the last time he smelled it. Today's smells all said BEACH—one of the strangest and most exciting places the Pack ever visited. One of Thor's all-time favorites.

Like the kids, he couldn't wait to hop in the car and get going, but like Mom and Dad, he was an adult, so he tried to control his excitement.

Mom and Dad kept checking and double-checking their pieces of paper and their piles of stuff; Mom and Dad did everything in slow motion. The kids collected their toys in no time, and in no time Debbie started whining, and Brett and Teddy got into an argument that threatened to escalate into a full-scale screamer. Dad yelled, "Hold it!" and hustled the kids and Thor in the direction of the front door.

"Teddy, do you have Thor's leash?" Dad said as Teddy opened the door. Teddy just held his hands out, palms up. "Well, get it. No, you don't have to put it on him now, but we might need it at the beach. And wait a minute." Dad ducked into the kitchen as if he'd just remembered something important. Thor heard a kitchen cabinet open, and the familiar rattle of dog biscuits against cardboard. Dad came back with a box of Milk-Bones. "Take these, too," he told Teddy, handing him the box. Thor appreciated Dad's thoughtfulness. "Now go wait in the front yard, and stay out of trouble!"

Thor, Brett, and Debbie burst through the front door, across the porch, and onto the lawn. Only Teddy sauntered casually onto the porch—Teddy was practicing to be an adult.

Brett and Debbie felt no such pressure of impending maturity. Debbie sort of bounced-ran across the lawn, carrying her plastic sand bucket with its plastic shovel and her favorite doll inside. Brett ran for the car at full throttle with Thor loping alongside, snapping at the Frisbee in his hand. As Brett reached the car, Thor tried to coax him into a game of fetch by playfully tugging at the plastic disc (he could easily pull it out of Brett's hand if he wanted to), but Brett wasn't in the mood. He was no good at throwing the Frisbee, and he didn't like to display his ineptitude in front of his big brother. Instead, he tossed the Frisbee into the station wagon and closed the windows so Thor couldn't hop in and get it, jump out, drop it at Brett's feet, and then bark incessantly at him to throw it.

With the Frisbee out of reach, Thor turned to Teddy, who was about halfway across the lawn, the box of dog biscuits still in his hand. Thor trotted over and sat down directly in front of him and vigorously scratched a flea. His claws found the flea and flicked it off on the second scratch, but he narrowed his eyes, let his jaw drop, and gave himself another ten or twelve scratches just because they felt so good. When he was done, he looked at Teddy to remember what he'd come over for. Seeing the dog biscuit box, he recomposed himself and looked directly into Teddy's eyes with a soulful, expectant expression. The aroma of the biscuits wafting out of the box sent a thin thread of saliva from his tongue to the grass below.

Teddy dug out a dog biscuit and held it up at shoulder level, out of Thor's reach (actually, Teddy wasn't tall enough to hold anything out of Thor's reach, but his posture told Thor he didn't intend to give it up yet, and Thor respected his intentions). Thor whined a little and waited for Teddy to give him a command, so he could earn the biscuit.

"You wanna Milk-Bone?" Teddy teased.

Thor *woofed* once in response.

"What are you gonna do for it?" Teddy asked.

Thor *woofed* again, a little louder. He was getting impatient with Teddy's teasing.

"Oh, you *do* want it, huh?" Teddy said, but showed no sign that he might give it up, trick or no trick.

Thor had had enough. He sprang up on his hind legs, put his forepaws on Teddy's waistband, and curled his claws around Teddy's belt. Then he delicately nipped the nearest button off Teddy's shirt.

Thor knew clothes weren't part of a person's body, and he knew if a Pack member annoyed him relentlessly, he could safely retaliate by damaging their clothes. Removing a button or two was his favorite way of getting even with the kids when they pissed him off. Even Mom and Dad gave the act tacit approval. Dad didn't want the kids teasing the dog—he'd made it clear when he first brought Thor home as a puppy that he wasn't a whipping boy. Dad wanted his kids to understand that cruelty is wrong no matter who—or what—is the victim. And he was only too aware of how annoying kids could be at times.

"Dammit!" Teddy said as Thor's incisors neatly sliced through the threads and plucked off the button. *"Here,* take it already!" he said, as if giving Thor a dog biscuit was some great sacrifice on his part.

He waved the biscuit up and down to show Thor he was going to throw it. Thor let go of his belt and backed away to give himself room to jump. Teddy tossed the dog biscuit in a high arc, and Thor leaped five feet straight up and snapped the biscuit out of the air. He landed with surprising grace for such a big dog.

He ate his prize standing up, savoring the feel of the hard biscuit cracking and crumbling under his jaws. It was gone in seconds, and Thor dutifully sat down to wait for the next one.

Teddy dug another biscuit out of the box and teasingly bobbed it up and down. Thor waited politely but impatiently, squirming on his haunches, his eyes locked on the biscuit. Wide ribbons of saliva ran freely from his mouth.

Then out of the corner of his eye he saw the Stranger with the unfamiliar (and unpleasant) walk, coming his way. All thoughts of dog biscuits abruptly left his mind as he turned to check out the Stranger.

The man wore a dark suit and sunglasses, carried an attaché case (like Dad), and was making good time up the sidewalk.

He seemed to be coming directly toward the Pack, ignoring the other houses on the way.

Thor licked the crumbs and drool from his lips, snapped his jaws shut, and faced the approaching Stranger at full attention.

A small, almost inaudible *woof!* escaped his throat before he remembered his manners. He took a quick look around to see if Mom or Dad had heard his rudeness, remembered they were still in the house, and turned his attention back to the Stranger.

Thor watched with mounting frustration as the Stranger continued up the sidewalk, carelessly passing all the trees Thor had marked with his urine to tell interlopers they were in Thor's territory and that they entered at their own risk. It was a source of ongoing frustration: Mom and Dad took him out every day to renew the markings, and yet they refused to let him enforce the boundaries. They acted as though the Pack's territory stopped at the edge of the front yard, or even at the front door of the house. Why did they take him on his daily perimeter patrol and then let just anyone invade their territory? They did so many inexplicable things, but this one was really maddening. It was as if they wanted to make Thor's life difficult.

Well, they weren't here now, but Thor and the kids were, and the Stranger would be here in seconds. Thor repressed the instinct to simply chase the Stranger away. He'd learned with great difficulty that Mom and Dad wouldn't tolerate such straightforward security measures.

So he stood and watched the Stranger approach, and tried to keep his fur down.

The Stranger came within a few feet of the driveway and slowed down. The Pack's house was obviously his destination. Thor trotted to the front edge of the yard, putting himself between the kids and the Stranger, though he knew the kids would probably follow him and he couldn't stop them. He walked briskly, but avoided any appearance of hurrying. He also avoided looking directly at the Stranger on his way over. Protocol demanded he not deliberately intimidate strangers without cause; the Stranger might turn out to be a friend of Mom and Dad's. And there was another reason for discretion: It demonstrated self-confidence. Thor was acutely aware of the importance of appearances.

While Thor maintained an outward posture of disinterest, he also tried to make it obvious to the Stranger that it was nothing more than a posture. He held himself erect and slightly tense, ears high and trained on the man, making his presence known—and felt.

But the Stranger didn't appear intimidated by Thor's presence. Very unusual. And not good.

The man came right up to the edge of the Pack's lawn without even slowing down, then stopped short as if he were testing Thor's reactions. He was finally close enough for Thor to pick up his scent: sweaty underneath his clothes, a little acrid, and no trace of soap perfume. Even people who went two or three days between baths bore a slight scent of soap.

The Stranger appeared to be looking at Thor, but his dark glasses hid his eyes, another thing Thor didn't like about him.

The Stranger said, "Nice doggie." Thor didn't like his tone of phony familiarity, either. "You're a big one, aren't you?" the Stranger went on. "Are you a dog or a horse?"

He answered the man with a low rumble from deep in his throat, but no show of teeth—no threatening behavior that Mom or Dad could see from the house.

"He's not a horse!" Brett huffed indignantly as he brought up the rear. "He's a German shepherd!"

"Well, he's a helluva big German shepherd," the Stranger said. "Are your mom or dad home?"

Thor casually studied the man's shoes and hands as he positioned himself for a clear shot at the Stranger, unaware that the fur on his shoulders had risen slightly. He took a step toward the Stranger, and the man inched back a little. The first good sign. At least the Stranger was no fool.

Before Brett could answer, the screen door on the porch

swung open and Mom hurried across the lawn, nervously pushing her hair in place as she walked.

"Can I help you?" she called to the Stranger. Thor heard tension in her voice, which she tried to conceal (and did conceal from everyone but Thor). Her tone told him the Stranger was not a friend or acquaintance of the Pack's. The hairs on Thor's back rose another half inch. The muscles in his hind legs flexed a little, and his claws gripped the ground. Adrenalin goaded him to action. He did his best to ignore it.

"Ah, you must be the lady of the house," the man said. Thor ignored the man's words, instead focusing on the inflections; there was a smug, easy familiarity in the Stranger's voice that sounded dishonest. His eyes locked on the man's feet and hands, which moved with ill-concealed nervousness.

"Yes, I am," Mom said, answering the Stranger's question without a trace of warmth. Her tension had not been eased by the Stranger's false friendliness.

Thor had observed that young kids often shared his ability to read intentions and emotions, but as they got older, their perceptions steadily faded. Teddy had already lost most of his natural sense of danger. People came to the door who would have sent Brett or Debbie running for cover, but Teddy stood and talked to them as if nothing was wrong, and called Mom to the door without warnings. As the kids grew up, their attention seemed to shift to *words,* away from tone of voice or the way people shuffled their feet and fidgeted with their hands, or kept themselves too still and spoke too smoothly. It was as if humans could only listen to one or the other—the words or the intentions—but not both. It was a problem Thor would never face. No matter how many words he learned (and he'd learned quite a few), he would never be distracted by them; the abstract nature of human conversation took care of that.

"Well, ma'am," the Stranger said, "I see you have three lovely children. Are you helping them get the best education possible? . . . " And off he went, into a spiel even Thor recognized as the product of rote memorization. Thor liked that. As the words tumbled automatically out of the man's mouth, his other thoughts came forward, and his intentions stood out more clearly.

The Stranger's emotional state shifted slightly. His weasely posture and hand gestures revealed an aggressive flirtatiousness, a sense of superiority and arrogance, and a desire to dominate Mom that Thor regarded as outwardly hostile.

Mom's tensions increased and Thor could see she wanted the man gone, but she felt powerless to rid herself of him. Thor's judgment hardened: The man was *enemy*.

Thor dropped all pretense of neutrality. The hair on his neck and shoulders rose to its full height and he curled his upper lip to show his dangerous fangs and let an audible growl escape his throat.

The man stood his ground as if Thor hadn't done anything.

Thor wasn't used to this. Most people made quiet, cautious retreats in the face of even the slightest displeasure on Thor's part. The Stranger's refusal to defer to Thor only heightened his alarm. He waited for the Stranger to make his move, ready to do whatever was necessary to protect his family.

Mom said something to the Stranger ("Go away," in so many words, Thor knew), and the Stranger ignored her, too. Thor looked up at the man's hidden face and growled at full volume and gave the man a single, vicious, snapping bark.

"Hey, look, lady," the man said, "you ever heard of leash laws? You better control your dog before he bites somebody. This is a public sidewalk, you know, and I've got a right to be here . . . " His tone was belligerent, challenging. Mom bent down to reach for Thor, taking her eyes off the Stranger for a moment. As her finger slipped into the metal ring on Thor's collar, the Stranger made a quick, flailing movement with his free hand over her neck.

That did it.

Brett yelled, "Hey!"

Thor lunged at the man's ankle, easily pulling free of Mom's grip. He snagged a few inches of the man's trouser leg in his teeth and barreled forward, throwing his body against the Stranger's legs with the pants still tight in his jaws, pulling the Stranger's foot out from under him—a maneuver he'd perfected during endless hours of roughhousing with Dad and the kids. The Stranger waved his arms in a desperate attempt to regain his balance, and went down on his ass on the strip of grass between the sidewalk and the curb.

Then all hell broke loose.

"Thor!" Mom shrieked.

"He bit me!" the Stranger screamed. "I'm suing!" He pointed an accusing finger at Mom, not Thor. "You got a dangerous animal there, lady, and you're gonna pay for it!" As he spoke, the front door of the house flew open with a bang.

"What's going on?" Dad shouted from the porch. He ran down the steps two at a time and crossed the yard in seconds. Thor quietly took his place next to Mom, his eyes on the Stranger, his body tense and ready to spring, a shred of the man's pants still stuck between his teeth. *No more warnings,* he silently told the Stranger.

Thor was relieved to see Dad. Dad would take over from here.

"You better get a lawyer, lady," the man said, ignoring Dad, " 'cause you're gonna hear from mine, toot sweet!" He sat on the grass and held his undamaged ankle as if in great pain. He made no move to get up. Then Dad arrived.

"You can talk to me," Dad said. He pulled a small white card from his wallet and contemptuously tossed it to the Stranger. "I'm a lawyer."

Before the Stranger could react, Dad reached down and jerked the torn pants leg away from the man's ankle. There was no wound. "I don't see what you're going to sue for," Dad said, "except maybe the price of a new pair of pants at K Mart." Dad's tone was openly hostile.

"Hey, listen, buddy," the Stranger said. "I don't care if you are a lawyer. Your dog attacked me, and if you don't want to settle, fine. I won't sue you. I'll go to the humane society and show them what he did. I'll get a court order and have him destroyed."

Thor understood none of it, but he saw that Dad was on the brink of violence himself. Thor let out another low growl, but Dad's hand came down like an avenging angel, slapping him hard on the nose.

Thor was shocked. He looked up at Dad in disbelief.

"Get in the house!" Dad bellowed, pointing at the front door. Thor had never seen Dad so angry at anyone before, least of all himself. Thor was only trying to help. He couldn't imagine what he'd done wrong, but he had no choice but to obey. Dad was the Pack Leader. His word was Law.

Thor reluctantly slinked away, head bowed, tail between his legs. About halfway to the house he stopped, turned around, sat down and watched, feeling guilty and not knowing why.

Meanwhile, the confrontation between Dad and the Stranger lowered in volume, but not in intensity.

"Did he bite your leg?" Dad asked, already knowing the answer. The Stranger, aware that he was talking to a lawyer, hesitated. " 'Cause if he bit your leg," Dad went on, "you'll have to see a doctor right away. Since you're on foot, I'll give you a lift to the nearest hospital emergency room right now." Thor could see the Stranger didn't like whatever Dad had just said.

"He . . . the bite didn't break the skin. . . . But I'm in pain!" the Stranger said. Then, improvising, he added, "I think I pulled something when I fell."

"Well, broken skin or not, if you're injured, we'll have to go to the hospital right now. C'mon," Dad said, reaching for the man's hand to help him up. "I'll take you to our family doctor."

"I got my own doctor!" the man said, recoiling from Dad's hand. Dad's attitude shifted abruptly from make-believe concern to open hostility.

"All right," Dad said angrily, "I think I've heard about enough, Flopsy." Thor had never heard the name Flopsy before, but he got the point. Dad said it with exactly the same inflections Teddy used when he called Brett "shithead" (something he only dared to do when Mom and Dad weren't around).

"There's no blood," Dad said, "there's no swelling, and you've been moving your foot around the whole time we've been talking. Your only damages are those crummy pants. So here's my first and last offer: I'm going to give you fifty dollars cash for the pants. Judging by the looks of them, you'll make a thirty-dollar profit on the deal. In return for the cash, you're going to sign a waiver right here and right now, stating that you deliberately provoked the dog, but suffered no injuries of any kind. Otherwise, I'm calling the sheriff and filing charges against you for molesting my wife."

Mom looked sharply at Dad but said nothing. Thor wondered what Dad had just said to produce such a response.

"I never touched your—"

"Two against one, Flopsy. Our word against yours. No other witnesses. Besides, I'd bet money you've got a record, and I'm sure I could satisfy a judge that your record would be relevant to determining the truthfulness of your testimony. Just between you and me, I think you'd stand a good chance of getting convicted, even if the judge and jury believe you're being set up. Now what'll it be, Flopsy?"

Thor felt great. Whatever they were saying, Dad was clearly dominating the exchange. The Stranger, whose name was apparently Flopsy, radiated anger and resentment, the emotions of the defeated. Thor half expected to see a tail appear between the Stranger's legs when he finally got up to leave.

The Stranger thought for a moment, then made a decision.

"You got the fifty now?" he asked sullenly. Dad pulled two twenties and a ten from his wallet, showed them to the Stranger, then stuffed them into his own shirt pocket.

"Okay," the Stranger said. "Deal."

"Teddy!" Dad said over his shoulder. "Go into the house and get my legal pad off my desk. Brett, get the Polaroid out of the car!"

"Wait a minute . . . " Flopsy said.

"No picture, no deal," Dad said, outwardly relaxed. "Take it or leave it."

"Awright," the man grumbled. Brett arrived with the camera. Under Dad's direction, the man pulled up his pants leg and allowed his ankle to be photographed from three angles. As Dad finished with the camera, Teddy arrived with the legal pad and pen. Dad gave the camera and photos to Mom while he scribbled on the pad. When he finished, he handed the pad and pen to Flopsy, who studied it carefully.

"I'm not signing till I have the money," Flopsy said. Dad responded by turning to his oldest child.

"Teddy, call Sheriff Jensen. Tell him you're my son, he'll take the call. Tell him we have a problem with a sex offender, and to send a deputy right away." Then he turned to Mom. "Honey, you were talking to him when you noticed he was fiddling with his pants. When you looked to see what he was doing, he was exposing himself. You were startled, you began to back away, he grabbed your wrist, and that's when Thor went for him. Got it?" He turned to Flopsy with a vicious grin. "It was nice knowing you, Flopsy. I'll visit you in the Big House."

The man stared back at him with undisguised hate. Thor tensed, ready to attack. If Flopsy made any move to attack Dad, Thor would take him out before he could get to his feet. It made no difference that he was halfway across the yard.

He let out a loud warning growl, which was a mistake. Dad looked around, saw Thor in the middle of the yard, and exploded.

"I said *get in the house!*"

Thor thought something like *What did I do?* and sullenly retreated to the porch. Dad's order was absurd. Thor couldn't go into the house unless someone opened the door for him.

He climbed onto the porch and lay down, still ready to intervene if necessary.

"Gimme the paper," Flopsy muttered.

"Let me see your driver's license first," Dad countered.

"What for?"

"Don't play dumb," Dad answered patiently, as if he were addressing a small child. "I have to see that the signature that goes on the paper looks like the one on your license. I'm sure you understand." The man trembled with rage as he pulled out his wallet, opened it, and handed it to Dad, who wrote down the name and birth date on a separate piece of paper, then gave the wallet back.

"Where's my fifty?" Flopsy demanded.

"You'll get it after you sign. If you don't like that arrangement, we can let the sheriff sort things out."

Flopsy signed, handed the pad and pen back to Dad, and waited. But instead of giving him the money, Dad stood up, folded the yellow paper, and stuffed it in his pocket.

"Okay, Billy-boy," he said, referring to the name on the Stranger's driver's license. All anger had left his voice, replaced by an impersonal, businesslike tone. "Here's the deal: As we both know, this agreement doesn't mean shit—you could always say you signed it under duress, which in fact you did. So if you want your fifty bucks, you can come into my office on Monday before ten A.M. and sign another copy in front of witnesses. You'll get your fifty then. If you come after ten, I'll be in consultation and the offer will be withdrawn. Understand? In the meantime, I am going to run a check on you for warrants and priors. Frankly, I won't be surprised if you don't show on Monday. And by the way, even though this paper isn't a legal contract, it's still evidence on my side, along with the pictures. The only reason I'm willing to give you the fifty at all is because I keep my word. Hey, as a father, I have to set a good example for the kids, right Billy-boy?"

"You son of a bitch!"

"Now, now, Billy-boy. You know, if you start getting abu-

25

sive, we might still have to call the sheriff. Now I suggest you get up, turn around, and walk away without saying another word and without looking back. And don't think of this as a total loss—you learned a valuable lesson: Don't mess with a lawyer on his own turf."

Dad turned his back on Flopsy and told the kids to get in the car and wait for him. He waited until Flopsy got to his feet and left, then he and Mom walked to the porch, where Thor lay on his stomach, nervously thumping the floor with his tail and wishing he could make it stop. Thor had no idea what to expect.

Dad watched him with hard eyes as he came up the porch steps. He opened the front door and said, "Get in!" with a voice like stone. A physical sensation of dread ran through Thor's body. He was sure he would be left behind—alone—while the Pack went to the beach. He barely lifted his body off the floor as he slinked into the house.

Thor had no idea where he went wrong, but he didn't ponder it. Life was full of rules, some minor, some major, many completely absurd. There was no point in trying to figure them out. The only important thing was to obey them whenever possible. Breaking a minor rule wasn't too bad—a little scolding, maybe a halfhearted swat on the rump with a rolled-up newspaper if someone was really annoyed—but no big deal.

It was the Laws that counted. The Laws were much more than rules—they were the Pack's foundations. When Thor obeyed the Laws, he was a Good Dog. When he didn't, he was a Bad Dog.

Nothing was better than being a Good Dog, secure in the warmth of the Pack's love and affection. And nothing was worse than being a Bad Dog. To be Bad was to be unfit to live with the Pack, and risk having all love and affection withdrawn.

And yet, there were times when it was hard to be Good. The problem was that there were two sets of Laws: Natural Laws, which came from the gut, and the Pack's Laws, which came from Dad. Natural Law Number One was Protect the Pack; it had guided all Thor's actions toward the Stranger. He'd tried to obey Natural Law within the framework of the Pack's Laws, but apparently he'd failed. Mom and Dad appreciated Natural Law, even if they didn't always agree with it. While it was clear to Thor that they expected him to protect the Pack, they were extremely nervous whenever he took direct action on their behalf. Now Mom and Dad would wrestle with the conflict between the Laws. No one would argue Thor's case for him, and there would be no appealing their decision. He just had to wait to find out whether he was a Good Dog or a Bad Dog.

If he were human, he would have thought his situation unfair and unjust. Being a dog, he thought his situation was normal, and for him, it was.

As Mom and Dad discussed his behavior, it became apparent that Dad was sympathetic to Thor's good intentions. But Dad was annoyed with Thor's disobedience, and he and Mom were worried. Very worried.

Thor couldn't imagine what was worrying them. Flopsy showed incredibly bad judgment, but he didn't seem very dangerous.

Finally, Dad picked up the phone, poked it, and spoke to it.

When Thor was young, the phone had been a bottomless source of mystery. Of all the strange things the Pack did, talking to the phone was the strangest. Sometimes the phone chirped, and they went for it like it was the last piece of meat in the world. Sometimes they picked it up unbidden, poked it a few times, and waited. In any case, they talked and listened to it as if it were another person. Usually Thor could tell who the other person was supposed to be, but that person was never actually in the room, or even in the house. Often the person talking to the phone was the only human in the house. Like all the Pack's mysteries, the phone ultimately became familiar without becoming understandable.

Dad talked to the phone for a few minutes, calling it "Bob." Thor had never met Bob, but Dad often spoke of him with admiration.

Thor listened intently, knowing Dad's verdict would hinge on this conversation. Dad told the phone what had happened on the lawn, read the piece of paper he and the stranger had scribbled on, and a few times said, " . . . a flop, yeah, I'm sure of it . . . "

Then the tone of his conversation changed. Dad listened, and with rising hope in his voice said, "Are you sure?" He listened again, and hope was replaced by relief, which gave way to gratitude. Whatever the phone was, it certainly possessed authority.

It had just acquitted Thor of Badness.

Dad put the phone down and sighed. All tension seemed to leave him, and he hunkered down next to Thor and leaned forward until they were almost face-to-face. Thor didn't like looking Dad in the eye. It wasn't his place; Dad was his superior. But Dad took Thor's head in both hands and forced Thor to look at him.

"Listen, stupid," Dad said earnestly, "I appreciate what you did. But you don't appreciate how close you came to a one-way trip to the carbon-monoxide room. So you're going to have to start wearing the leash."

Thor understood only one word of Dad's soliloquy—LEASH.

LEASH meant he wouldn't be allowed to run free. But it also meant he was going to the beach.

He tentatively wagged his tail, trying not to show too much of his relief. Unrestrained joy at this moment would be inappropriate, considering how close he'd come to being found guilty.

"Okay, c'mon, stupid," Dad said, standing. Thor had no trouble understanding those familiar words.

"And try to stay out of trouble, huh?" Mom and Dad walked

to the front door as Thor lay watching, pounding the floor with his tail. Dad opened the door and turned to him.

"C'mon!"

Thor ran to the door and leaped up to give Dad a wet kiss on the mouth. He knew Dad wouldn't like it, but he just couldn't help himself. Dad tried to dodge the kiss, but he was too late.

"Dammit, stop that!" Dad said, sputtering and laughing, and wiping his mouth with his sleeve. Thor ran to the car, where the kids held the back door open for him. He jumped in and spun around to face Mom and Dad, who seemed to be taking forever to walk across the lawn. He barked at them to hurry and wagged his tail so hard that the kids had to press themselves against the opposite side of the car to avoid getting swatted.

It was going to be a glorious day after all.

CHAPTER 2

"**I** THOUGHT you were pretty impressive back there," Janet said as the car barreled down the highway toward the Pacific Ocean.

"Right," Tom said sarcastically, "a couple more impressive performances like that and I'll be disbarred."

"Why did you keep calling him 'Flopsy'?" she asked.

"A lucky guess. I was in the living room when I saw him do something weird while you were bending over Thor. I couldn't see what he did, but it was so sudden and jerky, it looked like he was trying to provoke ol' brainless. So I thought he might be some kind of 'flop.' They're people who throw themselves in front of cars so they can sue the owners."

"You're kidding!"

"No, really, it happens all the time . . . well, not all the time, but often enough for lawyers to have a name for people who do it. Flops usually do their thing at big-city street corners, preferably in the rain, so it's hard for witnesses to see what happened. They wait for an expensive car to turn the corner—

that way it isn't moving very fast when it hits them, and it's easier to claim that neither one saw the other coming. Sometimes they even break a bone in advance, so they'll be sure to have something to sue for. It's about as slimy as scams get. But then, there's almost nothing people won't do for money.

"Anyway, when I saw him waving his arm over you, I thought maybe he was working a new angle. Like maybe he's less scared of dogs than he is of cars. I figured if he was pulling a scam, I wanted him to know I was hip to his act, so I took a chance and called him 'Flopsy.' And God, was I ever right. He came up with a cute angle: 'Settle or the dog dies.' That's one way to keep it out of court." Dad paused and shook his head in disbelief. "I still can't believe I threatened to frame him. Jesus. What if he'd called my bluff? We'd be up the you-know-what creek without a paddle. Or at least without a dog. Anyway, it worked. Apparently. But we're going to have to watch Thor a little closer from now on."

"What about Monday? I thought you had a meeting scheduled in Portland."

"I do. Bob is going to meet Mr. Scum for me, handle the whole thing. I really owe him one for this. I just hope everything works out."

"Are you kidding?" Mom said. "With Bob, the Terrible Tyrant of Torts on the case? If everything you've told me about him is true, I wouldn't be surprised if Flopsy pays *us* to drop the matter." Tom gave her a thin smile, but he knew she was just cheerleading. He decided to do his best to put the whole incident out of his mind, at least until the weekend was over.

They drove in silence for a mile or so and Dad said, "So how's my favorite brother-in-law?"

"He says he's doing fine," Mom said. There was no need to add that she didn't believe him. "He won't even consider seeing a counselor. He says he knows what his problem is, and a counselor won't help. And he was adamant that we can't visit him."

"Can't?"

"Uh-huh," Mom answered, "his exact words: 'Sis, I don't want any misunderstanding here. I'm not saying I don't want a visit, I'm saying you can't visit me. There's a chain across the road and it's staying there until I take it down. And if you hike the last mile, I won't let you in the house when you get here.'"

"Jesus," Dad said quietly. "It almost sounds like he's scared to see us."

"Why would he be scared?" Mom said defensively, though she'd thought the same thing while she was talking to him. How could he stand to be so alone after everything that had happened?

Tom took his eyes off the road long enough to see Janet holding her hair out of her face while she leaned her head on her forearm. It was a pose she unconsciously struck only when she was deeply worried. He decided to drop the subject. There was a lot more to talk about, but not in front of the kids.

Thor missed the entire conversation—not that he would have understood any of it. More important things occupied his mind, like the thrill of hanging his head out the window at sixty miles an hour, and the distant smell of brine that was already finding its way to his nostrils and making him squirm with anticipation.

Thor loved weekends. Tomorrow the Pack would laze around the house all morning with the Sunday paper spread out on the living room floor. Dad would sit contentedly in his chair, watching TV, reading the paper, dunking buttered hard rolls in his coffee and slurping noisily as he ate. And Thor would feel terrific, just lying around with his whole Pack all together. Later they would all go out, maybe to a park, maybe just to the yard, and someone would play fetch with Thor for an hour or more.

The next day, Dad would leave early and come home late for a number of days, and finally stay home for another two days.

Most of the year, the kids left too, like Dad, except they left later in the morning and came back earlier in the afternoon. Until a few months ago, when everything changed. The kids stopped going to school, and a month later, Dad stopped going to work. It was heaven while it lasted. Thor was just getting used to this wonderful new way of life—the whole Pack together all the time, taking trips to strange and exciting places—when one day, Dad went back to work.

But Dad still stayed home on weekends, and this was one of them, and the Pack was going to the BEACH. And they might even visit Uncle Ted later.

When Mom and Dad had first discussed the BEACH trip, Uncle Ted's name had come up often enough for Thor to relate Uncle Ted with the BEACH trip. Now the smell of salt air brought Uncle Ted to mind again.

The plan to visit Uncle Ted had gotten only as far as the phone. Mom and Dad had agreed to a visit, and Mom asked the phone for final approval. She spoke to the phone as if it were Uncle Ted, but the phone disapproved, which seemed to worry Mom. Still, Thor sensed they'd visit Uncle Ted soon, and the thought warmed him.

He'd met Uncle Ted a long time ago, when Thor was young. The two had hit it off immediately and been good friends ever since. Uncle Ted was Thor's favorite relative.

Through the roar of wind rushing past his ears, Thor heard the steady pounding of surf, and his hind legs did a little involuntary dance of anticipation. The car crested a hill and there it was: that glittering flat plane with its snarling, growling, churning edge. His old friend and playmate, the sea.

Dad parked the station wagon next to some sand dunes and the kids opened a door. Thor pushed past them and was, as always, the first one out of the car.

He scanned the beach briefly and saw it was deserted. Then he checked the Pack's reactions, especially Dad's.

He relied heavily on the Pack as a second set of eyes and ears. Despite the inferiority of their vision and hearing, they sometimes saw threats he missed, just as he frequently saw threats that were apparently invisible to them. But neither he nor they saw any danger at the beach. In truth, the Pack led a very secure life, and Thor had very little to do in the way of protecting them. But like a cop, Thor was never really off duty. His responsibility was too huge. The Pack was everyone he loved and everyone who loved him.

For now, though, he accepted the security of the beach and let himself think of the intense fun he was about to have.

He danced around the Pack as they trudged toward the water, whimpering at them to hurry and poking their bundles with his nose, looking for his Frisbee and a free hand to throw it.

Dad lugged a huge ice chest—no Frisbee there—and Mom carried a gigantic straw picnic basket. The food inside gave off stupefying aromas that momentarily blotted everything else out of his mind. Then he remembered what he was looking for, and checked the kids for the Frisbee. Teddy was dragging a huge beach umbrella. Debbie (who was worthless as a playmate) still had her doll in her plastic sand bucket with her plastic shovel, which smelled exactly like the Frisbee, and forced Thor to check her over twice before moving on. Brett lugged a large brown paper bag and an armful of beach towels. Thor stood on his hind legs for a second and poked his nose into the bag. He caught the scent of dog biscuits, leather—and vinyl.

Found you!

He barked, not very loud (he thought), and nuzzled Brett's right hand. He knew no one would play with him until the Pack found a spot and unloaded their stuff, but he wanted no doubt in Brett's mind about what was first on the agenda.

Brett stopped to dig out the Frisbee, and placed it in Thor's mouth to placate him. As long as Thor had something to carry (like everyone else), he was satisfied for the moment.

The Pack found a suitable spot and dumped the goodies. The kids stripped off their outer clothes while Mom and Dad spread a giant beach towel and anchored its corners against the breeze with jars of pickles, mustard, and mayonnaise. Thor dropped the Frisbee and stretched his back, lowering the front half of his body to the ground with his rump in the air and his tail wagging. He yawned and whined loudly, then picked up the Frisbee and bobbed from Teddy to Brett, pushing it into their hands. They refused to take it. Thor whined louder, dropped the Frisbee, and barked.

"Oh, shut up!" Teddy said, picking up the Frisbee. But Thor bit the other end and clamped down hard. If Teddy wanted to play, he had to play by Thor's rules; whoever wants the Frisbee has to fight for it.

"Doggone it!" Teddy said. "Do you want me to throw it or not?" Teddy put his face close to Thor's as they tugged on the Frisbee. *"You* want *me* to throw it, you dope. *I* didn't ask for it!" Though Teddy's words meant nothing to him, Thor thoroughly enjoyed having transferred some of his impatience to someone else. He shook his head violently, yanking the Frisbee out of Teddy's hand, then dropped it. He waited for Teddy to make a move for it, ready to snatch it away, or maybe just slap a paw on it to hold it down.

"Fine! Great! *You* keep it, moron!" Teddy said, turning his back on Thor.

"Thor," Dad said. "C'mere."

Thor answered with a *woof,* picked up the Frisbee, and flung his head back like a drum major. It wasn't every day that he got to play with Dad. He pranced over and dropped the Frisbee at Dad's feet, and waited to play his doggie version of quick-draw.

Dad reached lazily for the plastic disc. Thor snatched it away and took a few steps backward, inviting Dad to chase him.

"Uh-uh," he said, shaking his head. Then with quiet authority he said, "Give it to me."

Thor dropped the Frisbee a good two feet beyond Dad's reach and *woofed* sharply.

Try to take it!

Dad slowly shook his head. "Bring it here," he said firmly.

Thor whined, but picked up the Frisbee. He took one step in Dad's direction and dropped it on the sand, just an inch shy of Dad's outstretched hand. Dad sat with his hand in the air, palm up, waiting. "I said give it to me," he insisted. Thor stood his ground and barked twice.

I did! You can reach it!

Knowing this argument could go on all day, Dad gave in. He suddenly snatched the Frisbee and stood up. Thor wagged his tail and barked.

"Now let's see," Dad said, rubbing his chin meditatively. "Where would be a good place to throw this?" Thor barked as loudly and obnoxiously as possible.

"Shut up!" Mom screamed. To her husband she said, "Will you *throw* that damn thing?"

Dad's jaw dropped and his eyes widened in mock horror. "Such language! And in front of the kids, too!" Thor was still barking away, full blast.

"If you won't, I will!" she said. She reached for the Frisbee, but Dad jerked it out of her reach. She jumped him, tangling her body around his, clawing for the Frisbee. While Dad struggled to keep it out of her reach, she hooked an ankle around his leg and deftly swept his foot out from under him. They fell onto the sand together, Mom on top. She grabbed Dad's right wrist with both hands and pulled herself toward the Frisbee as if she were climbing a rope, but Dad passed it to his left hand. They wrestled in the sand, rolling and laughing and threatening to crush the food, or at least get sand all over it.

Thor lost it. The sight of his Pack's Mating Pair battling, even in fun, was too much for him. His instincts couldn't accept such irresponsible behavior; violence between Pack members was absolutely forbidden. Violence between the Mating Pair, even in jest, was unthinkable. It was up to Thor, as the Pack's only other adult, to stop them. He did the only thing he could do: He stood over them and barked frantically, urgently, *seriously,* to make them stop.

They might have rolled around for another five minutes, but Thor's distress finally got to them. Mom rolled off Dad (who was lying on his back, laughing helplessly) and turned to Thor.

"Oh, poor Thor," she said with overdone sincerity. "Are we fweaking out the poor widdew doggie?" Then, with lightning speed, she turned and snatched the Frisbee out of Dad's hand as he started to sit up.

"Got it!" she cried, and sprinted away from the blanket with her prize. She did the Church Lady's Superiority Dance, and turned to Thor. "C'mon, Thor," she said, *"I'll* play with you." She ran to the water's edge with Thor half following, half leading, and Teddy, Brett, and Debbie right behind.

Tom sat on the blanket and watched his forty-year-old wife acting like a sixteen-year-old.

He thanked his lucky stars that he'd ended up with such a rare and precious woman.

They stood at the water's edge, Mom facing the ocean, Thor watching her hands intently. She took a few practice swings, which just about drove Thor over the edge, then let it fly. Thor noted its direction and dashed for the water, keeping an eye on the sky for the Frisbee as it sailed overhead. Brett and Debbie ran after him, but Debbie squealed when the icy water splashed her legs, and did an abrupt about-face. Brett would've changed his mind too, but he didn't want to mimic his baby sister, so he waded in, shivering and covered with goose bumps, until the water was at his waist. Then he nonchalantly waded back out. Teddy watched the whole show and decided to stay dry.

Thor swam determinedly into the surf, doing his best to ignore the cold. It wasn't easy. The water immediately penetrated his fur and chilled him as no amount of cold air ever could, and rapidly drained him of energy. He snagged the Frisbee and quickly swam back, eager to get out of the water. He stepped out of the surf and shook himself violently, spraying Debbie and Mom. He dropped the toy at Mom's feet and barked for more while he shivered uncontrollably. Mom shook her head slowly at the foolishness of his request but threw the Frisbee anyway. It would take more than one freezing swim to make him calm down and give the family some peace.

After three more fetches, Thor was done. He still dropped the Frisbee in front of Mom and barked, but his insistence was forced and he looked like he was ready to drop.

"That's enough," Mom said as she turned to go back to the blanket. "Time to eat."

Thor scooped up the Frisbee and ran ahead of her, making a big show of the prize in his teeth, captured under such difficult conditions.

He was still panting from the exertion in the water when they arrived at the blanket, and he plopped down heavily on the sand. Both his blood and his muscle tissue stored oxygen for times when he used it faster than he could take it in. He'd used quite a lot of the stored oxygen out in the water, and it all had to be replaced before his chest would stop heaving.

As his metabolism gradually returned to normal (minus a few thousand calories), hunger hit him like a fist in the gut. It was unbearable to have to wait for the Pack to come feed him, but there was no way around it.

The kids arrived first, and Brett dug out a dog biscuit and tossed it to Thor. It was gone in seconds.

"Whoo!" Dad said as he and Mom arrived. "Looks like we've got a hungry dog here!"

Thor *woofed,* and the Pack laughed.

Brett tossed him another dog biscuit, which disappeared almost instantly. Thor watched intently as Dad fished a can of dog food and an opener out of the grocery bag, then stopped to search for something else.

"Did anyone bring Thor's dish?" Dad said, still digging through the bag.

"I did!" Brett said.

"Where is it?"

"It's in the car," Teddy said in his best condescending tone. He seldom missed an opportunity to point out his little brother's shortcomings.

"I'll get it," Brett offered glumly. The station wagon was about fifty yards away. Dad could see an open window on the passenger's side.

"Thor'll get it," he said. "Thor! Go get your *dish!* Get your *dish!*" Thor looked at him with his head cocked, confused. He knew what his DISH was, but he couldn't go all the way home for it. He got to his feet, eager to show off his smarts and eager to eat, but not sure what was expected of him. He *woofed* once in frustration, demanding a clarification.

Dad understood.

"In the *car,* Thor! Get your *dish.* In the *car.*"

Dad carefully avoided pointing; Thor invariably thought a person pointing was holding something in his outstretched hand. But he knew CAR as well as he knew DISH; two of his favorite things. His face brightened and he turned and ran to the station wagon, spraying the Pack with sand as he left.

From the beginning of the long partnership between dogs and humans, dogs' ability to understand large numbers of words has fascinated humans, tantalizing them with the thought of a talking dog. But dogs will never talk or otherwise communicate with words, not because they don't *understand* words, but because they don't *think* in words. No matter how many times Thor heard the word "yes," no matter how well he understood its meaning, he would never *think* "yes" when asked if he was hungry, or if he wanted to go out. He might *feel* yes with every cell in his body, but his mind would never "speak" the word, the way human minds do.

Unlike a human, Thor had no mental language to give structure to his thoughts; he could not use words to construct complex ideas, or formulate questions, or help him remember what he was just thinking about a moment ago.

For Thor, as for all dogs, words were strictly incoming, and thoughts always fleeting. Which was why he could seem so intelligent and mature, and at the same time, so childlike and simple.

Thor ran around the station wagon, looking for the dish. Dad shouted, "In the *CAR!*" and Thor saw the open window. "That's it! In the *CAR!*"

Thor put his front paws on the windowsill and stood on his hind legs to look in.

His dish lay on the floor behind the front seat. He barked at it, both to scold it for not being with the Pack, and to say "Hello" to his old pal.

There was no clear dividing line between the living and the nonliving in Thor's world, though the difference between the *currently* living and the *formerly* living was unmistakable. Life had a smell of its own, as did death; it was the things that didn't smell of either that were hard to figure out.

He was pretty sure his tennis ball was alive. How could it *not* be, the way it got so excited, bouncing gleefully off just about everything and hopping up and down at the slightest provocation? The odd thing about the ball was that it never acted on its own, but only reacted to others. Thor loved playing with it so much that sometimes, when there was no one else to play with, he tried to toss it himself. Taking it lightly between his teeth, he whipped his head up and let go. Assuming it would fly backward over his back, he spun around to chase it, but the ball invariably rolled straight down his neck to the floor.

Only once did he manage to fling it about three feet. Eventually he gave up on the idea. Still, sometimes when he played ball with Dad or Teddy he just couldn't resist giving it another try.

His Frisbee also enjoyed a kind of situational life. Like the tennis ball, it did absolutely nothing on its own, but when the Pack threw it, it flew. It wasn't just thrown, like a ball or a stick—it *flew!* Like a bird. Obviously alive.

Sticks, on the other hand, smelled of life but did nothing.

When thrown, they fell to the ground like a rock and sat there. And yet, sticks could swim, like the ball or the Frisbee. A tough call.

Was the ocean alive? Thor had never doubted it.

He didn't think of the ocean as a large body of water. It would never occur to him that rain or water from the Pack's lawn sprinkler were the same stuff as the ocean. True, they both got him wet, but in different ways—one gradually, from the top down, the other suddenly, from the bottom up. The lawn sprinkler came to life at times, like the Frisbee and the ball, but the ocean was always alive, a restless entity of awesome power. The ocean had dignity and strength and a clearly audible pulse. Sometimes almost deafening.

For the most part, Thor's *world* was alive.

He barked at his food dish again and kicked off with his hind legs as he hoisted himself up with his front legs, intending to get a foothold on the windowsill with his hind feet and push off into the car. But his feet missed the window and his claws scratched the door. He got it right on the second try and disappeared inside.

Janet was outraged. The station wagon was her car.

"Great!" she said, furious at Tom for encouraging Thor's reckless behavior.

Tom just said, "Oops!" and tried to keep from laughing—unsuccessfully. She picked up an onion roll and threw it at him. It bounced off his forehead, which sent the kids into hysterics. Teddy and Brett started throwing rolls at him, but he just sat there laughing and batting the missiles away with his hands.

Thor picked up his dish and leaped through the window with perfect grace, and proudly trotted back with his second trophy of the day. He dropped it squarely in Dad's lap, then pushed it with his nose.

"Well, what am *I* supposed to do with it?" Dad teased. Thor had had enough of this bullshit. He loosed a volley of ear-piercing, frustrated barks.

"Daaaaaaad!" the kids whined.

Mom threw an olive at Dad and yelled, "Dammit, Tom, feed the damn dog!"

Thor drooled freely as Dad opened a can of Alpo and spooned chunks of beef and beef by-products into his dish. He rudely poked his nose into the dish and started eating before Dad was finished emptying the can. His food never tasted better, nor vanished so fast.

After lunch, he got a special treat: a rolled strip of rawhide, as hard and stiff as fiberglass, knotted at both ends to look like a bone. It took considerable chewing to soften it up enough to eat. It kept Thor busy longer than anything else he ate.

But he still finished his rawhide bone long before the Pack finished their lunch. His stomach was reasonably full, but the smell of the Pack's food generated a lust in him that was totally separate from honest hunger.

He avoided staring at the Pack while they ate—only Bad Dogs begged openly. Instead, he settled down and watched out of the corner of his eye while he waited for them to finish. But his good manners were entirely superficial; he was perfectly aware that the Pack knew what he wanted. He went to great lengths to express his desire in ways subtle enough to fall within the boundaries of etiquette.

And it worked, as it usually did.

Dad pulled a slice of cold cut from his sandwich and dangled it in the air to catch Thor's attention. Thor was instantly on his feet. He sat on his haunches in front of Dad, waiting to earn the treat.

"You gonna give me your paw?" Dad asked. Thor's right paw shot forward and landed hard on Dad's thigh. When Dad didn't immediately respond, Thor dug his claws into Dad's leg. Dad slipped his fingers under the paw and pushed it back a little.

"How about the other paw?" Dad said. Thor withdrew his right paw and replaced it with his left, curling his claws a little harder into Dad's leg as saliva ran from his mouth. He didn't mind performing for his treats; on the contrary, his treats always tasted better when he had earned them.

And he enjoyed showing off his smarts. In addition to commands and tricks, he'd learned the most important lesson an education has to teach: that he was indeed intelligent and capable of learning. He found that the more he learned, the easier learning became. And when he learned a new trick and showed off his latest accomplishment, the Pack's pride in him was all the reward he could want. He'd grown to love learning, and actively sought new things to learn.

Somewhere along the way, he'd noticed that most other dogs didn't know much of anything. While Thor wowed crowds at the park with his many tricks, other dogs ran around like wild animals, too ignorant to even appreciate Thor's education. But humans appreciated it. Total strangers were highly impressed and lavished praise and affection on him as if he were their own. He came to see himself as smarter than other dogs and closer to his human family than to his own species.

But at the moment, his only thoughts were of the cold cut in Dad's hand. He drooled and whined a little, and Dad was finally convinced.

"Okay, here you go," Dad said. His hand moved only slightly in Thor's direction, but the gesture was clear. With an expression of intense gratitude, Thor leaned forward and touched the meat with the tip of his tongue, not to taste it, but to locate it precisely. His teeth grasped the meat at the exact point where Dad's fingers left off; Dad felt only the lightest touch of enamel against his fingertips. Thor was capable of extraordinary delicacy.

Normally, Dad enjoyed tossing high pop-ups to the World's Greatest Outfielder, and watching him snatch them out of the air with lightning speed. But not at the beach. Thor kicked up too much sand when he leaped. Thor missed the thrill of catching his treats, but he enjoyed having them handed to him, too. It wasn't much fun, but it made him feel adult—and human.

The taste of the meat was incredible, overwhelming.

He trembled with anticipation as he watched Dad pull another, larger piece of meat from the bread. The first piece was Danish ham; this one was rare roast beef with a smear of mayonnaise. The smell filled every corner of his mind, blotting out all other thoughts. His eyes locked on Dad's hands. Saliva ran from his mouth like syrup.

Dad passed him the roast beef, which Thor swallowed without chewing. The kids joined in, offering him scraps from the last bites of their sandwiches. When the meat was gone, they threw the leftover bread away (Thor wouldn't eat it) and showed him their hands, front and back, fingers splayed wide in the universal gesture of "All gone." Thor understood, but his mania for meat refused to die down. Knowing it was futile, he begged almost involuntarily.

After some petting and cajoling, his munchies finally subsided, and he settled down for a rest. He curled up between Mom and Dad with his head on Dad's hip. Dad scratched Thor's neck under his collar. Thor's eyes rolled back and drifted shut and his tongue lolled out. He turned on his back with his paws in the air, and Dad stroked his chest and tummy deliciously.

I offer my most vulnerable side to you, open and unguarded.

Only Dad fully appreciated the gesture.

No one else touched Thor like Dad. Everyone in the Pack loved Thor; he could feel it in their hands. But Dad's touch conveyed a deeper love. When Dad touched him, Thor felt totally secure, totally satisfied. When he was home, Dad's petting could put him to sleep in minutes. But today, something was different.

He lay on his stomach with his chin resting on his paws and stared at the horizon. Not the true horizon of the ocean, but the false horizon of sand dunes behind the Pack. He didn't really expect to see anything or anyone there, but he felt he should watch the horizon anyway. There was something in the distance, something to keep an eye out for. It suddenly occurred to him that he'd had the same sensation earlier. He'd been watching for something in the distance when he first saw Flopsy. But Flopsy wasn't it.

His thoughts, or rather his feelings, didn't last long. The kids, having been fed, were starting to get active again, and there was much to do, much to see, and much to smell. There were sand dunes to explore and strange animals to discover. Like the tiny fiddler crab that had held his attention for so long on his last visit; or the horseshoe crab he had once terrorized for five minutes, until the Pack dragged him away; or the tangled seaweed with all its hidden treasures and mysterious odors; or the occasional dead sea creature washed up on the shore.

And then his Frisbee would come out again, and it would fly over the sand, and Thor would run it down at full speed, overtaking its lazy flight, leaping with pinpoint accuracy and snatching it out of the air in a triumph of feet over flight!

The day had just begun, and every minute of it would be a thrill. Life didn't get any better than this.

The day went just as Thor expected. Nonstop action, nonstop excitement, and loads of new discoveries to tickle his curiosity.

The dreaded LEASH never came out. Although Thor would never know it, Dad hated the leash almost as much as he did.

Hours later, as the Pack prepared to leave, Thor pushed past the kids to be the first in the car (as always). He watched intently as the Pack got in, concerned that no one be left behind. Once satisfied that everyone was present and accounted for, he curled up on the floor behind the front seat and was sound asleep before the car left the parking lot. Snug inside the security of the Pack, the turns and occasional bumps in the road were unable to disturb his nap.

Fifteen minutes later, he woke instantly when the car pulled to a stop and the engine died. He hopped onto the back seat and crowded past the kids to the nearest window, and saw that the Pack had stopped at a supermarket.

He sat up on the back seat, alert and awake. It was hard to sleep when the Pack left him alone in the car, as they always did at supermarkets. Instead, he would guard the car and watch the front doors of the supermarket until they came out.

The Pack trusted him enough to leave a window open. He was proud of their trust, and had no intention of violating it.

It hadn't always been that way; as a young dog, he'd messed up badly on his first shopping trip. They'd left a window open for him, told him "STAY!" and left. As soon as they disappeared inside the store, he panicked. He leaped through the window and ran to the sliding glass doors of the store. An electronic motion sensor opened the doors with a *whoosh* that startled him. But he saw his chance and took it; he darted into the store, frantic to find his Pack.

When he found them, instead of being happy to see him, they were furious, especially Dad. He called Thor a Bad Dog and dragged him back to the car, painfully yanking on the choker collar the whole way. When they got to the car, Dad angrily repeated the "STAY!" command.

It was Thor's first lesson in a fundamental principle: Dad's Law overrides Natural Law.

Eventually Thor learned his lesson, and as time went by, the memory of his earlier mistake faded, replaced by memories of more recent, better behavior.

Now, years later, he only remembered how flawlessly he'd performed on these outings in the last year or so. Like a human, he used his memory to reinforce his Goodness instead of reminding him of his former Badness.

Of course, the earlier memories were still intact somewhere in his brain. He just didn't recall them.

When the Pack finally emerged from the supermarket, everyone carried a paper bag except Dad, who carried two. Thor barked once in greeting. Dad looked around to see if any cars were coming; seeing none, he called Thor, who eagerly leaped through the window and ran to meet them, barking for a bundle to carry.

It was a long-standing tradition. Since he was a pup, he'd always insisted on carrying a grocery bag with the Pack. It was one of the few chores he could help with, and he insisted on doing his part.

Dad took one of his two bags (the half-empty one he'd gotten specifically for Thor), and rolled up the top of the bag. He offered the rolled-up end to Thor, who took it gently in his jaws.

Thor strutted proudly with his bag, feeling completely adult, almost human. Few things felt better than full participation in Pack affairs.

He carried his bag to the car, and when they got home, he carried his bag into the house. It was a perfect ending to a perfect day.

As the Pack sorted the groceries and put them away, Thor curled up on the cool linoleum of the kitchen floor and sank into the deep, untroubled sleep of the innocent.

CHAPTER 3

"THOR!" Debbie called. "Here Thor! Heeeere Thor!"

Thor lay on the porch with his eyes closed and his chin resting on his crossed paws, breathing gently through his nose and smelling the world go by. He'd killed countless afternoons that way, but in the past he'd always let his eyes drift closed. Not today. Not for several days. His eyes had acquired a habit of scanning the horizon for something in the distance, despite his sense that it was quite far away. Something told him the thing in the distance mustn't be allowed to catch him off guard.

He listened closely to Debbie's voice but ignored her request. She could ask him to come, but she couldn't order him to come. He outranked her and was not obliged to do her bidding.

If she were to cry out in fear or pain, it would be a different story. Thor would be at her side in an instant, ready to offer whatever help he could. When it came to the Pack's well-being, every member was precisely equal. Rank did not figure into Pack security.

"Heeere, Thor! Heeere, Thor! Heeeeeeere, Thor!"

Her calls became a chant, which Thor actually enjoyed. It kept him updated on her whereabouts and condition, and he liked hearing the sound of his own name.

"Heeere, Thor."

She could call all day if she wanted to. Made no difference to Thor. As long as she was on Pack territory and she wasn't in trouble.

It was a weekday, and life was back to normal.

Mom and Thor had gone for their morning jog; afterward, Dad had come downstairs, smelling of soap and after-shave and dressed in his dark, creased clothes that somehow made him stand and move stiffly. He ate breakfast with Mom, kissed her at the front door, and left.

Thor hated to see Dad leave. It made no difference that he'd left practically every morning of Thor's life and returned practically every night. The fact remained, he *left the Pack,* and would be gone all day.

What if Dad met an enemy while he was out there? It could happen . . .

And Thor wouldn't be there to defend him. Dad could get killed, and the Pack would be without its male leader, without half its Mating Pair.

Thor stood at the living room window every morning and watched Dad leave, wishing he'd turn around and come back. And every night, he stood and waited for Dad's car.

And Thor always seemed to know just when Dad would return.

Sometimes Dad left for two or more days, and Thor didn't sit at the living room window until the day Dad came home.

Mom had noticed Thor's apparent awareness of Dad's schedule, but decided he was probably just picking up on her own expectations, which was partly right. Thor *did* notice Mom's lack of anticipation when Dad wasn't due home, but there was more to it than that, as she realized the night Tom got the flat tire.

The skies were dark with rain clouds as Tom got in his car to go home. He'd had a hard time getting out of the office, and hadn't looked at his watch until he was already in the car. He was a half hour behind schedule, due home in ten minutes, with a forty-minute drive ahead of him. He knew he should call to let Janet know he'd be late, but the nearest phone was in his office, six floors up, and he didn't want to go back. He'd told Janet he had a heavy schedule, so he figured she wouldn't worry too much, as long as he wasn't more than a half hour late. He figured he could make it home in a half hour if his radar detector didn't beep at him.

About halfway home, doing seventy and congratulating himself on his judgment, his left rear tire went out with a *pow!* that almost startled his bladder loose. The car lurched across two lanes before he managed to wrestle it onto the gravel shoulder and let it drift to a stop. He cursed under his breath, then thanked the stars there was no one else on the road when it happened. He took a deep breath and got out to survey the damage.

The left rear wheel was shot, torn to shreds. And then the down side of being alone on the road dawned on him. No one was going to stop to help, not even to give him a ride to a gas station or a pay phone.

Nothing but forest on either side of the road, not a building in sight, and, he knew, none within walking distance. Tom had never wanted a cellular phone in his car; he'd thought the whole idea was repulsive.

Until now. A car phone would sure be handy right about now.

He sighed, took off his suit jacket, rolled up his sleeves, opened the trunk, and bent down to haul out the spare and get to work.

By the time he had the lugnuts off the flat, his shirt and

pants were ruined, smeared with road grime, grease, and whatever else sticks to spare tires and jacks. He was pulling the flat off the axle when the skies opened and dumped what felt like Niagara Falls on him. He cursed and jumped into the car and waited for a break in the rain. It was a long wait.

He ended up spending forty minutes changing the tire.

Janet sat at the living room window the entire time, peering through the rain for headlights, trying to keep her fears under control. Thor lay on the floor at her feet, sleeping calmly. She tried to make Thor's disinterest into a good sign, but in reality, she wasn't sure what to make of it.

A minute before Tom pulled into the driveway, Thor suddenly tensed, sprang to his feet, and pressed his nose against the glass. Janet thought he must have heard the car coming. She squinted out the window, but saw nothing. Thor squirmed and whimpered. She looked again—still nothing. She decided Thor must have heard an animal outside; then she saw headlights through the rain, and Tom's car came crunching up the gravel driveway. Thor gave a little greeting *woof* and dashed off to the back door to greet his leader.

Janet wondered about the incident for a long time. For days, she watched Thor whenever Tom was due home. At first she thought Thor's hearing was just that much better than hers, but she couldn't convince herself. Thor had perked up a *whole minute* before the car arrived. A little arithmetic told her that if Tom had been doing thirty miles an hour (a conservative estimate, but considering the rain, he might have been going that slow) he would have been a half mile away when Thor first perked up. Even if Thor *could* hear the car that far away—through a closed window, in pouring rain—could he have distinguished it from all the other cars on the road?

The question gnawed at her until weeks later, when Tom was twenty minutes late. It was just enough for Janet to start worrying, but this time, she went into the living room to watch the road *and* the dog.

Thor had made himself comfortable in the window chair,

but he wasn't looking out; he was killing time. Janet sat a few feet away with her stopwatch in hand. A few minutes went by, and Thor sat up. She hit the stopwatch. Thor squirmed, pressed his nose to the window and whined, then sat rigid and alert. His ears were up, but they didn't twitch the way they did when he heard something in the distance.

The stopwatch ticked off twenty seconds, twenty-two, twenty-five. Thor didn't move. Fifty seconds. Thor stiffened slightly, his ears perked up, and he tilted his head to put his left ear a little closer to the glass. His eyes were locked on the street.

Thor squirmed, his ears twitched, and his face lit up. He'd heard the car for the first time. Janet stopped the watch. Fifty-five seconds. A few seconds later, she heard the car, too.

The hairs on the back of her neck stood up, and a chill ran down her spine. She'd witnessed something impossible.

Later, Janet told Tom about what she'd seen, but to her amazement, he wasn't surprised. His family had always had dogs, and he'd seen similar behavior in more than one of them. That kind of thing wasn't all that uncommon. His childhood dog, Harmon, for example, had always known when he was going to the vet, despite the family's careful avoidance of the "V-word." People casually referred to it as a dog's "sixth sense." When Tom was a teenager, he'd looked for other "psychic powers" in Harmon, but found none. If dogs had any other unexplained abilities, they kept them well hidden.

Eventually Tom accepted the explanation that dogs simply pick up *very* subtle cues from their masters. No big deal.

Janet was disappointed. She'd never been around dogs before, and thought she'd discovered something truly extraordinary. Thor might become famous, she'd imagined, the Psychic Dog.

But if this ability was so commonplace, why hadn't hard research been done on it?

"Well," Tom suggested one night, "assuming dogs *do* have

some psychic ability, maybe scientists feel it's beneath them to research. Who knows?"

Janet spent some time in the library reading all she could find about dogs, but never found any mention of a canine "sixth sense."

But she did find numerous stories about a mysterious ability of dogs to find their way home from hundreds, sometimes thousands, of miles away. Sometimes to homes they'd never been to before. In one case, a family moved cross-country, leaving the dog behind. Months later, the bedraggled pooch showed up on their new doorstep.

But as amazing as the stories were, they were just that—stories. Anecdotal evidence only. No research to back it up. *Why not?*

And Thor showed no other unusual insights. Just the apparent premonitions of Tom's return (and her own return from shopping, which she wasn't there to see).

In the end, Janet, like Thor, accepted what she couldn't understand.

Things seem normal because they're familiar, not because they make sense.

"Heeeeeeeeeere, Thor!"

"Thor? Here, Thor!"

Mom's voice, not Debbie's. Calling from the kitchen.

Thor sprang to his feet with his ears pricked up, listening for the next call to double-check her tone of voice.

"Here, Thor!" A little impatience, but that was normal for a second call. Overall positive, a little residual irritation (also normal at this time of day with the kids home). Her irritation probably wasn't directed toward him. Could be a trip. Could be anything.

He hopped to his feet and poked the front door with his nose, but it was latched, so he trotted around the house to the kitchen door, briefly checking on Debbie as he went by.

As he expected, she was playing with her plastic sand

bucket and shovel in the little grassy strip between the driveway and the house, chatting idly with her favorite doll, which sat watching from the sidelines. Her kitten was nowhere to be seen, which was not unusual. She'd brought some sand home from the beach, and was busy discovering that wet sand and dirt make better castles than the ones she'd made on the beach with wet sand alone.

He was glad to see that Debbie was on the Pack's side of the split-rail fence that separated the Pack's property from the neighbors'. The bottom rail was high enough for Debbie (or Thor, for that matter) to pass under easily, which she quite often did. Thor didn't care for that. He understood the meaning of the fence, and he agreed with it in principle. In fact, he reinforced its meaning every day with his urine.

The kitchen door, which opened onto the driveway toward the back of the house, was slightly ajar. Thor nosed it open and went inside, where Mom was talking to Teddy, who was trying to get out of the conversation.

"Look," she told her son sternly, "I don't want an argument. Now I want you to take the dog for a walk."

"Awwww!" Teddy whined. Thor didn't need to weigh the reluctance in Teddy's whine against the determination in Mom's voice. There was no contest. No matter what Teddy said or how long or loud he whined, he was taking Thor for a walk.

Thor was no more thrilled at the prospect than Teddy.

"And keep him on the leash," Mom added.

"Mom!" Teddy whined, stretching the word into several syllables.

Thor felt the same way. Why the leash?

Actually, Thor knew why. Relations between him and Teddy had been deteriorating lately, a situation Thor found extremely distressing. Unfortunately, there was nothing he could do about it.

Teddy was bucking for a higher rank in the Pack. Somewhere along the line, Teddy had noticed that Thor only obeyed him when he felt like it. It had always been that way, but Teddy either hadn't noticed or hadn't minded. Not any more. Suddenly he resented it; suddenly he wanted to outrank Thor. It had to do with his glands, Thor knew, but Teddy was getting ahead of himself, and his behavior was completely inappropriate. His attempt to assume a higher rank had made him a full-time pain in the ass, constantly asserting himself over Thor just for the sake of doing it.

It pained Thor deeply to be involved in any sort of strife within the Pack, but this situation was especially unpleasant, since he and Teddy had been best friends when they were pups. It had never occurred to Thor to wonder how he had gone through puppyhood, adolescence, and adulthood while Teddy remained a child; it had just happened, and now Thor was an adult and Teddy wasn't, and Thor could not be outranked by a prepubescent boy. Teddy could assert himself all he wanted, but he'd have to grow up before Thor would accept him as a superior.

Ironically, Thor could smell the first signs of hormonal changes in Teddy's crotch. He knew that Teddy would soon be a man, and as soon as he was, he would outrank Thor.

But in the meantime, Thor couldn't understand why Teddy resented Thor's rank. Thor was outranked by Mom and Dad, and it didn't bother *him* one bit. He didn't even resent it when they forbade him from having sex with bitches in heat.

Wolf packs are led by a couple, the Mating Pair, both of whom outrank all other pack members, male or female. The Mating Pair's authority even covers the sex lives of the others, and they often forbid mating between pack members. So Mom and Dad's prohibitions on Thor's sex life were in perfect accordance with Natural Law, and he saw no reason to resent them. On the contrary, Thor drew tremendous reassurance from knowing his Pack had a fixed hierarchy, regardless of his own station. A pack in which all members were equal would be chaotic. How could such a pack function? What would hold it together? How could it decide where to go, what to do?

And how could the members possibly be equal in the first place?

Teddy's foolishness was unfathomable, and Thor was not about to let the child meddle with Natural Law.

Meanwhile, Teddy showed no understanding of the situation. And worse, he seemed to blame Thor for his dissatisfaction.

Sometimes he teased Thor cruelly, without a trace of the love they'd shared for so long. Sometimes Thor took about all he could stand from the kid, though there was little he could do about it. Violence was out of the question. If a pack without hierarchy couldn't function, one in which pack members were free to injure or kill each other wouldn't last a day. Thor's only defense was to walk away from Teddy, something he did more and more lately. Walk away and ignore Teddy's outraged commands to come back.

And so the leash.

When Teddy (and only Teddy) took Thor for a walk, it was on the leash. Neither of them liked it, but neither of them outranked Mom.

But there was another reason for the leash today. The man Dad called Flopsy had not shown up at Dad's office on Monday, and Mom and Dad were worried. Mom had warned Teddy to be on the lookout for the man, and to keep Thor away from him if he showed up. It was possible that he might come back to provoke another incident.

All the way to the end of the block, whenever Thor stopped to renew the Pack's territorial markings, Teddy yanked on the leash and whined, "Come on! Hurry up!" At the end of the block (and, thankfully, the end of the Pack's territory), they turned right.

They were going to a mom-and-pop grocery store three blocks away. When they got there, Teddy would loop the leash around a fire hydrant and go inside for a moment, then he and Thor would go home by the same route. What a bore.

But when they got to the store, another dog was already tied to the hydrant. A small dog. Yapping. Thor hated being around small dogs.

He didn't exactly hate the dogs themselves; he hated the fate that had befallen them—that grotesque, unnatural, undoglike smallness. As for the dogs themselves, he felt painfully sorry for them. Their condition was so pitiful that it hurt to be around them.

Deep in his gut, Thor understood that dogs are predators, at the top of the food chain, meant to be strong and brave, not weak and helpless. Small dogs can't protect themselves, let alone their packs. All they can do is what the yapping dog was doing—yap for all he was worth, and hope to hell nobody calls his bluff.

Teddy tied the leash around a nearby light pole and went inside. The leash was long enough for Thor to go over and sniff the little dog by way of greeting, but instead Thor gave the yapper a wide berth and averted his eyes. He was deeply embarrassed by its behavior and its presence.

He wasn't too crazy about being tied to a pole, either—it was humiliating and dangerous. It put Thor at the mercy of any passing stranger.

It was moments like this when Thor understood that dogs are dogs and people are people, despite their feelings toward each other or their living arrangements. He never wondered why he lived among people—it was just the way things were—Mom and Dad and the kids were his Pack.

But they *were* different.

When he was a pup, Thor thought his dogness was part of growing up—a step on the road to humanness. When he grew up he would be human, like Mom and Dad. But now he *had* grown up—he was an adult and he knew it—and he was still a dog. The realization didn't come as a shock, because it never arrived at all. As he grew, he simply forgot the thought that he'd grow up human, and came instead to think of dogs as a different kind of human. A short, hairy, four-legged kind.

But on some level, when confronted with a mutation of breeding like the yapping dog, he *knew* he wasn't a short, hairy, four-legged person. He was a dog, totally and permanently different from the rest of the Pack. It was (mercifully) a fleeting thought, as were all his conceptual thoughts.

After a while Teddy came out, and they started home by a slightly different route.

About a block from the store, Thor stopped to sniff an unfamiliar turd.

"Come *on!*" Teddy said angrily, snatching hard on the leash. He acted like he and Thor were bitter enemies. The thought hurt Thor far more than the chain cutting into his throat.

Thor had worn a choke-chain collar as far back as he could remember. Dad had taught the kids not to use it to make Thor hurry (the way Teddy was using it now); the only reason Thor wore it was because it would be too easy for him to overpower the kids if he were to forget his manners—say, after seeing a cat hiss at him and run away. If he tried to run with the choker on, the collar would painfully remind him of the leash, and, hopefully, of the rules.

Thor knew Teddy's behavior was strictly against the rules, and he wished Teddy would grow up, so he could take his higher rank once and for all. Then maybe they could be friends again.

When they got home, Mom and Debbie were gone and so was the station wagon. The house was deserted. Thor understood immediately: He and Teddy had gone for a walk so he wouldn't be around to bug Mom about going with her. What a dirty trick.

"Later on, fur-face," Teddy said. He stepped out into the back yard and slammed the kitchen door behind him. Thor raced from window to window, watching Teddy walk away and hoping he might come back. He whimpered slightly as Teddy walked to the end of the block and turned the corner.

Then he ran through the house, upstairs and down, in a futile effort to find company.

Even Debbie's kitten was gone.

Deeply depressed, he went upstairs on the off chance that Mom and Dad's bedroom door might not be completely closed. He was in luck—the door popped open with a gentle poke from his nose. Mom and Dad's scents were strong here, so strong it was almost as if they were home. He hopped onto the bed and pulled the sheets back with his teeth to expose the place where their smells were strongest. He curled up on the sheets and drew in deep breaths. The reassuring fragrance melted his tensions, leaving him relaxed and tired. He lay his head on a pillow, among traces of Mom's makeup and Dad's after-shave, and didn't think about the scolding he would get when Mom returned. What he was doing was disobedient, but not Bad. He'd done it before and been punished every time, but whenever he found himself alone in the house, the reassurance of the bed was more important than a scolding or a slap from a rolled-up newspaper. If Mom had been thinking, she would have double-checked the door before she left, but she hadn't, and she didn't.

Thor was glad. He fell asleep with his head on Mom's pillow and his body sprawled across the open sheets.

CHAPTER

4

Tom slid naked into bed and noticed the sheets had been changed, after the previous sheets had only been on the bed one night. Janet left the door open and the dog got in the bed again, dammit. He almost said something, but decided there was no point in bringing it up.

"I'm really worried about Ted," Janet said, taking off her bra and panties and hurriedly slipping into a sheer black nightgown. Tom lay propped up on one elbow, watching her.

"I know," he said.

When they first married, Janet's discomfort with nudity had irritated him. He'd always been turned on by the thought that some wives walk around the house naked in front of their husbands, and he always assumed his wife would at least *sleep* naked with him. Hey, they were *married*, right? But Janet insisted on a nightgown at bedtime, and a robe before and after bathing—even though their bedroom had its own private bathroom. It wasn't being *seen* that bothered her—on the contrary, she enjoyed the hungry look in Tom's eyes when he watched her undress—it was the feel of fabric against her skin that she needed.

Now, three children later, Tom was eternally grateful for her apparent modesty. It had kept a little sexual distance between them, kept a little mystery in their love life. They had their own little bedroom games that revolved around Tom trying to pull off her nightgown, robe, or whatever, and Janet breathlessly but unsuccessfully trying to keep herself covered. In the end, her discomfort with nudity excited him in a way few husbands can be excited by their wives after so many years. And he'd always been turned on by black lingerie.

"He shouldn't be alone, Tom," Janet said. "Not now. Not after what he's been through."

"I agree, babe, but we have to respect his wishes. He's a big boy, you know." Saying that made him feel like a shit, but it had to be said. It was true.

Janet slid under the covers with her back to Tom, snuggling her bottom into his lap. He put his arm around her and pulled her close, cupping one breast in his hand and gently squeezing the nipple between his fingers.

They'd been together thirteen years, a year longer than Teddy had been alive.

"I think we should go visit Ted," Janet said, "whether he likes it or not." She pushed her fanny farther into Tom's lap, unconsciously using sex to sway her husband. Tom thought it was a cute move.

"I don't know," he said. "You might be right, but I'd still feel better if we at least called him and told him we were coming over first. Dropping in unannounced is awfully risky. And treating him like a child is downright . . . " He wanted to say "stupid," but there had to be a better choice of words. "It could make things worse instead of better."

Janet's brother Ted was a photographer, and a good one. Also a lucky one. The world is full of good photographers, but not all of them manage to make a comfortable living at their craft.

Ted had made much more than a comfortable living. He was what Tom called small-time rich—he never had to work again if he didn't want to, but he couldn't live on the Riviera.

Ted was a nature photographer who'd been in the right place at the right time on a number of crucial occasions, and he'd hit it off with the right people. His work had been published in *Life, National Geographic,* and a host of less well-known magazines specializing in the great outdoors. On rare occasions, his pictures even appeared in *Time* and *Newsweek,* two publications not known for nature studies.

To top off his good fortune, he'd met Marjorie. Marjorie spent three years with Ted. Together they climbed mountains, dove through coral reefs, hiked across deserts, hacked through jungles, and otherwise fought their way to that perfect picture. The only problem was that Marjorie was also a photographer, but it was always Ted's perfect picture they went after. Marjorie essentially gave up her career to be with Ted.

Tom liked Ted, but he also wondered about him. He didn't see why Marjorie's career had had to be sacrificed for Ted's, especially since they photographed the same kinds of things. Ted was a nice guy, but he always thought of himself first—and second, and third, and last. Tom never told Janet his doubts about his brother-in-law, and it was good that he didn't. Janet was absolutely devoted to her brother.

About a year ago in Nepal, Ted's luck changed. The gods, no doubt offended that a mere mortal should have such uniform good fortune, stole Marjorie away without a trace.

As Ted told the story, they'd been camping in the mountains, spending the days taking pictures and the nights in a small but remarkably warm tent. They went to bed side by side in thermal sleeping bags one night, but when Ted woke up the next morning, Marjorie was gone.

Ted had a painful lump on his head, a deep gash in his cheek, and several nasty-looking bites. The tent was torn open on one side and the camp was demolished. He couldn't remember anything from the night before.

Marjorie's sleeping bag had been ripped open from top to bottom. Some kind of animal tracks led down the mountainside, toward a bank of cliffs too steep and smooth to climb. Ted followed the tracks as far as he could, then hiked to the nearest village for help. As he arrived, a blizzard rolled over the campsite, obliterating it. In the days that followed, searchers were unable to find even a single tent pole. There was nothing to back up Ted's story.

The authorities suspected Ted of foul play. They had no proof whatsoever, but the very *absence* of proof—and the absence of a reasonable explanation—made them suspicious.

They were willing to believe in the yeti when some tourist claimed to have seen one, but not when a tourist claimed it ran off with his girlfriend.

They grilled him for two days—without a lawyer, without Miranda rights, and without results. And when, under pressure from the American Embassy, they finally let him go, they made it clear that he was no longer welcome in Nepal.

He returned to America, to a cabin he owned in the Cascade mountain range in Washington State, where he'd lived with Marjorie before the trip to Nepal. He'd never been terribly fond of civilization before, but after losing Marjorie, he became a full-fledged hermit, living completely alone in the house he'd shared with her.

He'd been like that for almost a year, and Janet was afraid he would never come out of his funk if he didn't start working again, and soon. She called him on a regular basis, but his mood never improved.

"I'll call him tomorrow," Janet whispered. Tom was nibbling her neck with unbearable delicacy. He'd slipped his free hand under her waist, and his fingers danced teasingly in the triangle of hair between her legs. She felt his erection pushing into the cleft of her buttocks, and was eager to wrap up the discussion without disrupting the mood. "We'll go visit him on Saturday," she breathed.

"Mm-hm," Tom murmured.

Janet reached around and pulled her nightie up until it was around her waist, then took hold of his hardness and guided him inside her.

CHAPTER

5

SATURDAY came, as Saturdays always did.

The kids watched cartoons while Dad sat with them in the living room, reading the newspaper from front to back. Mom sat at the kitchen table talking to the phone, calling it Uncle Ted.

Thor lay on the kitchen floor, listening to Mom's conversation. Almost everything she said was coaxing—"Are you sure?" "Oh, come on," "Why not?" "Please?"—but she was up against heavy resistance. The phone opposed her from the start, but Mom hung in there, and toward the end she wore it down. She got the phone to agree to a visit, then immediately ended the conversation and hung up. She didn't want to give it a chance to change its mind.

"It's all set!" Mom called to Dad as soon as the receiver was on the hook. Thor was delighted.

No one ever had to tell Thor that Uncle Ted was Mom's brother. He'd suspected it from the first moment he saw him, and his suspicions were confirmed in seconds. Dad hadn't even stopped the car before Thor spotted the resemblance between Mom and the man sitting on the front steps of the strange, pointy house. His posture and bone structure were the first clues. The man stood up as the car pulled to a stop, and as he strode toward the Pack, Thor immediately saw the similarity between Mom's walk and his. The man spoke, and though his voice was much deeper than Mom's, the cadences of his sentences, the way he put words together, the places where he paused to collect his thoughts, the words he emphasized—all were identical to Mom's speech patterns. By the time Thor got out of the car to sniff him, there was no question in his mind that the man belonged to the same pack that Mom had been born into.

But smelling is knowing. For Thor to decline to smell a new acquaintance would be like declining to open his eyes in the morning. Thor checked his scent, and sure enough, the man was Mom's sibling.

The two quickly became fast friends, and ultimately Thor came to feel closer to Uncle Ted than any other nonmember of the Pack. He and Uncle Ted seemed to share a secret understanding, and Uncle Ted's touch was exceptional. Uncle Ted seemed to know just where to scratch, where to rub, how hard and how soft, as if he were scratching himself. Thor wholeheartedly endorsed all visits to Uncle Ted. He could barely contain his excitement.

Thor hung his head out the car window, feeling the stiff breeze brush his fur and whip through his open mouth, cooling his tongue so fast that he didn't have to pant, despite the heat of the day.

The landscape rushing by was all hills and trees, with hardly a building in sight. The hills kept getting higher and higher as they went, and the buildings fewer and farther between. A dazzling variety of trees flashed past the station wagon, offering an equally dazzling variety of aromas, both floral and faunal. Thor was tantalized by the prospect of the animals he would find hiding behind the dense wall of leaves and pine needles that blanketed the hills. The thrill of discovery electrified him, and his hind legs and tail twitched with anticipation. The woods around Uncle Ted's house were denser and wilder than those behind the Pack's house; they were as exciting as any place Thor had ever visited, and the vague possibility of danger lurking among the trees only made the woods even more attractive.

Thor knew he was a feared animal, among the most feared animals in any environment. But he also knew there were animals out there that he would be wise to fear, and not all of them were bigger or stronger than he. As a young dog, he'd learned a painful lesson when he met his first porcupine. Now when he smelled porcupine tracks, he sniffed them out of curiosity only, and never hurried to catch up with their owner.

But caution didn't diminish his love of discovery. In fact, it heightened it. He couldn't wait to get out of the car and roam the woods around Uncle Ted's house, as free as any wild animal.

Which was another thing he liked about Uncle Ted. His house was all by itself, with no other humans around for miles, so there was virtually no need for Thor to think about Pack security. There were no restrictions on Thor's wanderings when the Pack visited Uncle Ted.

The trip seemed to take forever as the car snaked through the valley to Uncle Ted's house. It was strange, about the car. Humans did everything slowly; they walked slowly, they ran slowly, they ate slowly and they played slowly. The only thing they did fast was drive. And yet, no matter how fast they drove, it always took the car a long time to get where it was going. As if it, too, were going slowly.

Fortunately, the trip itself was fairly exciting. The smell and sight of dense forest (much denser than the woods behind the house) stirred something deep in his genes. The Pack had made this trip many times (though not lately) and Thor knew the route well. The sight of "almost there" landmarks encouraged a gentle flow of adrenalin that tingled his legs and chest.

The car turned off the two-lane blacktop and on to a gravel road, where it started its long uphill climb. There were five mailboxes at the mouth of the gravel road; some of their owners had to drive more than a mile from their homes to check the mail. Nothing else on the landscape indicated the presence of humans.

As they got closer to Uncle Ted's house, one of Thor's front paws kept stepping through the window involuntarily, as if he were about to jump out and run ahead. Brett kept grabbing his paw and pulling it back inside, which embarrassed Thor. He wasn't planning to jump, and wished he could control his paw's reflex action.

The car wound up a steep grade, high above the valley floor. The trees began to thin out somewhat, and eventually almost all of them were pines of one kind or another, with just a few leafy trees here and there. The hillside was cooler and darker than the valley, but the trees weren't dense enough to cut off the sunlight, and there were lots of bushes and scrub on the ground.

Then the road leveled off and followed the side of the hill. Eventually, they reached Uncle Ted's driveway and turned downhill. Finally an angular wood and glass structure appeared, and the car pulled to a stop. Uncle Ted's "cabin" was actually an airy, luxuriant, redwood A-frame, perched near the top of the hill, surrounded by redwood forest on three sides, and sky on the other. His nearest neighbor was two miles away. Above his house, a little-used hiking trail ran along the ridgeline of the hills for miles.

"Go for it, Thor!" Dad called over his shoulder as he stopped the car. Thor leaped through the window before the words were out of Dad's mouth. Mom punched Dad on the shoulder for encouraging rowdy behavior.

Thor hit the ground running, torn between his urge to sniff out the grounds and his desire to see Uncle Ted. Uncle Ted was nowhere in sight, so the urge to sniff won. His nose guided him to the edge of the pathway that led to Uncle Ted's house. He drew in a series of short sniffs of the ivylike foliage that carpeted the ground and shrouded the earth beneath its low-lying leaves. He sniffed aimlessly at first, both to familiarize himself with the smells of the area, and to overwhelm his nose with the ever-present odors of fresh and rotting pine needles, so their scents would fade into the background and allow fainter, subtler smells to be detected, categorized, and filed away.

The trees were different from the ones behind the Pack's house, and wildlife was *everywhere*. Scents of different soil types mingled with a kaleidoscope of animal smells—traces of fur, feathers, rotting carcasses, and waste products flashed through his nose and excited his imagination.

Thor's sense of smell wasn't just more sensitive than the Pack's; it was also more specialized. While he could detect *any* scent more easily than the Pack, he smelled some things better than others. Important things, like the fatty acids secreted by the skin of mammals, which tag each individual with a distinct and unforgettable signature. When it came to detecting and discriminating between these highly individual scents, his nose was supreme. He could find and follow a three-day-old scent trail, and identify it based on less than a millionth of the smallest amount detectable by humans.

The *experience* of smelling was also different. The wet end of his nose was extremely sensitive to temperature changes; it could determine the speed and direction of the slightest breeze with pinpoint accuracy. Thor's brain processed wind-direction information along with the odors in such a way that he smelled things *where they were,* outside his nose, the same way humans hear sounds where they are, instead of inside their ears, where the hearing is actually taking place.

Thor was deep in the ocean of aromas, finding and filing away new floral odors, acrid waste products from birds, insects, and small mammals, and the pungent, heavy mulch perfumes of the soil, when the front door of Uncle Ted's house opened, and he looked up.

Uncle Ted!

Thor forgot his explorations and ran to Uncle Ted with his head down, his ears flat against his head, his tail between his legs in respectful submission, wagging uncontrollably. He just couldn't get to Uncle Ted fast enough.

Uncle Ted smiled down at him just as Thor leaped up like a dolphin, lightly touching the bottom of Uncle Ted's chin with his nose and licking it with the tip of his tongue. He leaped and kissed him twice before Uncle Ted raised his hands to fend off the affectionate attack, then hunkered down to greet his old friend.

Unable to fully express his joy by wagging his tail, Thor's whole body wriggled and danced in delight at the touch of Uncle Ted's hands. Uncle Ted hugged him warmly, patting Thor's rump and stroking his head and neck to calm his twitching, squirming torso. Thor managed to control himself a little and politely kissed Uncle Ted's hands, in deference to Uncle Ted's wish not to be kissed on the face.

Then Uncle Ted spoke, and everything changed.

"Hi, Thor."

Something was wrong with his tone of voice. Uncle Ted was not happy.

Thor's concern overrode his sense of protocol, and he looked directly at Uncle Ted's face. He was sorry to see that his impression was correct. Uncle Ted was *terribly* unhappy. Thor kissed Uncle Ted's hands gently, tenderly, as he would kiss an injury. His kisses were intended to show his sympathy, to console Uncle Ted that whatever was wrong, he was still loved. The purpose of his kisses was more urgent than mere greetings, and he didn't let himself be put off by Uncle Ted's upraised hands. He easily pushed past them and kissed Uncle Ted's chin, then watched for some sign that his affection might have helped heal Uncle Ted's unseen wound.

It hadn't.

"Hi, Uncle Ted!" Brett and Debbie sang at almost exactly the same time. Uncle Ted stood up, a little relieved to escape Thor's emotional first aid. Brett and Debbie ran to him with outstretched arms, while Teddy leaned against the car, too cool for this scene. Thor let Brett and Debbie squeeze him out of the action, and soon the whole Pack was walking together up the stairs to Uncle Ted's house.

Thor muscled his way past the Pack (as always) and ran inside to sniff things out. He bounded into the house, looking for the scent of Uncle Ted's mate, Marjorie.

There were cardboard boxes on the living room floor, some filled with Uncle Ted's belongings, most empty. What was going on here?

He sniffed the boxes and the chairs and the sofa. He pushed his nose deep between the sofa cushions, where he picked up Marjorie's scent, old and faint and almost undetectable. Where was she? And where was the scent of sex that had never been more than a day old on previous visits?

Uncle Ted and the Pack came in the front door talking, which made their usually slow pace even slower.

"So where'll you go?" Dad asked Uncle Ted gently.

"I haven't made up my mind yet," Uncle Ted said. "But I can't stay here, not now. Maybe later. I'm putting my stuff in storage until I make up my mind where to go, which might take a while."

"Well, if you need help, all you have to do is ask," Dad said.

"No he *doesn't* have to ask," Mom said. "We're helping whether you ask or not."

"Hey, look, sis," Uncle Ted said, smiling lamely (but at least smiling). "No need to get bossy here. I'm a big boy. I can take care of myself." Dad elbowed Mom in the ribs at the sound of his own words.

Thor listened carefully to the odd-sounding conversation. Something was wrong with the way Uncle Ted was talking to Mom and Dad. Something disturbingly familiar, and at the same time, disturbingly out of place. Thor poked his nose into a box and didn't look up. He didn't want to be obvious about studying Uncle Ted, but his attention was riveted on the subtle nuances in Uncle Ted's voice.

He observed Uncle Ted for a few minutes, but still couldn't decide what was wrong. Uncle Ted was hiding something from the Pack, that much was obvious. First of all, he was both hiding and not hiding his emotional state. He was making it clear to the Pack he was terribly unhappy, but not allowing them to see just how unhappy he was. Typical human behavior.

But there was more to it than that, a deeper subterfuge that was obscured by the obvious one. *What was it?*

Thor's span of attention was stretched beyond its usual limit. An odd smell in one of the boxes caught his attention; he lost track of the mystery of Uncle Ted's secret and went back to his general-purpose olfactory investigation.

He finished with the boxes and sniffed the sofa again briefly, going back to the familiarization routine that had been interrupted by Uncle Ted's strangeness. Mom, Debbie, and Brett had made themselves comfortable on the sofa, which didn't make his job any easier. He picked up a whiff of Marjorie's scent again, which brought back the question of her whereabouts.

He followed his instincts to the wrought-iron spiral staircase that always gave him so much trouble. He climbed up the steps two at a time (his problem with the staircase was coming down, not going up). He wanted to check Uncle Ted's bedsheets.

He bounded onto the bedroom deck, an oversize balcony above the living room, and went straight for the bed, which was just a mattress and box springs on the floor. Unlike the Pack, Uncle Ted never made his bed, which made Thor's job easier. He stuck his nose deep in the sheets and snuffed around. He found only the faintest detectable trace of Marjorie, not on the sheets but on the mattress beneath. There was no detectable aroma of sex, which wasn't surprising. The smell of sex fades much faster than the smell of skin oils.

The picture was complete. There was almost no trace of Marjorie anywhere. Uncle Ted had been alone for some time. That must be why his emotions were so mixed up. Thor's sympathy went out to Uncle Ted. Nothing is worse than loneliness.

There was a cardboard box with laundry in the bedroom. Thor thrust his snout into it and got a surprise. Inside was the scent of a strange animal. The scent was strangely doglike, but the animal was not a dog. Its scent was wild, feral, unlike any animal scent Thor had ever encountered inside a house before. And even stranger was the fact that he hadn't picked up the scent anywhere else in the house. Just in the box. Uncle Ted must have encountered a wild animal outside and gotten its scent on his clothes, then left the clothes in the box.

"Thor!" Dad called from the living room. "Get down here!" Thor was glad to oblige. He'd found everything he was going to find up there.

He negotiated the first steps of the spiral staircase cautiously. The stairs were steep, and curved inward too tightly for his long, horizontal body. On top of that, they weren't solid. They were metal grids that Thor could see through, an unsettling quality he particularly disliked. He took three or four tentative steps with his front legs until his hind feet were on the top steps, then tumbled down in a kind of controlled fall, his feet guiding his descent rather than carrying him down.

The first time he'd gone up there, when he was a pup, he'd gotten stuck, afraid to negotiate the scary steps. Dad had had to come up and carry him down, which was humiliating beyond belief. The next time the Pack visited Uncle Ted, he bounded up the stairs again before remembering what had happened. When he realized what he'd done, he looked at the stairs, pulled back, recalled the embarrassment of being rescued, and forced himself down in exactly the same manner as

73

he did today. His technique was primitive—even Thor thought so—but it worked. He'd never improved on it.

When he reached the living room floor, Dad was in the kitchen area, holding the back door open.

"C'mon," Dad said. "Out you go." Thor needed no coaxing. He dashed through the door into Fantasyland. There was a lot of territory out there, just waiting to be explored.

His nose led him up the hillside. There was a path behind the house that got just enough use to keep it from being swallowed up by the underbrush. At the top of the hill it joined a more popular path that followed the ridgeline of hills through the area. The ridgeline path was older and, since it got more use, better defined. Hikers came through on a fairly regular basis, leaving garbage behind that attracted animals. It was a great place to sniff and explore.

Skyline Trail, as it was known, was almost a quarter mile up the hill from Uncle Ted's house, and hikers normally passed by without ever knowing anyone lived on the hillside below. Only at night could a hiker spot the house from Skyline, when light glowed dimly through the foliage below. But hikers rarely used Skyline after dark, and almost never took the little footpath down to Uncle Ted's house—Skyline was two miles long, with a hundred paths leading off; most of them led nowhere. Most hikers took Skyline all the way to the end, where it led out of the hills and into a state park, where friends waited to pick them up.

Thor had no idea why the myriad hikers along the summit didn't come down the hill, but his nose told him that was the case. Whenever he picked up a human scent on the path leading up to Skyline, it was invariably Uncle Ted's or Marjorie's. Now he picked up only Uncle Ted's scent, and an occasional hint of the Wild Animal he'd smelled in Uncle Ted's laundry.

He trotted up the path briskly, but not so fast that he might miss something interesting. In past visits, he'd frequently spotted animals off the path and gotten into some invigorating chases.

Less than halfway up the hill, he found the scents of raccoons, opossums, deer, squirrels, chipmunks, and a cornucopia of droppings. And the Wild Animal. Something about the scent made the hair on Thor's shoulders rise slightly, and he listened more carefully to the forest sounds around him.

The Wild Animal's scent got stronger as it went up the hill, which was odd in itself. Scents don't usually get more or less intense as they go along. They only get stronger if they're joined by the scent of another animal of the same kind, or if the animal stops and lies down, or does something to leave more of its essence behind, like scratching itself against a tree. But there was no sign that the Wild Animal had stopped, and no second scent. The scent just got stronger.

Very odd.

Thor wanted to sprint up the hill, follow the Wild Animal's trail to the end, see what he could find out about it, but some deep-seated instinct advised caution. Very strongly. He proceeded cautiously.

Just a few hundred feet below Skyline he picked up a fresh human scent. A woman. The scent appeared out of nowhere, as if the woman had walked down the path toward Uncle Ted's house, then turned around and gone back. He followed it up the hill for a few feet when he realized the Wild Animal's scent had stopped where the woman's scent started. He doubled back to find the end of the Wild Animal's path, and found his mistake: The scent trails didn't end, they left the path. The woman had been coming down the path while the Wild Animal was coming up. They met and left the path, into the dense underbrush on the hillside. Thor followed the overlapped trails.

About thirty feet from the path, the woman's trail entered a wide patch of berry plants whose stems were covered with sharp thorns. And here Thor picked up the unmistakable scent of human blood. The woman's scent was stronger here—she was probably struggling to get through the brambles, sweating, getting cut, and secreting more odor in the process. Thor stepped through the brambles carefully, lifting his feet high in the air and looking for an opening in the thorns before gently, tentatively setting them down.

Humans seldom stray from paths, Thor knew. Could the animal have led the woman off the path? But would a human follow an animal across a dangerous field of thorns? Would an animal cross the bushes in the first place? Everything seemed wrong. The questions fluttered through Thor's mind and vanished as quickly as they had appeared, but they changed the scenario in his mind.

The woman wasn't following the Wild Animal; the Wild Animal was chasing her. A trace of blood just inside the bushes confirmed his judgment. The woman was not being careful. She was in a hurry. A yard or two in, he found a different blood scent. The Wild Animal was in a hurry, too.

A few steps in, the thorns stopped him. Ahead the brambles were higher than his ears. Only a desperate animal, fleeing for its life, would run through this thicket. Its pursuer must have been either desperate or mad. He stretched his neck forward and sniffed, and confirmed a hunch—the Wild Animal's scent didn't follow the woman's scent through the thorns. The Wild Animal had turned back after running a few feet into them.

Thor carefully backed out of the berry patch and picked up the Wild Animal's scent trail. As he expected, it went around the thicket. He followed it to the edge of the berry patch, where the Wild Animal had circled around to the other side, to the spot where the woman had emerged from the thorns.

He found the place where the chase picked up again, and found another faint but familiar smell—that particular mixture of adrenalin, sweat, hormones, and enzymes that makes the smell of fear. *That* was a surprise. Fear is a fleeting scent, and the trails were at least a day old. For the scent to still be detectable, the woman must have been overflowing with it.

As her path led away from the berries, the scent of fear got steadily stronger.

This was where the Wild Animal had begun to catch up with her.

The trail led over a large fallen tree with lots of sharp branches, dangerous to negotiate. The woman had been looking for obstacles to slow her pursuer down. Thor picked his way through the maze of dead branches, and finally picked up the scent he'd been expecting for a while—the smell of death.

As a predator, he was not frightened by the smell; in fact, he liked it. It charged his blood with adrenalin and piqued his curiosity. But it also put him on guard.

He stepped onto the trunk of the fallen tree, mindful of the sharp branches that pointed at him like accusing fingers. As he hoisted himself up, he caught his first glimpse of his quarry, lying on her back on the grassy hillside, staring at the sky with dead eyes. There were no other predators around. He cautiously stepped up for a closer look.

She wore hiking boots and shorts, and her bare legs had been horribly lacerated by the thorns. The cuts must have been painful, but they hadn't killed her. She'd died when the Wild Animal ripped out her throat. Afterward, he'd torn her shirt apart and opened her torso from her neck to her navel. The ground was sticky with blood, which thousands of ants were busy cleaning up. Some of the ants marched into her body, where they fought with maggots for her remains. Thor didn't like the idea of setting his paws down in the writhing sea of insect life that surrounded her, so he leaned as far forward as he could and sniffed from a distance.

His nose picked up the odor of liver, one of his favorite foods, and curiosity got the better of him. He stepped lightly over the ants and leaned his nose into the opened torso.

The Wild Animal had ripped through her thorax in search of an organ, but somehow he'd missed the best part—her liver was still intact, untouched except for a few maggots and ants. The smell of liver, even with the odor of decomposition setting in, was intoxicating. But Thor resisted the temptation to eat.

He was no dummy—he'd learned a few things about meat in his time, and he knew better than to eat meat found outside.

It had been a painful lesson. He'd been on a walk with Dad one weekend in the woods at home. Dad had brought Thor's tennis ball, and they walked to a little clearing where Dad threw the ball to the far end, behind a big tree. When Thor got there, he found a thick, raw, chuck steak lying in the grass like a gift from the gods. Thor helped himself to the succulent meat—and his mouth and throat caught fire. He yelped and howled and whined and vomited, but nothing put the fire out. He ran back to Dad, who was unable to help, then back to the creek behind the house. He drank as fast as he could, but it hardly helped. As soon as he stopped drinking, the fire started up again. It seemed to burn forever.

In fact, he was back to normal in about a half hour, but it was the longest half hour of his life. The next day, out with Dad again in a different part of the woods, the ball again landed near a tempting treat.

Beef liver. Irresistible. He drooled uncontrollably, but held back for a moment, remembering the chuck steak. But steak is steak, and liver is liver. He succumbed to temptation, only to have the same horrible lesson repeated. Since then, he'd twice found meat in the woods and passed it by both times.

He'd never found meat in the wild again until today, but the lesson held. He sniffed the woman's liver and passed on.

"Thanks, Ted," Tom said, taking the offered mug of coffee. Tom usually didn't allow himself more than two cups a day, but he always made an exception at Ted's place. Ted ground his own beans for every cup, and the beans he ground weren't cheap. There was nothing else like it in the world. Certainly not the canned coffee Janet got at the supermarket.

"So, let's talk," Janet said. The three of them sat around the small kitchen table. Reflected sunshine bathed them in a diffuse light that made their faces look angelic. Only Ted's face was imprinted with a sadness the soft light couldn't wash away.

"So talk, sis," Ted said. He didn't resent their intrusion, but he wasn't eager to spill his guts, either.

"Ted," she said earnestly, her hand on his, "We know you've gone through a lot. And we respect your desire to be alone. But we . . . I . . . I'm afraid for you. You've been holed up here for *months*, Ted. You can't go on like this forever. You need to put your life back together."

Tom looked away from the table, embarrassed. He could understand why Janet wanted him to be with her during this discussion, but he wished she could have done it by herself. It wasn't his place to hear this. It was too intimate. He felt like an intruder.

"I don't know what I need," Ted said sullenly. Then he snorted bitterly and said, "Actually, I *do* know what I need. Only I don't have the guts to do it."

"Ted!" Janet gasped.

Tom cringed. This was exactly the kind of thing he didn't want to hear.

"I don't want to hear that kind of talk," Janet said.

Well, Tom thought, *at least we're in agreement there. Now can I leave?*

He almost laughed, and desperately made himself think of something else before he got himself into trouble he could never get out of. He stood up from the table and sauntered over to Uncle Ted's bookshelves for a browse.

Uncle Ted didn't respond to Janet's outburst, so she picked up the discussion without him.

"Ted, I know you loved Marjorie, but there are other women in the world. You'll find one you love some day, if you'll just go out there and meet them. You're just digging yourself into a hole in this place."

"Not deep enough, apparently," Ted said, and snorted. Janet bit her lower lip and tears welled in her eyes. Ted saw her expression and was immediately sorry for what he'd said. He put his hand on hers and held it tight.

"I'm sorry, Janet. You know I didn't mean that. It's just that . . . I have to make up my mind. I . . . right now, I really don't know . . . I don't know what I want to do with my life . . . I don't know what I *can* do with my life anymore . . . There are things you don't know about . . . I just can't say more than that. Not now. Okay?" Janet said nothing. A tear rolled silently down her cheek. She bit her lip a little harder.

"Okay," she said in a barely audible whisper.

Tom noticed something odd about the books in Ted's shelves. He opened his mouth to say something about it, then closed it. This wasn't the time.

Thor had learned about as much as he could from the carcass. The Wild Animal had eaten some part of the woman's body, but left a dizzying array of organs untouched, organs Thor would have eaten first. There was a lot of damage to the woman's left rib cage and the lung underneath it. Whatever the Wild Animal had taken had come from under her left lung.

Thor passed no judgment on the killing of the woman. As guardian of the Pack, he himself might be called upon to kill a human someday. Other humans, those not associated with the Pack, were not his friends and not his concern. If Thor were to see a strange dog attacking a strange human on the street, he would not assume the human was Good and the dog was Bad. He would look to the Pack for cues. If he were by himself, he would simply watch.

Still, he didn't like the idea that there was something in the woods that could kill a human by itself—not with the Pack nearby.

Fortunately, all traces of the Wild Animal were a day old; there was no sign that it was still in the area. If there had been, Thor would go back to Uncle Ted's house immediately, just in case.

Thor turned his attention to the trail the Wild Animal had

left after the attack. It wasn't hard; the Wild Animal's scent stood out in the potpourri of aromas like garlic in a pot of spaghetti sauce. Except that Thor liked the smell of garlic. He didn't like the Wild Animal's scent, though he wasn't sure why. There was something about it that almost worried him.

He picked up the trail a few feet from the corpse and followed it down the hill.

"Ted," Janet said, "I want you to stay with us. For a while. Until you sort things out."

Tom held his breath when he heard that. He was still perusing the books, and wasn't too sure if he should even be in the house. Trouble was, he couldn't think of an excuse to leave.

"Sis, I really appreciate your offer, but I just can't." Tom silently let out his breath. "I have things to work out on my own, and it has to be that way."

"You can stay with us and be by yourself," Janet insisted. "We have a garage with an apartment on top. You wouldn't be in our way, and you'd have all the privacy you need. But we'd be there if you need us."

Well, that's better than putting him in the guest room, Tom thought.

"I don't know . . . "

Uncle Ted got a faraway look in his eyes, and for just an instant his expression changed to one of calculation. He pressed his lips together in a grimace of inevitability.

"You might be right," he said, so softly that only he heard the words. Tom didn't hear anything at all, and Janet only heard him mutter something unintelligible. But she knew her brother, and she accepted the murmur as capitulation.

She felt infinitely relieved.

Thor stopped what he was doing and raised his head. The hairs on the back of his neck rose to attention, and he stood absolutely rigid, smelling the air without sniffing it. Without realizing it, he held his breath for a moment to listen in total silence.

He heard nothing and smelled nothing. It was neither sound nor smell that had alerted him, but a feeling. The same kind of feeling that told him Dad was coming home, only different. That feeling was Good. This feeling was Bad.

Something Bad was coming. Something very, very Bad.

He looked down the hill in the direction of Uncle Ted's house, but it was too far away to be seen.

He'd wanted to follow the Wild Animal's trail, but it would have to wait. He couldn't look around anymore. He belonged with the Pack.

He retraced his steps back to the body, over the deadfall, around the berry bushes and back to the path. He ran all the way down the hill to Uncle Ted's house.

Tom sat down at the kitchen table, thinking the heavy stuff was over, just as Thor came bounding into the room through the open back door.

Thor glanced at him, and at Mom and Uncle Ted, then dashed into the living room to see if anyone else was in the house. Satisfied there was no one else inside, he ran back to the kitchen table to look them over again.

Lacking the ability to count or compile mental lists, he had to imprint his mind with the images of those present, looking back and forth from person to person until his gut told him no one was missing. His job was made more difficult by the fact that the Pack was split up.

Having imprinted the adults in his mind as best he could, he ran through the front door and onto the deck, where he was relieved to find the kids playing right in front of the house. He stood on the porch and looked at the kids, then turned to look back at the grown-ups, then back to the kids. In about four passes, he was satisfied; everyone was here.

He returned to the kitchen to check the mood of the adults.

He didn't need to watch the kids as long as he could hear them, but he wished they would come inside.

Inside the house, the adults had a quiet little laugh watching Thor go through his head count. Then they settled into an awkward silence, waiting for someone to restart the conversation. Thor finally calmed down and trotted into the kitchen area. He plopped down next to Dad's feet and grunted.

Dad figured it was time to make small talk.

"What happened to your book collection?" he asked Ted innocently.

"I thinned it," Ted said with finality.

Not much of an answer. If Uncle Ted had said, "Marjorie took some of them," Dad would have dropped the subject. But he hadn't said that. Surely this couldn't be a painful, personal topic, could it?

"I noticed," Dad said. "Ansel Adams, Minor White, the Westons . . . There's not one book on the shelves that's more than twenty years old."

"I decided to bring myself into the twentieth century," Ted said, shrugging. Thor took the defendant's side. He walked over to Uncle Ted and sat at his feet with the weight of his body against the man's legs. Uncle Ted reached down and patted him appreciatively.

"I thought maybe it was something else," Dad continued casually. He couldn't understand why this had suddenly taken on the feel of an interrogation. What was going on here? "It looks like you got rid of all the black-and-white books. Every photo collection on the shelf is in color. Every single one."

"Well, you caught me, Sherlock," Ted said. "You're right. They're all color." He paused for a moment and said, "I don't like black and white anymore."

"What?" Dad said. "Is this the same guy who lectured me for an hour on the beauty of black and white? About how it's a whole world to explore, and you don't know if you'll ever discover all its secrets?"

Ted shrugged. "That's what I thought then. I don't now. I'm

83

fed up with black and white. I've seen all the black and white I ever want to see."

"Ansel Adams and Edward Weston?" Mom asked, incredulous.

"I don't care *who* shot it, I don't want to look at black and white! I want to see color, that's all. I . . . had a . . . an unpleasant experience. And black and white reminds me of . . . things I don't want to remember."

Mom and Dad just looked at him.

Ted turned his attention to Thor, scratching the dog's neck roughly, deliciously. Thor threw his head back, mouth open, tongue hanging out, eyes narrowed to slits, and panted his approval. Thor had no idea what Uncle Ted had been talking about.

Neither did Mom or Dad.

They dropped the subject, though, and Ted relaxed a little and focused his attention on petting Thor.

And that was the moment when Thor first noticed the change in Uncle Ted's touch.

When Uncle Ted petted or stroked or scratched Thor, his touch spoke only love. There was tremendous love in Mom's and Dad's hands, but their touches conveyed other feelings as well. Commitment. Obligation. Consolation. The other feelings didn't bother Thor—on the contrary, he was reassured by them; Mom and Dad *should* feel those things. Mom and Dad were, after all, the Pack's Mating Pair.

But Uncle Ted was not part of the Pack, no matter how close he might come. He and Thor were friends, not relatives. Their relationship was based solely and exclusively on love; no responsibilities, no debts. It was the kind of single-emotion relationship that could only exist with an outsider. Relationships within the Pack could never be so simple.

But now Uncle Ted's touch was different—no longer the pure, uncomplicated affection Thor knew so well. And it wasn't just Uncle Ted's sorrow, either. There was something new, something different in Uncle Ted's relationship to Thor. Other feelings had crept in. Respect. Caution.

Caution?

Could Uncle Ted be afraid of Thor? The thought shocked him, and he whipped his head around to look into Uncle Ted's face, confused by the ambiguity of his own feelings.

Thor's sudden movement startled Uncle Ted. He snatched his hand away from Thor's neck, realized there was no danger, and put it back.

As if Thor might have turned around to bite Uncle Ted's hand!

He *was* afraid of Thor. But why?

The wordless question evaporated, and Uncle Ted scratched Thor's neck some more. But Thor didn't drop to the floor and turn his underside to Uncle Ted, as he normally would have done. Something had changed, and he didn't like it.

"Well!" Uncle Ted said sharply, startling Thor. "Let's talk about something else! You guys must be hungry by now. How about trying a little recipe I picked up in Nepal, huh? You'll love it!" Thor was glad to hear the conversation lighten up, but he wished the oddness in Uncle Ted's tone (and his touch) would disappear. It was subtle, but bothersome. And it didn't change when Uncle Ted put on a happy face.

Thor made no connection between Uncle Ted's oddness and the body outside. He'd completely forgotten the body for the time being, and would not remember it until he went outside again. The sensation that something Very Bad was coming was also fading.

Uncle Ted opened a kitchen cabinet and pulled out an enormous wok. "The dish I'm going to make isn't normally cooked in a wok, but I can't remember how to cook with anything else . . . any objections?" he said with forced bonhomie. There were no objections—Mom and Dad loved Uncle Ted's stir-fried delicacies.

He put the wok on the stove and poured a puddle of oil into

it, lit the burner, and only then opened the refrigerator and rummaged through it for ingredients.

The smell of oil heating in the wok was more than enough to start Thor's salivary glands working.

Uncle Ted emerged from the refrigerator with a treat dangling from his fingertips. Thor immediately recognized the savory odor of hard salami. His eyes locked on the slice of meat. Uncle Ted abruptly tossed it without warning. Thor leaped, snapping it out of the air almost before it cleared Uncle Ted's fingers. It disappeared down his throat before his feet touched the floor.

"Well. Impressive," Uncle Ted said. Thor noticed the nervousness in his voice, the feeling of something being concealed, and something else, too. When his mouth had approached Uncle Ted's fingers, Uncle Ted had pulled his hand back as if it were in danger. Thor had taken meat from Uncle Ted's hands many times in the past. Sometimes his teeth had actually touched Uncle Ted's fingers, but he always knew exactly where his teeth were, and he always had time to pull back if they touched the wrong thing. *And Uncle Ted knew it.* He'd *never* pulled his hand back like that before.

What was with Uncle Ted?

Thor didn't like the feeling the unanswered question gave him. It had now come up enough times to fix itself in Thor's mind. From now on, whenever Uncle Ted was around, Thor would discretely keep an eye on him, until he understood what was with him. He would not enjoy the complete abandon he'd known on previous visits with Uncle Ted. It was a big loss.

Uncle Ted showed Thor his empty hands, fingers splayed, and turned to serious cooking. Thor dropped himself onto the floor. He was a little disgruntled about only getting one measly treat, but he knew Uncle Ted would give him more later on.

He listened carefully to the kids playing outside, and kept Uncle Ted in his peripheral vision.

Soon the house was filled with the smells of burning oil, garlic, onions, meats, and a multitude of vegetables that Thor would never eat by themselves, but which somehow made the soup of aromas smell even better. Thor waited patiently, knowing there was no rushing a cooking human—you can only annoy them and get yourself into trouble. If he begged now, they'd feed him dog food. The treats would come only when the humans felt like doling them out.

Uncle Ted announced that he was almost done, and Dad called the kids in. Thor watched them enter to be sure they were all here.

"So how are things with you guys?" Ted asked over his shoulder, still cooking. Tom decided to take another stab at small talk. Maybe he'd do better this time.

"Well, we had a few nervous moments for a while. Someone in our neighborhood was poisoning animals."

"You're kidding!" Ted said. The oddness was in his voice again.

"I wish," Tom said. "Thing is, it was so general, we couldn't tell if they were trying to kill pets or wildlife or what. You know, I thought it was such a great place for a dog, with the woods behind the house and all. Then some asshole—" Janet kicked Tom's shin under the table "—some jerk starts in with something like that. I sure didn't want to keep Thor on a leash, but what could we do? Fortunately, I saw a nature show on PBS that solved everything. Some forest rangers had the same problem with coyotes: Ranchers were poisoning them. So the rangers flew over the coyotes' territory in a helicopter and tossed out slabs of red meat, laced with cayenne pepper. The idea was to teach the coyotes not to eat meat they find lying around, and it worked. So poor Thor had to learn the same lesson." He looked at Thor sympathetically and grabbed a hunk of the loose skin on the back of his neck, kneading it like dough.

It felt like heaven to Thor. What difference did it make what they were talking about?

"Anyway, it worked for Thor, too," Tom said. "He won't go near a piece of meat outside." Uncle Ted seemed particularly interested in that not-quite-correct statement. He nodded knowingly.

Before Uncle Ted finished cooking, Dad told Teddy to get Thor's food and dish out of the car. What a letdown. Thor had carefully avoided showing his hunger, in the vain hope the Pack might forget the rules and let him snack from Uncle Ted's feast. But Dad never forgot the rules. Everyone else in the Pack might forget or decide to forgo the rules at times, but not Dad.

And the rule was: Eat the Food in Your Dish First—Treats Later. As much as Thor wanted to skip the rule today, he felt a deep respect and admiration for Dad's unfailing adherence to rules. Dad was a good Pack Leader.

Mom and the kids were terribly lax compared to Dad, and not just with the rules. Sometimes they forgot to stock Thor's dog food, for example. Dad believed in getting a variety of canned foods for him, assuming (correctly) that dogs get bored with the same old stuff, just like humans. Knowing dry dog foods are generally better balanced than canned (but that dogs invariably prefer canned food), he made sure Thor got a different canned food each day, mixed with dry.

Only sometimes Thor ran out of canned food, and he got a full bowl of dry food instead. Thor hated that, but the Pack always made up for it by giving him extra leftovers after he finished his dry food.

On one such day, Thor got what he thought was a brilliant idea. His bowl was next to the clothes dryer in an alcove off the kitchen. The bottom of the clothes dryer was about an inch off the floor. Thor pushed the boring dry food out of his bowl with his nose and shoved it under the dryer. Then he pranced into the kitchen, where the Pack was finishing its dinner.

It was a good plan, but for one little problem. Thor's conscience. As he entered the kitchen, he couldn't pull his wagging tail up from between his hind legs. His ears refused to unflatten from his head, and his neck refused to hold his head high. Thor was a lousy liar.

As soon as Dad saw him, he knew something was up. Thor might as well have worn a neon sign saying, BAD DOG!

When Dad discovered what he'd done, he tried to be mad, but he was no better at acting angry than Thor was at acting innocent. He said all the right angry, scolding words, but laughter kept bursting out of him, completely spoiling the effect. Thor got off easy.

So he tried the trick a few more times. He got a little better at concealing his guilt, but never good enough to commit the perfect crime. Besides, after the first time (unknown to Thor), the Pack had learned to listen for the telltale scraping and rattling sounds he made as he nosed the kibbles onto the floor. He eventually gave up on the idea.

From then on, when the Pack fed him dry food by itself, he rebelled by refusing to eat it. At all. No matter how many treats were offered.

That strategy, although harder on Thor, worked better. The Pack's performance in the area of cuisine improved greatly.

Now, he knew, he'd have to eat his food before he got samples of Uncle Ted's cooking, but he didn't mind. The food was canned (they didn't bother lugging dry food along on trips), and Uncle Ted was a soft touch. Thor always gorged himself on treats at Uncle Ted's house.

Teddy opened a can of dog food and dumped it unceremoniously into Thor's bowl on the kitchen counter. He was about to put it on the floor when Dad stopped him.

"Teddy!" Dad said with a trace of annoyance, "Will you break that up, please?" Teddy had let the food stand in the bowl in a solid cylindrical mass, as if it had been squeezed out of a giant Chap Stick.

Teddy had begun to resent his share of the doggy chores, and he'd been making a point of doing things in the most perfunctory manner possible. Unfortunately for Teddy, he almost always got caught in the act and had to do everything over until it was done right. He only succeeded in making trouble for himself, but he always seemed to blame his problems on Thor.

Teddy made a big show of wearily lifting the bowl back onto the counter. He broke the food up into large chunks and gave the bowl a little contemptuous toss as he dropped it on the floor. Thor did his best to ignore Teddy's nonsense.

Surrounded by the Pack with his nose in his dish and his mouth full of beef and beef by-products, Thor didn't much care about anything. Not Teddy's attitude nor the required meal before snacks. The food was *his* food, after all, and his exclusive ownership of it compensated for its comparative lack of flavor.

No one else ate his food. The thought that the Pack might consider it beneath them never entered his mind. His bowl, his food. No one else's. A place for everyone, and everyone in their place. Very reassuring. He ate heartily and felt good.

When he finished, he walked casually to the kitchen table without once looking at it or anyone who sat there. He sat on the floor a few feet from the table, facing slightly away from the Pack, looking straight ahead at nothing. It was his way of making his presence known without being rude.

Uncle Ted and the Pack weren't even close to being finished (naturally). Dad told Thor to back off, but Thor knew better. He'd played out this scenario many times. He was within his rights.

"Oh, it's okay," Uncle Ted said, warming to the task at hand: Spoil the dog. "Here ya go!" Ted said, tossing a sliver of cooked meat in Thor's direction. Thor hadn't glanced toward the table the whole time, but his peripheral vision was precise. His head snapped around instantly and plucked the meat out of the air as if he'd been watching Uncle Ted's hands the whole time. He moved so fast that the motion was almost invisible—his head seemed to be in one place at one moment, then another the next. If a small dog had done it, it would have been impressive. But to see a dog of Thor's size and power move with such speed was absolutely awesome, even to the Pack. Thor was good, *damn* good, and watching him at his best was a little like watching a champion gymnast—no matter how many times you saw it, you could never quite believe your eyes.

Uncle Ted leaned over Thor with another piece of meat in his hand, not intending to throw this one.

"Here ya go," he repeated in a more subdued voice, expecting Thor to come over for it. Thor looked worriedly at Dad, who frowned and said, "Go ahead." Thor stretched his neck to reach the treat without moving from his polite seated position, and took the meat from Uncle Ted's hand with consummate delicacy.

He felt tension in Uncle Ted's bearing. The man's manner somehow reminded Thor of his own failed attempts at subterfuge. Uncle Ted offered Thor the treat the way a Bad man might—to establish a false friendship, to get Thor to drop his guard, to make Thor forget his Duty.

Thor boldly looked straight at Uncle Ted's face, ready to look away immediately when Uncle Ted returned his gaze, but to his surprise, Uncle Ted didn't look back. He certainly saw Thor staring at him, and each time he looked in Thor's general direction Thor began to turn his head away, but Uncle Ted never looked directly at Thor. Not for an instant. Thor found the experience strangely disorientating.

To look at someone in the eye is a statement of position. Thor looked at the kids eye-to-eye all the time; he outranked them. But for Thor to lock eyes with Dad would be a challenge to Dad's leadership. Thor could never conceive of doing such a thing.

Uncle Ted, on the other hand, wasn't a Pack member, but he *was* a Pack insider, and in a strange way, he both did and did not outrank Thor. Their relationship seemed to work itself out on a case-by-case, moment-to-moment basis. But Thor's immediate behavior was so challenging that it could only be regarded as insubordination, regardless of their unclear relationship.

And yet Uncle Ted refused to exercise his authority and put a stop to Thor's rudeness by looking back at him.

In a flash of recognition, Thor realized *Uncle Ted was behaving just like a Bad Dog.*

And he was avoiding Thor's gaze, *as if Thor were a human and Uncle Ted were a dog.*

Suddenly the room turned upside down. Everything stayed in place, but Thor *felt* it, the world was upside down, the ceiling was below him and he would fall into it at any moment! He tried to dig his claws into the slippery hardwood floor, and an involuntary whimper escaped his throat. Panic raced through his mind for an instant—then the bubble burst, and the room was right side up again.

Throughout the whole disconcerting experience, Thor never took his eyes off Uncle Ted's, and Uncle Ted never looked back. A convulsive shiver ran through Thor's body.

He made a decision: He would stay close to Uncle Ted for the rest of the visit, never leaving him alone with any Pack member.

And for the first time ever, he would be glad when the visit was over.

CHAPTER 6

THOR lay on the living room floor like a sphinx—head erect, paws straight ahead, still as a statue, waiting for the attack. Only his eyes followed the movements of the pure white ball of fur crouched on the rug about two feet from his head.

The kitten's eyes were locked on Thor's, her face a mask of psychotic concentration. Her body squirmed and twitched with barely controlled energy. Any second now, she would fling herself at Thor's head. If her attack was successful, she would wrap her legs around his face and cover his forehead with sharp, frenzied play-bites.

A passerby, unfamiliar with the two animals, would probably wonder what the dog had done to the tiny kitten to produce such passionate hatred, such a lust for revenge. In fact, he'd done nothing more than what he *was* doing—lying on the floor, providing a tempting target for her to attack. That alone was more than enough to drive the kitten over the edge.

The kitten had only been with the Pack a few months, about

as long as she'd been alive. Where she came from and how she joined the Pack had been intriguing mysteries at first, but Thor had long since forgotten the riddle of her origin. She was Pack now, and nothing else was really important.

Their game had evolved quickly once they'd established mutual trust. Thor had tried chasing her (the most basic kind of dog play), but without success: When he chased her in the open, he ran right over her in one or two strides, and when he chased her in the house, she scrambled under the nearest furniture and the chase was over. And Thor could see that she didn't *like* being chased.

But she liked to play, and she understood that Thor was trying to play with her, so she played with him on her terms, ambushing him from behind furniture. Thor loved it. He walked through the house slowly, stopping right in front of her hiding places, looking the other way and pretending not to know she was there. His invitations to attack were so obvious that she eventually got up the nerve to walk right up to him on the open floor and jump at his face, which was slightly bigger than her body.

To make it a fair fight, Thor opted to lie on the floor and not use his paws. It wasn't as much fun as chasing or being chased, but it was better than nothing. A lot better.

So he lay in wait, paws on the floor, while the kitten's energy reached the boiling point.

Thor vaguely understood that Kitty was Debbie's pet. It was always Debbie, and never Mom or Dad, who carried her around and petted her and fed her (with a little help from her brothers). Thor was a little unsure how a small child like Debbie could have her own animal, but it wasn't important. What was important was that Kitty's presence in the Pack had (thankfully) not affected Thor's status in any way, so there was no reason why they shouldn't get along.

He accepted her as part of the Pack, and they got along fine. If necessary, he would defend her to the death, as he would any Pack member.

Kitty tried to back a little deeper into her crouch, but there was nowhere left to go. She was already pressed flat against the carpeted floor, ready to catapult herself to the dog's face. Her ears flattened against her head and the intensity in her eyes reached pure madness. Whatever Kitty saw in front of her existed only in her blown-out imagination. Her body trembled as her tense muscles waited for the right moment, the moment when the dog would be most vulnerable.

Thor taunted her by tilting his head down until his nose touched the carpet, holding it vertical, like the cat's scratching post. A perfect landing pad for a flying kitty.

Come get me.

He peered up at the cat without lifting his face, like a schoolmarm looking over her reading glasses.

His mockery worked. The cat exploded.

She flew at Thor's head, covering the distance between them in an instant. Somehow during her short flight she managed to bring her legs forward, to wrap them around Thor's skull.

But Thor outmaneuvered her. The moment the furry white ball left the carpet, Thor jerked his face up in a sudden sweeping motion, so it was horizontal when Kitty reached it. He continued the upward sweep as her legs touched his face, and flung her over his shoulder and onto the carpet behind him.

Plop!

Thor hadn't really reacted to Kitty's attack—even *his* lightning reflexes weren't that fast—he'd anticipated it. He'd watched her intently, and made his move when his gut told him she was about to spring.

It was a good maneuver; it worked this time. It didn't always. Thor felt smug.

Kitty was furious. She scrambled into position for another attack.

Thor waited, mouth slightly open and curled at the corners in an unmistakable smile.

Kitty psyched herself up like an Olympic sprinter at the

starting line. Thor started to lower his head in the same mocking gesture, but Kitty surprised him. She shot at him as soon as he moved his face, anticipating *his* move this time.

Splat!

She wrapped her legs around his face as she landed, looking like the creature in the movie *Alien*.

Thor growled and twisted his head around, vainly trying to throw her off. If the attack was successful and he couldn't dislodge her, he could always wipe her off with one paw—and send her flying across the room in the process. She wouldn't mind; they both understood that when Thor used his paw, it meant Kitty had won.

But this time something went wrong.

As Kitty grabbed his face, the point of one needle-sharp claw narrowly missed Thor's eye and went into a tear duct. Both animals realized the problem immediately, but neither was sure what to do. Kitty tried to gently pull her claw away, but the hooked end refused to let go of the delicate tissue. Thor mewled in panic and she stopped. He couldn't wipe her off his face with the claw anchored in such a sensitive spot.

They sat perfectly still and Thor whined as loud as he could, calling for help from someone big, someone on two legs, someone who always knew what to do in difficult situations.

Mom heard Thor's cries from the kitchen and ignored them at first. Thor often complained loudly at the cat when they played. But when his whining grew desperate she went into the living room to investigate.

"Ouch!" Mom cringed when she saw them.

She knelt next to Thor and gripped the patch of skin around the tear duct in one hand and Kitty's paw in the other. Gingerly lifting the claw out like a fishhook, she removed it without harm.

Thor was so relieved that he jumped up and gave Mom a big wet one right on the mouth, just the way she didn't like them.

"Oh, *yuk!*" She wiped his saliva from her lips and sputtered like a cigar smoker trying to spit a piece of tobacco off the tip of his tongue. "Dumb dog!" she said, without real anger, and went back to the laundry.

Thor and Kitty picked up the game where they'd left off.

Thor looked away from Kitty, daring her to take advantage of his vulnerability, secretly watching in his peripheral vision for that last-minute squirm, the one that always came right before the pounce.

There it was!

He closed his eyes and ducked as Kitty flew overhead and skidded across his back. She tried to grab hold of his back, but her claws weren't long enough to penetrate the thick fur, especially at the speed she was doing.

She sailed over him and onto the floor with a dull *plop*.

Now she was *really* furious. She jumped onto Thor's head from behind and bit the skin behind his right ear, kicking his neck with her hind feet. Then, having asserted herself, she scampered down and got into position for another launch. That was cheating, of course, but Thor didn't mind. Her little bites and scratches felt kind of good.

Suddenly something distracted Thor. A feeling. He tilted his head slightly and listened intently. Nothing. Mom was doing laundry—nothing else was happening that he could tell. Without knowing why, he looked at the phone.

Something was coming. Something Bad. He remembered the feeling he'd had at Uncle Ted's, and suddenly felt the need to check on the Pack. He stood up abruptly, just as the cat leaped. He didn't even notice her attack until she crashed into his now-upright legs. The impact startled him a little, but he looked down and prodded the cat gently with his nose, gave her a lick, and went to the living room window.

The phone rang just as he hopped onto his lookout chair. He ignored the electronic chirping and peered out the window.

Whatever was coming was far away. Too far to see and too far to hear. Still, he watched the street for any sign of an approach. The thought of checking other windows never entered his mind. When the Bad Thing came, it would come by the road.

Mom answered the phone.

"Ted! How are you doing?"

Silence. Mom gasped.

"What? How far? When we were *there?* Oh my God!"

Silence again.

"So what do they think did it?"

Silence.

"What are they going to do?"

Silence.

"I understand. Of course. No, I wouldn't want to, either. Of course."

Silence.

"No, of course not, you know that. Do you need any help?"

Thor listened distractedly to Mom's distressed tone of voice, but his attention remained focused on the street. He was listening for something that made no noise. Not yet.

"Are you sure? Okay, if that's the way you want to do it. We'll see you then. And Ted . . . I don't want you to feel you're imposing on us, okay? Stay as long as you want, you're welcome here. Okay? Okay. See you then. Bye."

She put down the phone and sighed heavily. Her poor brother. What next?

At the window, Thor felt the Bad Thing pause in its advance.

It would not come today, but it was coming. Thor felt it.

Mom picked up the phone, poked it, and spoke briefly to Dad's secretary. Thor sat and watched the street until she went back to her laundry.

Thor resumed his watch at the living room window early that evening. He wished Dad would come home soon. He would feel much better with Dad home. Even more so than usual.

When Dad arrived he offered Thor only a perfunctory greeting and went straight into the kitchen to talk to Mom. Thor followed and quietly lay on the kitchen floor. The tension in the air was almost palpable.

"I got your message," Dad said. "What's this about a body?"

"A woman," Mom said. "A hiker. She was camping out on Skyline Trail last weekend, and she didn't show up on Monday. A search party found her body just below the trail, just off the path that connects Ted's property with the trail." Mom paused and took a deep breath. "Apparently, she was there while we were visiting Ted."

"Jesus!"

"Here's the weird part," Mom continued, "the coroner says she was killed by a wolf."

"What?" There hadn't been wolves within a hundred miles of Ted's house for decades, maybe more.

"Ted says the place is crawling with hunters. The sheriff's department and the forestry service have parties trying to find the wolf, and as he put it, 'Every jerk with a rifle is out there, shooting at anything that moves.' He says he's not afraid of the Big Bad Wolf, but he doesn't feel safe with the hunters. He wants to stay here for a while, until they kill it. I told him he could."

"So when is he coming?"

"Saturday."

"Does he need help moving?"

"He says he's just going to toss some essentials in boxes and leave everything else there—most of his stuff is already in storage. He's letting the sheriff's department use his house as a base of operations."

"He sure has a dark cloud following him, doesn't he?"

Mom said nothing.

Thor was disappointed. Mom and Dad's concerns were strictly for Uncle Ted; they didn't appear to know the Bad thing was coming.

He got up, walked back to the living room, and climbed into the lookout chair to watch the street and worry.

CHAPTER

7

THOR'S sense of foreboding steadily intensified over the next two days, and he became increasingly uneasy. He tried to conceal his anxiety from the Pack, but Mom saw it, and so did the kids.

It made Mom nervous to see him spending the bulk of the day in his lookout chair, staring out the window. Whatever he was waiting for, he wasn't looking forward to its arrival. At night, he listened more carefully to the footsteps of neighbors and strangers on the street, and barked at faraway sounds more often.

When the kids were home, he shadowed them. He tried to do it surreptitiously, tried to act casual and make it look like pure coincidence that he happened to be hanging out wherever they happened to be playing. He didn't want the Pack to see how worried he was.

Without realizing it, Mom began to mimic Thor's behavior: She kept the kids a little closer to home, paid more attention to people in the neighborhood, and picked up a habit of glancing out the living room window for—who knew what?

As Saturday approached, Mom's nerves got steadily worse. It didn't help to see Thor getting more nervous, too. She made up her mind that the whole thing was ridiculous, that *she* was the one who was imagining things, and the dog was probably just picking up on her irrational fears, caused by her anxiety over Ted. She resolved to ignore her misgivings, but it was easier to make the resolution than to keep it.

By Saturday, Thor was unbearably jumpy. Mom held her breath and watched him closely as Ted's car pulled up, and when Ted stepped out and Thor still scanned the street, she felt a great weight lift off her. Uncle Ted was *not* what Thor was watching for, after all.

Thor watched Uncle Ted's arrival with interest and confusion. Uncle Ted wasn't the Bad Thing he was waiting for; and yet, when Uncle Ted arrived, the Bad Thing's journey was also complete. The Bad Thing was no longer en route to the Pack, *and yet it wasn't here*. It was here and not here at the same time.

???????

Could Uncle Ted be the Bad Thing? Thor hopped off the lookout chair and paced from window to window as Dad and Uncle Ted got out of the car. He would give Uncle Ted a thorough sniffing as soon as he came through the door.

But when Uncle Ted entered the house, Thor knew immediately that he wasn't the Bad Thing. The Bad thing was closer, *much* closer, so close it might arrive at any moment—but it wasn't Uncle Ted. He ran back to the chair and urgently scanned the street. The Bad Thing might be across the street, hiding in the neighbor's shrubs, or it might be in a car about to turn the corner and pull up to the Pack's house, or it might sneak into the woods behind the house, waiting for nightfall. . . .

A hand touched Thor's back, startling him, and he wheeled around snarling, teeth bared, and snapped savagely at the air.

"Jesus!"

Thor was horrified by what he'd done. He'd gotten lost in thought, feeling the shapeless, nearby danger—and he'd snapped at Uncle Ted!

All thoughts of the Bad Thing left his mind as the enormity of his faux pas washed over him. Even showing teeth to a guest of the Pack's was forbidden; to snap was unthinkable.

Years ago, when Thor was full-size but still young and impetuous, Mom and Dad had thrown a party. Thor had never seen anything like it. The house was packed with strangers, and though Thor didn't know a single one of them, Mom and Dad appeared to be comfortable.

But Thor wasn't. The sheer size of the crowd made him nervous. And to make matters worse, there were people in the crowd who radiated untrustworthiness, and some who even struck him as downright malicious. One of the guests reached to pet him—one of the untrustworthy ones. Thor was not interested in developing a relationship with such a person, so he growled just loud enough for the creep to hear.

But Dad was standing right behind Thor, and he heard it too.

Dad quietly grabbed the loop in his choker and dragged him into the kitchen, to the cellar door. He opened the door and pushed Thor through. Only then, away from the guests, did Dad tell Thor he was a Bad Dog. Then he slammed the cellar door.

Thor spent hours at the top of the cellar stairs, mewling and whimpering through the door. But no one let him out or consoled him in any way. No one even stopped to listen to his pleas. It was as if he'd ceased to exist.

He was a Bad Dog, unfit to live with the Pack.

He worried for the Pack's safety with the untrustworthy guests, but he worried more about his own position in the Pack. What if they *never* let him out? What if he was banished from the Pack *forever*?

By the time the party was over, he'd been in a state of total panic for hours.

It was a terrible lesson he never forgot.

And now he'd not only growled at a guest, he'd snapped at Uncle Ted, Mom's own brother.

Dad spoke the awful words he knew were coming.

"Bad Dog!"

Dad picked up a newspaper, rolled it up, and slapped Thor hard on the snout. It stung his nose a little, but the pain was nothing compared to the effect of Dad's words. It was bad enough to snap in panic and discover he'd offended a Pack relative, but nothing was worse than Dad's disapproval.

"What's the matter with you?" Dad demanded angrily. He grabbed Thor's collar and dragged him off the chair and over to Uncle Ted. Thor crawled as close to the floor as he could and looked left and right as if for an escape route, as his tail wagged involuntarily. He didn't want to face Uncle Ted. He knew what he'd done. He was terribly ashamed of himself.

He wished he could make his tail stop wagging, but he couldn't even slow it down. The best he could do was restrain it a little, so it thumped the floor a little less loudly. His tail wasn't wagging from pleasure, of course—far from it. It was the intimacy of his engagement with Dad that made his tail move. For this awful moment, only he and Dad existed. There was a certain terrible excitement, almost a sexual feeling to the situation. As miserable as he felt, he almost got an erection.

Dad took Thor's head in one hand and held the choker collar in the other. He lifted Thor's face up to look at Uncle Ted. Thor tried to avert his eyes, but with his nose pointing directly at Uncle Ted's face, he couldn't avoid meeting Uncle Ted's disappointed gaze.

Dad slapped his snout with the newspaper and chanted: *"Bad! Dog! You understand me? Bad!* Don't you *ever!* do anything like that again, you *hear me?"* Thor trembled, but deep inside he was tremendously relieved. He knew this would be the limit of his punishment. He would not be exiled to the cellar.

His place in the Pack was not at risk.

Uncle Ted felt bad about Thor's predicament, but he knew better than to interfere in family affairs. He put on a sympathetic face for Thor's benefit, but Thor didn't see it—he was too ashamed to look.

When Dad finally finished scolding him, Thor was overcome with relief and a desire to make amends. He tried to kiss Dad's hands, still keeping his rump near the floor and his tail between his legs to show his contrition.

"Don't apologize to *me*," Dad said, pointing to Uncle Ted. "Tell *him* you're sorry!"

Thor understood immediately and turned to Uncle Ted, who turned out to be a much more receptive audience. Uncle Ted knelt down and stroked Thor's neck.

"That's okay, Thor," he said. "You're okay. You're a Good Dog."

Thor appreciated the sentiment, but he wondered how Uncle Ted could be so wrong on such an elementary point. Thor couldn't be a Good Dog and a Bad Dog at the same time. He was a Bad Dog until *Dad* said he was a Good Dog, and not before.

Feeling he'd done his duty to Uncle Ted, Thor turned again to Dad, and again tried to lick his hands. He dared not leap up for a face kiss before he was forgiven.

Dad was moved, but not very far.

"You gonna be a Good Dog?" he demanded. "Huh? Are you?" Thor answered by desperately kissing his hands. Dad accepted his answer. Almost. He wagged a finger reproachfully at Thor as he said, "You *better* be. Asshole."

Thor was back in the fold. He wasn't a Good Dog yet, but he wasn't a Bad Dog any more. He would be a Good Dog soon enough. He leaped once and kissed the corner of Dad's mouth.

"Stop it!" Dad said, annoyed but not angry. Dad opened the front door and pointed to the front yard.

"Go on out for a while, Stupid." Thor was more than happy to oblige.

The incident pushed the Bad thing out of Thor's mind, and it didn't return for the rest of the day. He retained a sense of increased caution, but nothing like the nerves he'd been experiencing for most of the week. It was as if the Bad Thing had come and gone.

Dad came out and moved his car into the garage so Ted could park his car under the staircase to the garage apartment.

Thor spent the rest of the afternoon watching Dad and Uncle Ted unload Uncle Ted's boxes and carry them up the stairs. He followed them up and sniffed at the contents of the open boxes as they put them down, then ran back down the stairs to watch them take more boxes from Uncle Ted's car.

Finally Uncle Ted got the last item, a suitcase. Dad sat at the top of the stairs, watching Uncle Ted lug the suitcase up with Thor at his heels. Mom stepped out of the kitchen with some beer cans in a plastic six-pack web.

"You guys look like you've earned a reward," she said, holding the six-pack up for their approval.

"Great!" Dad said. "Bring 'em up. I don't even want to walk down the stairs until I take a little breather!" Then, to Uncle Ted he said, "I thought you were only bringing a few essentials." Uncle Ted just laughed and pushed past Dad and disappeared into the apartment, followed closely by Thor.

Thor had picked up a surprising scent emanating faintly from Uncle Ted's suitcase: the scent of the Wild Animal. The smell sent a thrill through him; under normal circumstances he would have whined and poked his nose at the suitcase. But he restrained himself.

Uncle Ted was acting guilty, like a Bad Dog again, only much more so. And once again, no one else in the Pack seemed to notice. So Thor concealed his own emotions. No particular reason; it just felt like the right thing to do under the circumstances.

He watched Uncle Ted out of the corner of his eye, kept his distance, and tried to sniff and poke through his belongings as unobtrusively as possible.

And, though he would never know it, he was right to be surreptitious. If Uncle Ted had suspected that Thor smelled the Wild Animal in his belongings, he would never have let him near his things. As it was, Thor's subterfuge worked perfectly; Uncle Ted blithely tossed the suitcase on one of the two small beds in the apartment, and opened it with Thor standing no more than three feet away.

As he cracked the case, the smell of the Wild Animal wafted out, almost as strong as it had been near the woman's body. Uncle Ted lifted some clothes out and walked to a dresser opposite the bed, and Thor put his front paws on the bed and poked his nose deep into the suitcase, into the stifling, overwhelming odor of laundry detergent, looking for the source of the Wild Animal's scent. Uncle Ted turned around and saw what Thor was doing.

"Hey! Get out of there!"

Thor was almost there, almost to the source of the smell. He pushed aside clothes with his muzzle and uncovered the scent carrier just as Dad stepped forward. Thor jumped off the bed, withdrew to the door, and innocently sat down. He was eager to see the source of the scent, but he wasn't eager to get on Dad's bad side again.

He didn't miss much. If he had seen it, he wouldn't have known what it was.

But Tom saw the shiny police handcuffs in the bottom of the suitcase. They'd been hidden among Uncle Ted's underwear until Thor uncovered them.

For an instant, Tom had to stifle a laugh. He and Janet sometimes acted out harmless fantasies. Occasionally he tied her up, and would let Janet tie him up if she wanted to, but she didn't. He almost made a joke about it; then he remembered Uncle Ted's tragedy.

At a loss for words, he finally said, "Well." And then, "Thor, you've got to have more respect for Uncle Ted's privacy."

Of all the mementos to a lost love, Tom thought, *handcuffs are an awfully grotesque choice. No matter how innocently they might have been used.*

Thor watched Dad and Uncle Ted closely as they looked into the suitcase at the source of the scent. Their reactions would probably tell him more than seeing the thing firsthand.

Dad went through an unusual set of emotions; first amusement, then confusion, then embarrassment. And a faint shadow of guilt, too.

But the real show was Uncle Ted. His face, his hands, his whole body took on the heavy guilt of the Bad Dog again, much stronger than before. Dad saw it (for once!), but he didn't seem surprised or curious. He seemed more guilty himself for having noticed it.

Uncle Ted's Badness had become a cause for concern. It hadn't mattered much at Uncle Ted's house; the Pack was only visiting. But now Uncle Ted was living here (joining the Pack?) and he obviously planned to stay for a while. His Badness could not be ignored any more.

And then there was the smell of the Wild Animal; it reminded Thor of his feeling that something Bad was coming. The two seemed somehow connected. He wondered what Uncle Ted's connection with the Wild Animal could be. The scent only meant the two had made some kind of contact. The Wild Animal might have attacked Uncle Ted, or it might have entered his house while he was away, and left its scent on whatever was now in his suitcase. Uncle Ted might not even know the Wild Animal.

But that Bad-Dog look on Uncle Ted disturbed Thor deeply.

For the first time, Thor considered Uncle Ted a possible threat to the Pack.

But if Uncle Ted joined the Pack, what could Thor do, other than keep an eye on him?

CHAPTER

8

"WOULD you feed the dog, Ted?" Mom said, and quickly added, "*Little* Ted, I mean. And open a can of cat food for Debbie."

Teddy was once again stung by his new title, "Little." Thor saw how he hated it, but no one else in the Pack seemed to notice. Teddy did a fair job of hiding his feelings.

Thor wasn't confused by the similarity between "Uncle Ted" and "Teddy," but since Uncle Ted moved in, Mom and Dad started calling him "Ted." Even that wouldn't have been so bad if Teddy hadn't recently requested that he be called "Ted" instead of "Teddy." Of course, that was before Uncle Ted arrived, but now his new name caused problems. So Mom started calling them "Big Ted" and "Little Ted." Little Ted didn't complain much (not enough to make a difference), but he seethed inside, and this latest indignity seemed to make him more determined than ever to outrank Thor.

Thor was well versed in the myriad names the Pack used. The kids could be "kids," "children," "guys," or "brats" when they were bad (but not as bad as a Bad Dog—the kids were never that bad). Mom and Dad were also "Tom" and "Janet." Anyone in the Pack might be "Honey," if Mom was talking to them. Thor especially liked it when Mom called him "Honey." Her voice was indescribably sweet when she said it. Thor himself could be "Bozo," "Stupid," "Horse," or "Nose," in addition to his real name. He was proud of his nicknames. They meant nothing to him, except to remind him how well loved he was.

Sometimes when Mom and Dad were the only humans around, Mom wore a black nightie and Dad called her "Sweetcakes," and she called him "Sailor." Whenever they used those names, they either shut themselves in the bedroom and mated, or they shut Thor out in the backyard and mated in the living room or the kitchen, or wherever they happened to be. Afterward, Thor could smell what they'd done, even when they showered and the sickly perfume of soap masked the musky perfume of sex. And he smelled it in their bed, or on the kitchen table, or on the living room rug. And he could always spot that special contentment they felt afterward. The whole house was happier after they mated.

Thor was happier too, knowing they had reinforced their bonds, and were doing their Duty as the Pack's Mating Pair.

But for the moment, the only thing on Thor's mind was food. The heady bouquet of aromas from the Pack's dinner put a sharp edge on his appetite, and he waited impatiently for "Little Ted" to serve him his dinner. Dad was on his way into the kitchen, and "Big Ted" sat at the kitchen table, playing the part of the good brother, keeping Mom company. He was obviously going to eat with the Pack again, which Thor didn't like one bit. Every time Uncle Ted ate with the Pack, it brought him a step closer to Pack membership. He'd been here for days, and he still had the look of a Bad Dog. And Thor was still the only one who could see it.

A permanently Bad Dog in the midst of the Pack. At least he

didn't sleep with the Pack. It was bad enough that he slept in the Pack's territory.

Thor wanted Uncle Ted gone. He had to concentrate on protecting the Pack from the Bad Thing that was coming. He didn't need the distraction of Uncle Ted's guilty behavior, precisely because it *was* so distracting: He couldn't tear himself away from it. As long as Uncle Ted acted guilty around the Pack (and he only acted guilty around them, a bad sign in itself), Thor was stuck guarding two fronts. He could only hope that when the Bad thing arrived, Uncle Ted wouldn't be around.

To make matters worse, Uncle Ted appeared to notice Thor's surveillance. Uncle Ted seemed to understand Thor better than the rest of the Pack. On the rare occasions when he looked directly at Thor, it felt as if he looked *through* him, to see Thor's very thoughts. Thor found the sensation unnerving. Thor and Uncle Ted went about their business as if they were invisible to everyone else in the Pack, Thor secretly watching Uncle Ted, Uncle Ted hiding his guilt from everyone but Thor, and secretly watching Thor.

Uncle Ted had been doing things in the night, too.

Thor stood watch at the kitchen window long after the Pack was asleep, listening to the sounds in the garage. He heard Uncle Ted cry out in his sleep and he heard him talk to himself when he was awake. Occasionally, Thor heard the metallic *clink* of handcuffs locking shut, though he had no idea what the sound was. Thor took to sleeping in the kitchen, as close to the garage as possible.

And now Uncle Ted was sitting with the Pack again, about to have another meal, further solidifying his position within the Pack.

Uncle Ted didn't go to work, like Dad; he was around all the time. Thor didn't like that either. If anyone should be around all the time, it should be Dad. Who did Uncle Ted think he was?

Teddy finally finished with the dog food and opened a can

of cat food for Debbie. Kitty was Debbie's pet, but Debbie couldn't handle the can opener yet, so she did what she could—she spooned Kitty's food into her dish and put the dish on the floor for her. Teddy gave Thor his food, and he began to chow down as Mom herded the rest of the Pack into the kitchen for dinner. Debbie carefully put Kitty's cat food on the floor about ten feet away from Thor. Thor issued a low, whining growl, just to remind Kitty whose food was whose.

He'd had a problem with the cat over food a few days before Uncle Ted arrived, and the memory still rankled him. It had worked out all right (no thanks to Dad), but it was most unpleasant while it lasted.

The Pack kept the dog food and cat food together in a kitchen cabinet under the sink. The cabinet doors were held shut by magnets, not latches, and the kitten, in her tireless search for small, dark places to explore, had discovered she could pull the cabinet door open with her paw. She grabbed the edge of the door and pulled, and the cabinet opened about a half inch before slamming shut again. She repeated the operation twice before she swung it far enough to stay open. The noise brought Thor into the kitchen just as she disappeared into the cabinet. Thor was aghast. He ran to the open cabinet and barked at the trespassing cat. Kitty had no idea why he barked. She backed deeper into the cabinet.

Thor lost it. The cat was cringing between his food cans! What if she opened them and ate his food! Something had to be done! He growled at her to get out, but she just scrunched herself deeper into the corner.

Thor's mind swam in confusion. If the cat weren't a Pack member, he'd simply kill her—no problem. Kitty might get in one or two painful scratches, but she would be dead before she could do serious harm.

But the cat *was* a Pack member. Violence was not an option.

Thor whimpered and whined, hoping Mom or Dad would hear him and come punish the cat for its criminal behavior.

Nothing happened. He tried growling at the cat again, but the cat (who was just starting to relax) shrank back at the sound of the warning.

There was only one thing to do.

He stuck his head into the cabinet, turned it sideways, and gently took one of his dog food cans in his teeth. Then he backed out, walked across the kitchen, and put the can on the floor at the farthest point from the cabinet, whimpering for help the whole time.

He returned to the cabinet and Kitty was still inside, still threatening the security of his food. He tried growling again (what else was there?), and the kitten dug in. He switched from growling to whining as he lifted the next can of dog food out.

He repeated the process about four times before Dad came in to find out what all the fuss was about.

At first, Dad couldn't figure out what was going on. He watched Thor remove a can, then looked in the cabinet to see what Thor was growling at. When he realized what was happening, instead of helping Thor, he fell on the floor laughing.

Thanks a lot, Dad!

Dad watched Thor empty the entire cabinet of dog food, a can at a time. Thor then removed a box of dog biscuits with extra care (but still managed to spill some on the floor). He growled extra loud as he went back to pick up the precious biscuits and drop them on the floor next to the box and the cans.

Dad finally intervened, but only after Thor had cleaned out all the cat food cans and started on the people food on the shelf above. Thor had looked to Dad the whole time, imploring him to step in and end this awful situation, but Dad just laughed. When Dad finally took action, it wasn't to help Thor, but to stop him from removing the Pack's food. He shooed Thor away and pulled the cat from the cabinet, then put the dog biscuits back in their box, and the box and cans back in the cabinet.

The very next day, Thor was distressed to discover the cat inside the cabinet again. But after a few replays of the incident (the kitten never did understand what was happening—she just enjoyed opening the cabinets and sneaking in), Dad got some tools from the cellar, worked on the cabinet for an hour or so, and domestic tranquillity was restored. Once again, only humans could open the door to the dog food cabinet. Thor's faith in Dad's leadership was restored.

Thor finished his dinner and strolled over to the kitchen table to see what treats he might pick up—and to watch Uncle Ted. As he approached the table, without warning, Uncle Ted tossed him a scrap of meat.

Thor was startled by the sudden move, but his reactions were up to it. He lunged, snapping it out of the air flawlessly. His performance was awe inspiring, as always.

He hoped it would demonstrate to Uncle Ted the foolishness of contemplating any Bad behavior toward the Pack.

"My watchdog," Uncle Ted said sardonically.

"He's not your dog!" Debbie objected. "He's *our* dog!"

Uncle Ted laughed ruefully. "Oh, I know honey. That's not what I meant. He's your watchdog because he watches *for* you. But he *watches* me."

Dad looked at Mom quizzically. Mom gave him a look that said, "I'll tell you later."

Thor ignored the conversation. He could see there were no more treats forthcoming (the Pack was still eating, and except for Uncle Ted's oddball behavior, treats came after dinner only). He made himself comfortable on the tile floor, facing slightly away from the dinner table, slightly away from Uncle Ted, but keeping an eye on both.

CHAPTER

9

Dusk.

Uncle Ted had been living with the Pack for almost a month now, and Thor was miserable. His relationship with Uncle Ted, once his favorite relative, could best be described as a truce, and Thor didn't have the slightest idea why.

Dad still wasn't aware how deep the tension between them ran, but he knew something was wrong. Mom was painfully aware, but for reasons she didn't understand, she hadn't spoken to Dad about it. Thor was aware of Mom's discretion and felt tremendously grateful to Mom for it, but like her, he wasn't sure why. He had no idea what was happening. He only knew that the longer Uncle Ted stayed, the less Thor trusted him.

And it wasn't just his feelings toward Uncle Ted that confused him; his feelings about *himself* were changing.

He used to enjoy the clicking sound his claws made on the tiled kitchen floor and the hardwood floor in the dining room. Now he hated it. It announced his every move, and made it difficult to shadow Uncle Ted without being obvious. And

Thor's constant pacing from room to room was getting on Mom's nerves. Thor didn't like being a source of annoyance, but what could he do?

He did what he *had* to do. He did his Duty. He kept an eye on Uncle Ted. He paced nervously when he was stuck inside the house, and on the rare occasions when Uncle Ted wasn't on Pack territory, he sat in the lookout chair, staring at the street.

And now Uncle Ted was doing something at night; something more than just rattling around in his apartment.

He'd been getting more active every night for days, more fidgety toward sundown, and more eager to get away from the Pack before dark.

And every night Thor felt the Bad Thing come closer. The Bad Thing was always out there somewhere during the day, but it was very close at night. In the last few nights the Bad thing was not only closer, it was bigger and stronger. Thor hadn't slept at night for the last three days, and his daytime naps were so long and constant that Dad was getting worried about his health.

He wouldn't sleep tonight either. Tonight, the Bad Thing was so near, Thor almost thought he could smell it. Tonight, Thor was frantic.

Uncle Ted had retired to his apartment at sundown, then left his apartment just after the sky became dark, as the kids were bedding down, and Mom and Dad watched the TV in their bedroom.

He walked down the stairs quietly, surreptitiously, and he glanced back at the house as he went. Thor pulled away from the window and into the shadows of the kitchen as Uncle Ted looked in his direction, but he knew Uncle Ted had seen him. It didn't matter; Uncle Ted didn't have to catch Thor in the act to know he was under surveillance. They both knew their parts in this little play.

Uncle Ted walked quickly into the woods behind the house, wearing clothes Thor had never seen before: a sweatshirt, sweatpants, and running shoes. Something at his waist glinted in the moonlight; the handcuffs. Thor made a mental note of the sound they made: the distinctive, high-pitched jingle of metal on metal.

Thor watched him disappear into the woods as the moon began to rise. The moon had been getting brighter lately, and once it cleared the horizon, Thor would be able to see almost as well as if it were daytime. Thor's night vision was far superior to a human's.

But light or no light, once Uncle Ted disappeared into the woods, Thor had no way of knowing where he was or what he was doing. He didn't like it. He paced nervously from window to window, watching for Uncle Ted. Uncle Ted might circle back and approach the house from any angle.

Thor *woofed* quietly to himself. He'd learned, painfully, to refrain from barking at night. In the last few days, Uncle Ted had emerged from the apartment almost every night, always just as the sun was going down, and after the Pack was in bed. Each time, Thor had felt the Bad Thing come closer, *much* closer, as if Uncle Ted were calling it. Each time, Thor had sounded a warning, and each time Thor had been punished when it was discovered that the intruder was only Uncle Ted, going for a walk.

So he *woofed* to himself when he saw Uncle Ted leaving, and he *woofed* to himself in frustration when he couldn't see where Uncle Ted went.

But now he *woofed* to himself for another reason.

The Bad Thing was here.

It was no longer here-and-not-here, it was *here*. *Now*. He could feel its presence in the woods behind the house. It had finally arrived. An unusual emotion passed through Thor, one he almost never felt: fear.

He mentally shrugged it off, and it was gone. But for a moment it had really shaken him.

Thor stared out the window at the forest, where he knew

the Bad Thing was. His hair was high on his back and a low growl rumbled in his throat.

He saw nothing.

But something was happening.

Something not good. The Bad Thing was out there, and it wanted to get at the Pack. He felt its evil as strongly as he felt the Pack's love, and he couldn't keep silent any longer.

He barked as loud as he could, steadily, relentlessly, determined to wake the whole Pack. They were all in terrible danger.

"What the *hell!*" Tom said angrily. He'd just been drifting into a pleasant dream when the barking woke him. "That damn dog!" He listened for a moment until he was sure it wasn't going to stop, then *really* cursed as he threw off the sheets.

"Don't assume," Janet said quietly. She wasn't angry like Tom; she was frightened.

"What's that supposed to mean?"

"It means remember the boy who cried wolf," Janet said. "We don't know what he's barking at, so let's find out first. Okay?"

"Okay," he said. "I'll find out what's up first, *then* I'll kill him." He heaved himself out of bed, wrapped his wife's bathrobe around himself, and trudged off to find out what was freaking out the damn dog *this* time. But on the way down the stairs, the urgency of the barking got to him, and he found himself seriously considering what Janet had said, and wondering if he shouldn't have some sort of weapon.

Thor's barks bounced off the hard kitchen walls and floor like a sledgehammer. He stood with his front feet on the kitchen door, watching the woods as he repeated his warning to whatever was out there. He barked so loud he didn't even hear Dad come down the stairs. But he felt the vibration of Dad's heavy steps on the dining room floor, and he darted to the kitchen door to meet him, glad to have finally wakened someone who could open a door.

But Dad wasn't glad to see him.

"Be quiet!" he shouted, barely audible over the constant barking. Dad squinted through the kitchen window at the moonlit backyard and the woods beyond, and saw nothing.

But Thor refused to stop. The danger in the woods was far more important than mere disobedience. He dashed to the back door, put both paws up, looked through the glass, and barked to show Dad where the problem was.

"Be quiet!" Dad said again. His open hand came down hard on Thor's rump. Thor got down off the door, feeling bad about his disobedience, but the sense of urgency refused to go away. He stood his ground on the kitchen floor, looked straight at Dad, and barked at him.

The Pack is in danger!

Dad bent down to grab the loop in Thor's choker collar, but Thor backed away, stood his ground, and continued to bark.

A look of concern crossed Dad's face and he looked out the window again. Still he saw nothing. By now, Mom, Teddy, and Brett were on the stairs. Teddy and Brett were excited, as if they were going to a new Spielberg movie. Mom was terrified.

"Don't you go down there!" Mom told the kids. Brett stopped on the landing, but Teddy, as if imitating Thor, ignored her and kept going.

Dad wasn't sure what to do. This, after all, was one of the reasons he got the dog: to guard the family. But from what? Was Thor losing it? He looked out the window again, pondering the wisdom of letting the dog out. He decided to try silencing him once more.

"Bad Dog!" he shouted angrily, and walked to the cellar door, opened it and pointed in. "Get in there! *Bad Dog!*" Thor stood his ground and barked, then ran to another window, away from his angry master. He barked more warnings to the thing in the woods, looking over his shoulder at the family that

refused to take him seriously. His throat was beginning to feel sore.

"All Right!" Dad yelled over the din. He opened the kitchen door wide. "Go on! Get out!" Thor dashed for the opening, running low to avoid letting Dad snag his collar as he went by. And in fact, Dad tried to do just that. Thor had seen his intentions as clear as day, but it didn't matter now.

He was out, and the only thing that mattered was finding and neutralizing the threat to the Pack.

Thor charged across the cool, silvery, moonlit grass, leaped the little creek that separated the yard from the woods, and vanished into the trees. As he reached the point where he last saw Uncle Ted, he slowed to a fast trot, found his scent trail, and followed. It wasn't hard. The scent trail was strong with Uncle Ted's sweat, and strong with Uncle Ted's fear.

The woods were dark, much darker than the yard. The moon was still low in the sky and very little moonlight penetrated. The shadows were deep and dangerous.

From time to time the sound of a twig snapping or a leaf rustling in the shadows made him stop, head and ears erect, ready for action. But the noises were just small animals; the Bad Thing was still in the distance. He pushed ahead and tried to ignore all but the most distant sounds.

Uncle Ted's scent trail followed a well-worn jogging path, but there were loads of small side paths running off the main trail. The small paths often ran under the branches of tall bushes, resembling tunnels through the foliage more than paths. They frequently led into large clusters of bushes that hid small clearings in their midst. Kids used these natural hideouts for all sorts of things; like smoking cigarettes and stashing girlie magazines. Thor had investigated plenty of them. He could run through them like a bullet in the daytime, but at night their shadows were too deep for even his eyes to penetrate well. Fortunately, Uncle Ted's trail didn't take a side path. He was too tall for them.

But Uncle Ted had a long head start. Thor had hoped to

catch up with him right away, but the man was nowhere to be seen or heard. Could Uncle Ted have run through the forest in the dark? It didn't seem possible. Even Thor risked spraining or breaking an ankle if he ran too fast.

Thor picked up his pace until he was trotting as fast as he could without losing the scent trail. The trail left the familiar jogging path that ran along the edge of the woods, and turned in toward the forest's interior. Soon he was a quarter mile from the house, in unfamiliar territory, much farther than he thought the chase would take him. The new surroundings sent another surge of adrenalin through him that mingled with the exhilaration of exercise, anticipation—and a touch of fear.

He both did and did not look forward to a confrontation with the Bad Thing. He knew the Bad Thing was a danger to himself as well as to the Pack, and he sensed that the meeting would be extremely dangerous, and yet the thought of fighting the Bad thing aroused him.

At long last, he would fulfill his destiny and use his formidable strengths and skills to do his born Duty: Protect the Pack.

He didn't fear danger nearly as much as he feared failure.

Uncle Ted's fear-laced scent led him another quarter mile into the woods, where it began to fade and another scent gradually took its place—the scent of the Wild Animal. Thor slowed down to check it out, but before he learned anything, a noise up ahead startled him.

It was a violent thrashing sound, accompanied by a low, angry growl. He knew immediately, deep in his gut, that it was the Bad Thing he'd dreaded for so long.

Thor stopped dead in his tracks and came to attention like a pointer. He held his head high and trained his ears in the direction of the sound. Nothing. He scanned the landscape for similar sounds from other directions. Nothing. If whatever made the noise heard Thor coming, it could try to circle around him.

Then the sound came again, from the same direction. The foliage around him muffled the noises, so he went to the nearest tree and stood on his hind legs with his front paws high on the trunk to give himself some altitude.

From his improved vantage point, he pinpointed the direction of the sounds. A struggle of some sort was going on, but it was stationary, and only seemed to involve one animal. Through the dark web of leaves and branches, he caught sight of movement in the distance. Something was shaking violently, apparently attacking a tree. Thor hopped down and cautiously crept toward the commotion.

His blood was charged with adrenalin, and the fur on his shoulders and neck stood high. He padded quietly toward the noise with his body close to the ground. His ears wanted to flatten against his head in the presence of danger, but he held them up through force of will. Crouched down as he was, he couldn't see more than a few feet ahead. He couldn't afford to miss sounds in the dark.

The closer he came to the noise, the more he felt danger, and the more cautiously he proceeded. He was not there out of curiosity or a sense of adventure. He was there to defend the Pack; he could not defend the Pack if he was dead.

Thor was well acquainted with ambushes. When he was a puppy, Teddy and Brett had played a game in which Brett jumped up and down on his bed, calling Thor and teasing him. When Thor ran into Brett's bedroom, Teddy sprang out from behind the door and tried to catch Thor's head in a pillowcase.

The game only worked once—Thor was a quick study. It had been years since they'd tried to ambush him like that, but Thor hadn't forgotten.

He picked up Uncle Ted's scent again as he crept toward the Bad Thing. It was disturbingly faint, and seemed to go straight to the Bad Thing. Thor thought Uncle Ted must have gone somewhere else, but when he tried to find where Uncle Ted's scent left the path, he came up empty. The fading scent on the path was the only trail. It didn't make sense.

As Uncle Ted's scent faded, the scent of the Wild Animal

(which he now knew was the Bad Thing) got stronger. It was as if Uncle Ted had faded away and the Bad thing had gradually appeared out of nowhere to take his place. The abnormality of the situation frightened Thor in a way that was unlike any fear he'd known before. It was not fear of death or injury or pain, nor fear for his own well-being or even the well-being of the Pack. A silent voice deep inside him seemed to say that what lay ahead was *wrong*. It was too strange, too different. More different than birds or cars or telephones or all the other strange things in the world.

It didn't belong here. Or anywhere else.

Fear heightened Thor's attention to his surroundings, and he noticed for the first time there were no other sounds around him—at all. Small animals in the woods always made sounds, night or day. Even if they weren't nocturnal animals, they often scooted out of their hiding places when Thor passed by a little too close for comfort. He'd heard them tonight when he first entered the forest. Field mice, birds, possums—they all made noise as they fled Thor's approach. But not here, not now. It was as if Thor and the Bad Thing had the forest all to themselves. As if all the other animals had felt the strange new fear Thor felt, but unlike Thor, they had no Duty to perform. Their instincts told them only to flee.

Thor continued his approach, inches at a time, as the Bad Thing struggled in place. If the Bad Thing broke and ran, Thor would give chase, but as long as it stayed put, there was no reason for Thor to announce his presence by charging in.

He was about fifty feet from his quarry when the underbrush gave way to a small clearing, and he got his first real look at the Bad Thing.

Every hair on Thor's body stood on end. The Bad Thing, whatever it was, was hideously unnatural. It smelled like a dog, but it was not a dog. It was taller, longer, bigger than a dog, and its body was not a dog's body. Covered with fur, it stood upright on its hind legs, with its front legs wrapped around a tree trunk, held together by Uncle Ted's handcuffs.

123

It wore Uncle Ted's sweatpants and the ragged remains of his sweatshirt, and a small metal object dangled from a shiny chain around its neck. It had torn away as much of the sweatshirt as it could reach with its sharp teeth and the two grotesquely long fangs that protruded from its mouth. What remained of the sweatshirt lay limp and tattered around its waist. Its face, though covered with fur, was human-shaped—its mouth and nose were separate structures, not a snout.

Its fangs were sharp and long and dangerous-looking. It had been trying to cut through the tree trunk with them, and had gnawed a big hunk out of the tree before giving up on the idea.

The Bad Thing hadn't seen Thor yet, though Thor had a feeling it knew he was near. Thor backed slowly, silently, into the surrounding bushes and circled around it from behind the cover of low-lying foliage. He carefully worked his way through the forest until he was behind the Bad Thing, then edged in for a closer look.

Fortunately, the Bad Thing was chained to the lone tree in the clearing, and the full moon, now high in the sky, beamed down on it like a spotlight. The Bad Thing's attention seemed torn between the moon and the handcuffs that bound it. It struggled for a while, got tired, and gazed upward. Thor kept expecting it to bay at the moon, but it didn't. Instead it glowered at the moon, its face a picture of hate. The only sound that came from it was the same constant low growl Thor had heard in the distance.

Thor was almost directly behind the Bad Thing, but not quite. He'd chosen an approach that kept the handcuffs in his line of sight. He wasn't at all sure he could kill the Bad Thing if it got free. He smelled something in the undergrowth as he advanced, and stopped to check it out. Uncle Ted's sneakers lay on the ground. They smelled of Uncle Ted and the Bad thing.

Had Uncle Ted tried to put them on the Bad Thing, as he had his sweatpants and shirt? Why? And where *was* Uncle Ted?

The questions passed through his mind and were forgotten, and he turned his attention back to the beast on the tree.

He crept to within a few yards of the Bad Thing when it heard him and snapped its head around to see the interloper.

At the sight of Thor, the Bad Thing flew into a mad rage. Thor tensed and bared his teeth, ready to fight, but the handcuffs held—the Bad thing couldn't attack. Instead, it twisted itself around the tree to face him, snarling, growling, pulling at the handcuffs and snapping at the air the whole time. The Bad Thing's fury made it foam slightly at the mouth, and despite its helpless state, it showed no fear, only rage. It was acting like a small dog on a leash, but with a big difference: It wasn't faking anger or hiding fear. Its rage, its hate, were completely genuine. It wasn't afraid; it gave off no scent of fear. Even helpless, locked to the tree, it wanted Thor to come closer, wanted any opportunity to try to kill him.

It was utterly mad.

Their eyes met, and Thor froze. The Thing's eyes were neither canine nor human, but resembled both. It looked straight into Thor's eyes, and Thor looked back as he would never look at a human. Its eyes seemed to beckon to Thor. They bore an invitation to join the Bad Thing in its wildness, in its freedom, in its madness. To enjoy the taste of blood and the smell of death, to revel in the power each of them possessed in such abundance—the power to kill.

Thor had never killed. He'd never experienced the godlike rush of triumph as a victim's struggles ceased between his jaws, the smell of the prey's blood filling his nostrils. But the Bad Thing's eyes seemed to tell him just how good it felt, to mock him for his unfulfilled destiny, to draw him into its circle of madness and bloodlust.

Something deep inside Thor told him this seduction was wrong. Wild or domestic, wolves do not kill for pleasure. They kill for food, and they fight to defend their packs, but even when a pack's existence is at stake, they fight until the enemy is vanquished and almost always allow the defeated enemy to escape with its life. The Bad Thing's lust to kill was without purpose, without design or reason. It wanted to kill only for the love of killing.

And yet its gaze, its bloodlust, its fury were so *appealing*. It offered freedom from all hierarchy, freedom from all rules and laws, freedom to run wild, even wilder than wolves.

Thor and the Bad Thing stood motionless, eyes locked. Thor's mind swam with intoxicating images of blood and strength and triumph and death.

Until a far-off sound distracted him.

From hundreds of yards away, the shrill voice of Thor's dog whistle called to him in the forest, and the strange sensations vanished, washed away in a flood of reality.

The Bad Thing's bloodlust was without focus or purpose or meaning; given the chance, the Bad Thing would gleefully kill the entire Pack. And if Thor were to surrender to its bloodlust and join it, he would, too. A wave of guilt and revulsion washed over him, and the curiosity and fear Thor had felt toward the Bad Thing were replaced by white-hot hate.

Thor barked savagely, furiously at the Bad Thing.

And heard an unexpected response in the distance.

"Thor! Here, Thor!"

It was Dad, and he was coming closer, homing in on Thor's barks. The Bad Thing heard Dad and turned to look in the direction of the house. Its eyes gleamed with an insane lust that sent a ripple of unnatural terror through Thor. But he stood his ground and barked, and didn't attack.

As dangerous as the Bad Thing might be, it was clearly helpless, and a helpless animal is not a threat. All Thor's defensive instincts were geared toward attacking an *active* threat, not a potential one. There was nothing in this bound creature that invited attack.

Besides, Dad was coming. Dad would know what to do.

Thor barked steadily, as he had in the kitchen, announcing the presence of danger and telling Dad which way to come.

"Thor! Get over here!" Dad was too far away to see the Bad

Thing, and he wasn't coming any closer. Thor turned around to bark at him.

You come here!

"Thor! Dammit, *get over here! Now!"*

Dad's voice was a mixture of fear and anger. Thor was torn between obedience and Duty, but his Duty wasn't clear in this situation.

The Bad Thing growled in anticipation of Dad's arrival, but Dad either couldn't hear it or didn't care. Or maybe he did hear it, and that's why he kept his distance.

"Get over here!"

Thor knew he was on the brink of being a Bad Dog. It was a line he didn't want to cross.

Snarling and showing his teeth to the Bad Thing, he circled it cautiously and started back toward Dad, glancing over his shoulder at the nightmarish creature as he left.

The Bad Thing snarled back at first, but when it saw that Thor was leaving, it exploded. It opened its mouth wide, showing its teeth, and issued a loud, voiceless, hateful hiss. It thrashed its head and shoulders from side to side in mindless fury, frantically trying to break the handcuffs or the tree trunk itself. The handcuffs bit into its wrists and it attacked the tree trunk with its teeth again. It took as much of the trunk into its jaws as it could, then lifted its hind legs and kicked against the tree like a cat. Thor stopped for a moment to watch its maniacal display and see if it might break free after all, but the tree trunk held. The Bad Thing would not escape.

"Thor!"

Thor turned toward his Pack Leader, still worried for the safety of the Pack, but unable to disobey any longer. He trotted briskly through the dark to the distant flickering flashlight beam, trying to make up for lost time.

He approached Dad deferentially, head, ears, and body low, tail wagging apologetically between his legs. Dad stood waiting for him in Mom's bathrobe and slippers, hands on his hips, the leash dangling from his wrist.

Thor glanced over his shoulder. The Bad Thing was too far away to be seen. If only he could show Dad . . .

"Get over here!" Dad said again. He was furious. Thor was in Big Trouble. He nearly crawled to his leader, and when Dad bent down to put on the leash, he cowered as if he expected to be hit. But when Dad grabbed his collar and held it in place for the leash clasp, Thor noticed his hand was trembling. Dad acted angry, and he was—but he was also afraid.

Thor's heart sank. There was no chance of showing Dad the Bad Thing; Dad didn't want to see it. That was why he'd hung back and called Thor from a distance.

Dad gave the leash a sharp jerk and started off toward the house. Thor knew better than to resist. Behind them in the woods, faint sounds of the Bad Thing's struggle filtered through the forest.

Thor sniffed the air as they walked back to the house. At the spot where Dad was waiting, the Bad Thing's scent was barely detectable. A few yards closer to the house the scent vanished completely, replaced by the ever-strengthening scent of Uncle Ted. As always, Dad was totally oblivious to the scents. Even if Dad had a real nose like Thor's, his head was much too high to follow the trails.

Did Dad know Uncle Ted was out there somewhere? If so, he didn't seem to care. Dad and Thor were about a half mile from the house, and the Bad Thing had never come near the Pack. Was Thor crazy to go so far to meet a potential enemy? The closer they got to home, the less afraid Dad became, and the more Thor doubted his own judgment.

Maybe Dad was right. Maybe the Bad Thing was too far away to pose a threat. Maybe Thor had wakened the Pack for no reason. He began to feel that awful Bad Dog feeling. But his instincts still told him the Pack was in danger.

He felt miserable; guilty for having been disobedient, guilty for waking the Pack in the night, guilty for dragging Dad into the woods for nothing. And guilty for not protecting the Pack.

For not killing the Bad Thing when he had the chance.

He almost wished Dad would punish him, to cleanse him of his guilt, but he dreaded punishment. He dreaded Dad's anger and the possibility of losing Dad's love more than anything else. But if he were punished, Dad wouldn't be mad at him anymore. If he were punished, Dad would love him again.

Halfway back to the house, Thor noticed the occasional sounds of small animals scurrying away as he and Dad approached. They were no longer alone in the woods with the Bad Thing. They were in safe territory. Dad's nerves seemed to quiet down, too. The leash no longer transmitted tremors or twitches from Dad's hand. But he didn't slow down; he was understandably eager to get back to the house, back to his warm bed.

They emerged from the forest and crossed the little creek into the backyard. Dad walked straight toward the house, ignoring Uncle Ted's scent trail as it veered away toward the garage. It was the trail Uncle Ted had left when he went into the woods. Uncle Ted hadn't come home. Thor glanced up at the apartment windows above the garage. The lights were on, just as they had been when Uncle Ted left.

Dad gave the leash an angry jerk as they approached the back door, and pulled it as Thor climbed the stairs. The moment of truth was approaching. Once inside, Thor would face judgment. He wished he could sink into the kitchen floor and vanish.

They entered the kitchen and Dad closed the door behind him. Dad unhooked the leash from Thor's collar, and Thor slinked into the farthest corner of the room, which also happened to be the farthest corner from the cellar door.

Dad walked over and squatted down, then lifted Thor's jaw in his hands to make Thor look at his face. Thor's nose pointed directly at Dad's, but his eyes refused to meet Dad's. He felt extremely uncomfortable. It was not his place to look Dad in the eye.

"Just what the fuck is wrong with you?" Dad said with equal parts of anger and curiosity. Thor had no answer.

"I want you to *be quiet!* Understand?"

Thor wanted to be quiet, wanted to be a Good Dog. But what could he do if the Bad Thing came back? Dad didn't want to punish Thor, but his demands for obedience left him in the same quandary as before. Thor almost *wanted* to go to the cellar, just to absolve himself of this whole mess. Almost, but not quite. He couldn't imagine being so bad that he would *want* to go to the cellar.

He just wanted to lie in the corner and feel miserable for as long as it took for this incident to blow over.

But Dad had other ideas.

He dragged Thor by his collar to the cellar door, opened it, and pushed his nose into the opening.

"You *be! quiet!* or you're going into the CELLAR! You understand me?" Thor trembled violently. He got the message; this was his last warning.

Dad let go of the collar and closed the cellar door. Thor thumped his tail loudly on the floor and licked Dad's hands in thanks for his reprieve.

Normally, Dad would have forgiven him. He would have patted his head and repeated his warning without anger, then gone to bed. But this time he didn't. He was still angry. He stood up, not allowing Thor to make amends, wagged his index finger at him sternly, and repeated his orders.

"Be *quiet!* Got it?" Thor half-leaped to kiss his hand. "You *better* be good, dammit," Dad said, and turned to go to bed. Thor watched him walk to the kitchen door, waiting for him to pass through before leaving the kitchen himself. But Dad didn't let him.

"No!" he said. "You're staying in here tonight. And if you're not quiet, you're going in the CELLAR." He pulled the kitchen door closed behind him and snapped the latch shut, and Thor's fate was sealed for the night. He wasn't in the cellar, but he wasn't allowed to be with the Pack, either. It was a kind of halfway house, a purgatory. He slinked back to his corner and lay down, defeated.

Sleep was out of the question.

He spent the rest of the night with his front paws crisscrossed under his jaw, staring at the glass window in the back door, listening for unusual sounds from the woods. About a half hour before sunrise, his feelings about the Bad Thing began to fade. As the sky began to lighten, his gut told him the danger had passed. For the moment at least, the Pack was safe.

As the sense of menace faded, sleep settled over his thoughts like a warm blanket. He slept for two hours before the sound of Mom coming downstairs woke him. Thor was desperately tired, but he had to go jogging with Mom. He could never again let her go into the woods alone.

As tired as he was, he was relieved to be wakened. His sleep had been filled with disturbing dreams consisting of hideous images of the Bad Thing and Thor and the Pack. Images that, mercifully, he forgot upon waking.

CHAPTER 10

"WELL, if it isn't the *asshole*," Janet said, confident that the kids were still upstairs sleeping. She felt like she'd been up all night, but she was still glad Thor had been on the alert. As much as she loved jogging in the woods, she didn't always feel safe living so close to them. And it wasn't animals that worried her.

She'd considered skipping her morning jog today, but decided if Thor wasn't worried, she wouldn't worry. If last night's uproar proved anything, it was that no intruder could sneak up on Thor.

"You better be careful when Dad comes down," she warned. "He wasn't very impressed with your little performance last night."

Thor watched and listened expectantly as Mom spoke, and though her words meant nothing to him, her tone was soothing. She was trying to sound stern (and thinking she was doing a good job), but her voice revealed her inner forgiveness. Thor wasn't surprised. He and Mom shared a powerful common bond: They both worried about the Pack's safety every day.

Thor kissed her hands to apologize for last night, and they stepped out together into the early-morning sun.

Thor sprinted across the yard, nose to the ground, occasionally looking up as if he expected to see someone coming. Instead of crossing the creek and starting into the woods, he stopped just short of the water, sniffed the ground for a second, then followed his nose back to the garage stairs.

He'd picked up Uncle Ted's latest scent trail, mixed with traces of the Bad thing. It was a fresh, strong trail, only an hour or two old. Uncle Ted must have returned while Thor was sleeping. The new trail backtracked along the original trail precisely. Thor followed it up the stairs and sniffed around the edges of the apartment door as Mom stood watching him, bewildered.

As far as he could tell, Uncle Ted was inside the apartment. He could hear heavy snoring inside, and though he'd never heard Uncle Ted snore before, he assumed it was him. There was, after all, no other scent trail on the stairs.

Satisfied that he'd learned all he could, he hurried back down the stairs and carefully urinated on all the fence posts in the driveway, stopping to sniff each one to be sure it was well marked. He crossed the creek and marked all the nearest trees in the same meticulous fashion, then started back to rejoin Mom. About halfway across the yard, he had an afterthought. He trotted back to the base of the garage stairs and urinated on the banister.

"Hey!" Mom yelled, more surprised than angry. Thor ignored her. He finished the job in seconds and sauntered up to her, smiling and wagging his tail as if nothing unusual had happened. She shook her head in wonder at his odd behavior and together they started off into the woods.

She felt a strange mix of reassurance and apprehension at the way he never left her line of sight and frequently doubled back to be close to her. He didn't seem worried—his hair didn't stand up on his shoulders—but he'd never acted that way before. Whatever had bothered him in the woods last night was obviously gone, but Thor was still being cautious.

And her own feelings agreed. She'd *felt* something last night, a sense of imminent danger that she'd tried to shrug off as nerves or imagination. But this morning was different. Neither she nor Thor felt anything today.

They jogged together as if nothing were out of the ordinary. Except that Mom found herself running slower than usual so she wouldn't have to stop for breathers. And Thor took an inordinate interest in the scents he found. And they both stopped and listened to sounds in the distance.

They finished their run in a little more than half the usual time, and were both glad to head back to the kitchen.

By the time Dad got up, Mom was already plucking bacon out of the frying pan and laying it out on paper towels.

The smell filled every space in Thor's brain, and he almost forgot about last night. He was just about to beg for a slice of bacon when he heard Dad's footsteps on the stairs and remembered he was *canis non gratis*. He quietly went back to his corner and waited.

Dad came into the kitchen and looked straight at Thor as if Mom weren't even in the room. Thor thumped his tail tentatively and looked at the floor near Dad's feet.

"So," Dad said. "I hope you slept well. Shithead."

He turned to Mom and put his arm around her waist and kissed her cheek. His mood seemed to change completely, but Thor wasn't fooled. Dad hadn't forgiven Thor.

But forgiveness was on the way, and would probably come before Dad left for work. The tightness in Thor's chest loosened a notch. He almost felt ready to go back to sleep.

But something kept him awake. A feeling of unfinished business. He wanted to go out to the woods by himself and check on some loose ends from last night.

Teddy and Brett came downstairs, bleary-eyed and cranky.

"Stupid mutt," Teddy said contemptuously.

"Yeah," Brett chimed in, "thanks for waking us up,

stoopid!" Thor ignored their derision. He had more important things on his mind than disapproval from those he outranked.

"Oh, leave him alone," Mom said. "He can't help it. He heard something outside, and he thought he was protecting us. You guys should appreciate him more."

"But he's so stupid!" Teddy whined. "Does he have to wake us up every time a raccoon comes within a mile of the house?"

"Look, I hate to admit it," Dad said, "but your mother's right. He thought he was protecting us, and that's what we bought him for, so maybe we should all lighten up a little."

Mom looked open-mouthed at Dad.

"What do you mean, 'I hate to admit it, but your mother's right'?" she demanded.

"That's not what I meant," Dad said wearily. "I meant I hate to admit that we should lay off the dog. Okay?"

"I'm sorry," Mom said, realizing she was just possibly a little cranky herself. Like Thor, she'd been unable to sleep, even after things had calmed down. She'd lain awake in bed for what seemed like hours, waiting for the sound of an intruder, or Thor barking at one.

"You see the trouble you caused?" Dad said, looking at Thor. He laughed ruefully in spite of himself and said, "C'mere, stupid."

His tone of voice, his posture, and his face all said: You're forgiven.

Thor scrambled awkwardly to his feet on the slick tile floor and trotted over to Dad's outstretched hand. He planted a wet kiss in Dad's palm, and Dad grabbed a hunk of the loose skin on the back of his neck and pulled him closer. It was such a relief to feel Dad's hands loving him again. His tail pounded against Dad's chair as Dad patted the side of his chest.

Thor even dared to lie down on his back and offer his underside to Dad, and Dad stroked his chest and stomach deliciously.

He was back in the fold.

* * *

135

Uncle Ted missed breakfast, which had become standard; in the last few days, he'd been sleeping in later and later. Thor nonchalantly watched the back door while the Pack ate, taking his eyes off it only when someone tossed him a scrap of bacon. And even then, after catching it, he went back to watching the door without acknowledging the donor. That was a first. He usually made a point of thanking his benefactors.

Dad noticed his preoccupation with the door. He got up and walked over to it, just to see what Thor would do.

Thor immediately stood at attention. Nothing unusual there, but there was something oddly businesslike in Thor's attitude. He didn't look *happy* about the prospect of going out. Dad wondered for the umpteenth time what the hell was going on.

"You wanna go out?" he said, speaking the words Thor knew as well as his own name. Thor flinched at the sound of the word "out," but lay back down again.

"No?" Dad said, a little befuddled.

Thor's Duty had taken on new dimensions. He could not guard the Pack as casually as he once had. From now on, he would stay as close to them as possible.

Later, when Dad left for work, Thor was shocked by his own reaction. He was actually *relieved* to see Dad go. And when Teddy left to play softball, he felt the same unprecedented sensation, and hoped Mom and Brett and Debbie would go shopping soon; then they, too, would be safe. Then maybe he could get some sleep.

But Mom and Brett and Debbie didn't leave, and Thor didn't catch up on his sleep.

Instead, he lay on the kitchen stoop watching Debbie ruin her shoes in the creek, and watching the garage. Brett was fooling around in the driveway and Mom was doing the laundry. Since he couldn't stay near all of them, he watched the garage and wished Debbie would play somewhere else.

* * *

A little past noon, Uncle Ted came out, looking like hell. He tried to act casual, but Thor saw the mantle of the Bad Dog on him more clearly than ever before. Uncle Ted walked guiltily to the kitchen door where Thor lay watching him. A few feet from the door he greeted Thor as if he'd just seen him for the first time.

"Hello, Thor," he said, with a slight quiver in his voice that a human would have missed. Thor lay in place, watching him intently. A formless question had taken hold of his mind. Most of Thor's questions only lasted long enough to amount to a sensation of wonder before evaporating. But this question was different. This question, as wordless as the others, stuck in his mind.

Is Uncle Ted a member of the Pack?
He eats with the Pack.
He sleeps in Pack territory.
He lives with the Pack.
He's Mom's brother.

The thought suddenly occurred to Thor that Uncle Ted hadn't simply gone out and met the Bad Thing; he had somehow *brought* it to the Pack, and if the Bad Thing returned, it would be because Uncle Ted went out and got it again. Even now, under all the soap and deodorant and too much cologne, faint traces of the Bad Thing were on him.

Uncle Ted stepped over Thor and into the kitchen. Thor got up and followed him in, but walked over to his empty food bowl and stuck his nose in to mask his intentions.

"Long sleeves?" Mom said when she saw him. "On a day like today?" It was eighty-two degrees, and the forecast called for highs in the nineties. Mom sat at the kitchen table with a mug of coffee, waiting for the dryer to finish with a load of laundry.

"Yeah," Uncle Ted said self-consciously. "It's, uh . . . it's laundry day for me, too. Besides, I don't want to get skin cancer."

"Well, it's about time!" Mom said. She'd been on his case for years to stop tanning. "I'll be through in a minute if you want to do a wash. Or you could give me your stuff and I'll wash it. I'm going to be here anyway. God, you look awful!" she said suddenly, with the tactlessness of a sibling. She made a sympathetic face and asked, "Did Thor keep you up, too? I'm awfully sorry."

Uncle Ted seemed startled by her question.

"Oh! Yeah, but . . . I probably wouldn't have gotten any sleep anyway. I've got . . . things on my mind lately."

"Anything you want to talk about?"

"Not really. But thanks."

"Want me to take care of your wash?"

"I'm sure I can manage."

Thor felt a flash of recognition as he watched Uncle Ted with Mom. Uncle Ted was acting exactly like a dog who's dirtied the living room rug while the family was out, and is trying to act nonchalant while he waits for the inevitable discovery of his incriminating turd.

Thor wondered where Uncle Ted's turd was hidden.

Uncle Ted took Mom's empty laundry basket and walked out to the garage, glad to be away from the awkward conversation. Thor followed him as far as the kitchen door. He made himself comfortable on the back stoop and watched the man go up the stairs and into his apartment. A few minutes later, Uncle Ted came out with the full laundry basket in both hands. As he crossed the yard and came up the kitchen steps, Thor caught a strong scent of the Bad Thing from the pile of laundry.

Uncle Ted's hidden turd.

Thor followed him through the kitchen door and watched him toss his clothes into the washing machine. The machine, Thor knew, would erase the scent of the Bad Thing, as it erased almost all scents.

Uncle Ted seemed to breathe easier now that his turd was safely hidden. But he still bore the demeanor of a Bad Dog.

He leaned over and patted Thor's head.

Thor didn't move. He issued a low growl, barely loud enough for Uncle Ted to hear, too low for Mom to hear. Their eyes met, and Thor didn't look away—Uncle Ted did.

Uncle Ted slowly, cautiously removed his hand from Thor's head and straightened up. He didn't want Mom to see him snatch his hand away in fear. Good. Thor didn't want Mom to see their little exchange, either.

"So," Uncle Ted said, nervously tucking his shirt into his pants and sounding as innocent and nonchalant as Eddie Haskell, "what-all happened last night? I missed most of it."

"I don't know, really," Mom said over her shoulder as she set up the ironing board. "Thor thought he heard something in the woods, I guess, and he just about threw a fit. Woke the whole house up. You're lucky you were in the garage." She laughed in spite of herself. "You'd think World War Three started. Anyway, Tom finally let him out, and he ran into the woods and didn't come back. He tried calling him with the dog whistle, but he just barked. I told Tom to forget it, let the dog come home when he wants, but he was afraid the neighbors would complain, so he trudged out there in my robe to find him. You should have seen it. I think I'll get him a robe like that . . . it really shows off his"—she lowered her voice a notch—"ass."

Uncle Ted's face went white with fear, but Mom's back was turned and she didn't see it. "So . . . what did he find?" he managed to say.

"Nothing." Mom answered. "It took some effort, but he finally got Thor to come in. He was really pissed when he got back to bed."

"So what do you think it was all about?" Uncle Ted asked, a little too nonchalantly.

"I have no idea, but I'm not too worried. Thor barks at practically everything."

"Well, I don't know, sis. Big predators can travel awfully long distances if their habitat runs dry. Just because the woods here haven't had anything dangerous *recently,* doesn't mean they'll always be safe. If I were you, I wouldn't let the kids play out there for a while, until—" He stopped short.

"Yeah? Until what?"

"I don't know. I must be getting confused. I was thinking for a second about the wolf near my house. I was going to say, 'until this thing blows over.' But anyway, it just proves my point: There aren't supposed to be wolves where I live, and look what happened to that girl. I just think you should be more cautious, all of you, and take the dog more seriously. And don't let him go out there, either."

"Ted, don't you think you're overdoing it a little? Thor isn't exactly helpless, you know."

"How big is he? In pounds, I mean."

"Are you ready for this? Ninety-three pounds!"

"You know how big gray wolves get? Up to a hundred seventy-five!"

"Ted, give me a break! The dog starts barking in the night, and now you've got a hundred and seventy-five pound wolf at the door! It's not exactly like dogs never bark in the night. Are you feeling okay?"

She put down the iron and looked at her brother. "Listen, Ted," she said, "I know you've been going through hell for a while now, but you've got to try to take it easy. Relax. You're turning into a bundle of nerves. Ever since you got here, you've been as jumpy as a cat, and the last couple of nights it's gotten worse. I really think you should think about . . . seeing someone."

Uncle Ted snorted. "And I don't suppose you mean a girl-friend, do you?" Mom looked at the floor, took a deep breath, then met his eyes.

"No, Ted, I don't. I'm afraid for you. I've never seen you like this, and I don't know what to do. You're drifting further and further away, and I don't mean from me. I mean from everybody and everything." Tears welled in her eyes and her voice wavered. "Oh, Ted."

She choked back a sob, then broke down and cried, face in

her hands, knees trembling. Uncle Ted rushed to her and took her in his arms.

Thor snapped to alarmed attention, his fur standing on his shoulders. If Mom cried out or tried to get away from Uncle Ted, Thor was ready to kill him without hesitation.

But Mom took succor from Uncle Ted's embrace. Uncle Ted gently guided her to the kitchen table and sat her down, then went to the stove and turned on the burner under the tea kettle. He looked over his shoulder at her as she dabbed her eyes with a napkin, then turned his face to the stove. He gripped the stove with both hands and spoke to the burners.

"Oh, Janet. I wish there was something you could do to help me, but you can't. If I weren't such a selfish, cowardly bastard, I wouldn't even be here." He took a deep breath and let it out slowly. "I'm leaving. Today."

Mom looked up, startled.

"No, Ted! You can't! Where would you go?"

"I don't know," he said with his back still turned to her. "But I have to. It's not right, me being here, taking advantage of you."

"You're not—" Mom began, but Uncle Ted cut her off.

"I *am* taking advantage of you, and the fact that you don't realize it doesn't make it any better." He took another breath and said, "I have to go."

Mom got up and tentatively put a hand on his back to massage the muscles between his shoulders. Uncle Ted didn't respond. She leaned against his back and ran her hands down his arms and took hold of his wrists, and he flinched and gasped. She immediately let go and decided against asking why his wrists were sore. She was afraid to find out.

"Ted, don't go," she pleaded. "Stay for me. Please. If you go now, it'll kill me. Please don't." She knew her brother well enough to understand he was talking suicide. She countered the only way she knew how, by threatening in kind.

Thor understood the conversation better than almost any other he'd ever heard. The depth of Uncle Ted's guilt and

141

despair, and the desperation and terror and love in Mom's response left no doubt that they were discussing Uncle Ted's possible demise.

But unlike Mom, Thor wasn't bothered by the prospect. Uncle Ted's departure would solve all of Thor's problems.

What *did* bother Thor was the strength of Mom's attachment to her brother. Every word that passed between them seemed to cement Uncle Ted's position in the Pack.

"Promise me," Mom whispered demandingly. "Promise me you'll stay here until . . . until you work things out. Please."

Uncle Ted let go of the counter and covered his face with his hands, unconsciously imitating his sister's pose from moments before.

But he didn't cry. He just stood that way for what seemed like an eternity, thinking. Finally, he said, "I'll try."

CHAPTER

11

Uncle Ted kept to himself for the rest of the day, retreating to his apartment after his laundry was done. Thor spent the day on the kitchen stoop, watching the door to Uncle Ted's apartment. Dad got home early for a change, and under orders from Mom, he dragged Uncle Ted out of hiding and into the house to "be with the family." The Pack seemed determined to make Uncle Ted a full-fledged member.

Uncle Ted worked hard to conceal his depression in Dad's presence, and he did a good job, too. The two of them sat together in the living room, drinking beer and talking while they ignored the TV news. After a while, Uncle Ted seemed as relaxed as any Good Dog. At one point, Dad grunted himself out of his chair and grabbed the remote control. He muted the set and flipped through the channels and found a National Geographic special, which he left on with no sound.

"You were there, weren't you?" he asked Uncle Ted. The screen showed the Serengeti Plain in Africa.

"No, but I could've gone. I got an offer last year." Dad was sorry he'd asked. Uncle Ted had turned the offer down because he was in mourning. Uncle Ted deftly changed the subject.

"Check this out," he said, and he nodded his head toward the dog. Thor, who was lying between them on the floor like a library lion, had just straightened his posture a little to get a better view of the TV. The image on the screen was a cheetah stalking a wildebeest. Both animals appeared in profile. Their shapes and behavior were unmistakable, and Thor was fascinated.

"Well, how do you like that?" Dad said. "I always wondered if they can see what's on the screen. I guess he just isn't interested in car chases and bouncy blondes."

Uncle Ted laughed.

"For sure!" Uncle Ted said. "It was proved conclusively on Stupid Pet Tricks, on David Letterman. This lady had a dog who watched TV all the time, and he was totally cool as long as there weren't animals on screen. Humans yes, animals no. As soon as he saw a dog on screen, he went crazy. It was wild! He was jumping and snapping at the set like a maniac. And as soon as the animals left the screen, he calmed down. Fucking amazing!"

The profile views of the cheetah and the wildebeest were gone, and so was Thor's interest in the TV.

"I wonder what he thinks of the stereo," Dad said, almost to himself. "You know, it doesn't matter what's playing, classical, jazz, noise-rock—he acts like he doesn't even hear it."

"Oh, he does. He just knows it's irrelevant, that's all."

"But how does he know it's irrelevant?" Dad said. "I mean, some of Teddy's records sound like the end of the goddamn world; people screaming, cymbals crashing, bombs going off. And he plays them *loud*. But the dog just lies there like he's deaf."

"It's directional," Uncle Ted said without a moment's thought. "He's learned that the meaningless sounds, the ones that never result in anything happening, always come from the

144

exact same spot in the room, no matter what they sound like or how loud they are. So he learns to ignore any sound that comes from that spot." Uncle Ted noticed Dad looking at him wonderingly. "I'm . . . speculating. I've wondered about it myself, given it a lot of thought."

Dad thought that was an odd answer, considering Uncle Ted had never owned a dog. And he didn't *sound* like he was speculating. But Dad didn't say anything about it.

"Hey, I've got an idea!" Uncle Ted offered. "Hey, Janet! Call the dog, will you?"

"Here, Thor!" Mom answered from the kitchen. Thor looked up but didn't move.

"Thor!" Mom repeated. "C'mere!" Thor sat up at attention, but still didn't budge.

"Hey!" Dad snapped. He reached down and gave Thor a light slap on his rump. Thor looked around, startled. "Get out there!" Dad said, annoyed. Thor stood up and sullenly walked into the kitchen. The slow click of his claws on the hardwood floor spoke eloquently of his reluctance to leave the living room. As soon as he was in the kitchen, Uncle Ted called, "Now put him out!" Mom opened the kitchen door, and after some ordering, reordering, and angry foot stomping, she dragged him onto the back stoop.

"Okay," Uncle Ted said, rubbing his hands mischievously and hunkering down in front of the the stereo cabinet. "Where's the microphone for your cassette deck?" He and Mom always mailed each other cassette-letters when he was out in the boondocks, so he knew there was a mike around somewhere. Dad opened a drawer next to the cabinet and pulled out a cheap plastic Radio Shack microphone.

"Okay, here's what you do," Ted said conspiratorially, explaining his plan in hushed tones as if there were a spy in the room.

Mom thought it was odd that Thor didn't want to go out. He *always* wanted to go out, and yet this time he'd resisted. And when she finally got him out, there was another surprise; instead of joining the kids, who were playing in the backyard, he ran around the house and onto the front porch, for no apparent reason.

Mom went back to the stove, turned down the gas under the instant mashed potatoes, and started toward the living room to see what was going on.

Dad and Uncle Ted were snickering in front of the cassette deck as she entered the room. Dad had the microphone in his hand. He was about to record something.

"Look at that," Mom said, pointing to a window. Thor stood on the porch with his paws on the windowsill, watching them.

"What the . . . ?" Dad said. He'd never seen Thor do anything like it before.

"Hm," Uncle Ted said, sounding disappointed. "We can't do this with him there. Let's see if the kids can get him to stay in the backyard."

Mom gave Dad a look that said, *What's going on here?* but Dad just shrugged. He was having fun and obviously wanted to try whatever Uncle Ted had suggested.

It wasn't easy, but they finally got Teddy to drag Thor into the backyard on a leash, where Teddy tethered him to a fence post. Throughout the operation, Thor's eyes and ears never left the house. He thought he heard Dad calling him at one point, and he barked and strained at the leash, choking himself in the process. Brett wanted to unleash him, but Teddy wouldn't let him.

"He's doing it to himself," Teddy said callously. "If he doesn't want to choke, he can stop pulling."

The muffled sound of Dad's voice inside the house faded. Thor lay on the ground as close to the house as he could get, with the leash pulled taught. He never once looked around at the kids playing in the yard.

Uncle Ted had not only insinuated himself into the Pack, he'd also managed to separate Thor from his Duty. Things were bad and getting worse. He watched the house and worried.

A few endless minutes passed, and Mom stuck her head out the kitchen door.

"Okay, you can let him go!" she called. Brett undid the clasp at Thor's collar and he dashed across the yard and through the kitchen door, which Mom thoughtfully held open for him.

He ran into the living room in a state of high alert. When he saw everything was normal, he excitedly kissed Dad's hands and wagged his tail as if he hadn't seen him all day. He hardly glanced at Uncle Ted. His only concern was that Dad was okay.

Whatever they'd done, it didn't show. Everything looked and smelled the same as before. Dad and Uncle Ted sat in the same chairs, watching TV. Thor relaxed and made himself comfortable on the floor between them, and forgot about their mysterious behavior.

The rich soup of aromas from the kitchen became overwhelming and Mom called everyone in for dinner.

Thor lay on the floor a few feet from the table, ignoring the food in his dish. He didn't have much appetite lately, and even the promise of table scraps for dessert couldn't arouse his interest.

"So what's the big secret?" Mom asked Uncle Ted after settling into her seat.

"You'll see," Uncle Ted said, smiling mischievously. "After dinner."

Dad asked Uncle Ted about the Amazon Basin, where he had once spent over a year photographing insects, and the table conversation quickly led off into geography. The big secret was almost forgotten by the time everyone finished eating. Mom was collecting the plates when Uncle Ted brought the subject up.

"Okay," he explained, "the best way to do this is to move the table, so we can all see the living room from our seats. That way, we can act like nothing is going on while we watch." He and Dad lifted the table and scooted it into position as the kids followed with their chairs. Brett got Mom's chair for her while she put the last dishes in the dishwasher.

"Ted," Uncle Ted said (winning a few points with his nephew by not calling him "Teddy" or "Little Ted"), "would you go into the living room and press the 'play' button on the cassette deck? Everything is set up, so all you have to do is start the tape, then come back and have a seat. Janet, come on and sit down."

Teddy did as he was asked and joined the family at the table. No sound came from the stereo.

Then, after about thirty seconds, Thor was startled by the sound of Dad's voice in the living room.

"Here, Thor!" it called out cheerily. "C'mere, Thor!" Thor scrambled to his feet, looked briefly at Dad, then dashed to the living room, looked around, and looked back into the kitchen, where Dad sat smiling at the table. From behind him in the living room, Dad called again. "Thor! Come here! C'mere, Thor!"

Thor ran to the left stereo speaker and peered at it quizzically with his head cocked at a forty-five-degree angle. Except for the difference in breed and color, he looked just like Nipper, the dog in the old RCA Victor trademark, "His Master's Voice." But just as Thor was examining the left speaker, Dad's voice said, "Over here, Thor!" from the right one.

Thor jumped and ran to the right speaker, just as Dad's voice came out of the left speaker again. "No, no. Over here!" Thor stayed put and looked into the kitchen, where Dad sat at the table, laughing with the rest of the Pack. "Come here, Thor!" Dad's voice said from behind him. Thor spun around and barked angrily at the speaker cabinet. The Pack laughed so hard they appeared to be in pain. Tears rolled down Mom's cheeks, and Brett was literally rolling on the floor, holding his stomach.

As Dad's voice continued to beckon him, first to one speaker then to the other, Thor decided the correct response

148

was to ignore the stereo as he'd always done. It wasn't easy. The voice in the speakers wasn't Dad, and yet it sounded just like him. The timing, the inflections, the pitch and timbre . . . But it still wasn't Dad. Dad was in the kitchen, in plain sight. With great difficulty, Thor resolved to ignore the phantom voice of Dad.

Besides, he didn't like being laughed at.

Thor did plenty of things that made the Pack laugh, but it was never like this.

The first time he pulled Teddy's buttons off for teasing him, Dad had just about laughed himself to death. But Dad's laughter wasn't ridiculing him—on the contrary, it told Thor that Dad was proud of him, impressed by his resourcefulness.

This laughter was different; it said that the Pack was amused by his confusion.

Thor did nothing to show his feelings, but inwardly he was mortified.

He walked back into the kitchen, ignoring the laughter and trying to act as if nothing had happened, while the tape-recorded calls continued to beckon from the living room. Thor grunted and plopped down sulkily on the floor, and Dad told Teddy to turn off the stereo.

"That's the funniest thing I ever saw," Dad said as he wiped tears from his face.

"Yeah," Uncle Ted agreed. "It was nice to get a little reprieve, too."

Dad looked at him oddly.

"What do you mean?"

"Haven't you noticed?" Uncle Ted asked.

"Noticed what?" Mom said.

"Watch," Uncle Ted said. He got up and nonchalantly walked to the living room window, where he stood gazing at the street. A few seconds later, Thor got up as if he were bored and just looking for a change of scene. He wandered into the living room and lay down on the floor with a view of Uncle Ted.

As soon as Thor made himself comfortable, Uncle Ted turned away from the window and walked back into the kitchen. Thor immediately got up and followed him back, with his nose not more than six inches behind Uncle Ted's heels. Thor never took his eyes off the floor the whole time.

Uncle Ted sat down, and Thor dropped himself onto the floor. Uncle Ted got up and walked back to the living room. After a moment's pause, Thor got up and followed. Before Thor had a chance to sit down in the living room, Uncle Ted came back into the kitchen. He followed so closely that Mom was afraid Uncle Ted might accidentally kick Thor's nose with his heels. Uncle Ted sat back down, and Thor sat behind his chair.

"What the hell is going on here?" Dad asked without a trace of amusement in his voice. He'd never seen the dog do anything like it before.

"I don't know," Uncle Ted lied. "But he's been following me around all day. Even when I'm over the garage, he's on the back stoop, watching the apartment door."

"Jesus," Dad whispered, and slowly shook his head.

No one else said anything, but Brett's skin broke out in gooseflesh. He'd been feeling funny about Uncle Ted lately. It wasn't a strong feeling at first, and he'd tried to shrug it off. Even when it blossomed into a genuine sense of foreboding, he hadn't told anybody about it. Hell, he was supposed to be outgrowing his childhood fears, not adding to them—he was still afraid of the dark, for example, though he would eat hot coals before he'd admit it.

Thor's actions seemed to confirm and legitimize the shapeless dread Brett felt around Uncle Ted. Without knowing why, Brett was secretly glad Thor was shadowing his uncle.

"I can't believe this," Dad said. He rubbed his chin and thought for a moment, then said, "Teddy, go follow Uncle Ted, but don't let Thor leave the kitchen. Ted, do it again."

Uncle Ted got up and left the room, this time with Teddy. As Uncle Ted walked through the kitchen door, Teddy hung behind. Thor got up and started toward the living room. Teddy stood in the doorway and blocked his path. Thor tried to use his snout as a wedge to push his way through, but Teddy held fast to the door frame. After a few tries, Thor grunted and plopped down on the kitchen floor just inside the doorway. He made no show of watching Uncle Ted, but he'd positioned himself in line of sight with the man.

"Let him through," Dad said. Teddy stepped aside. Thor didn't move. "Step away from the doorway," Dad said. "Come in here and sit down." Teddy returned to the kitchen table. By the time he reached his chair, Thor was in the living room.

"Now go back to the doorway and this time, keep him out," Dad said. Teddy positioned himself and Dad called Uncle Ted back to the kitchen.

Uncle Ted came back, and as before, Thor was right on his heels. But as Uncle Ted stepped through the kitchen door, Teddy stepped into the doorway.

This time Thor was not so easily put off. It was one thing to let Uncle Ted go off by himself unsupervised, but quite another to let him be alone with Mom and Debbie and Brett. Thor pushed hard with all his weight, and Teddy had to grip the door frame with all his strength to keep from being pushed aside. The harder Thor pushed, the tighter Teddy held.

Uncle Ted stood watching about halfway between the doorway and the kitchen table. He took a step toward the table and Thor growled. Mom's eyes opened wide and Uncle Ted stopped. Thor stepped away from the door and barked sharply at Teddy. Teddy was startled by the unexpected rebuke, but held his ground.

Uncle Ted took another step toward the table and Thor barked viciously. It sounded like a last warning. Teddy held firm.

What happened next took less than five seconds from start to finish.

Uncle Ted walked to the table and sat down between Mom and Debbie. Thor lurched at the doorway and pushed his head through before Teddy's thigh slammed his neck hard against the door frame. Teddy reached for the ring in Thor's collar. In a move as fast as any the Pack had ever seen, Thor withdrew his head from the doorway and snapped at Teddy's hand. He caught the boy's wrist with a bite calculated to hurt without breaking the skin. Teddy shrieked in alarm and snatched his hand back. Thor knocked him over and shot through the doorway as Teddy pulled back. He charged into the kitchen as Dad leaped from his chair.

"What the fuck?" Dad yelled, springing at Thor and slapping his face in a blind rage. *"What are you doing? Bad Dog! Bad Dog!"*

Before Thor knew what was happening, Dad had snagged his collar and yanked hard, cutting off his wind and lifting his front legs off the floor.

Dad was flying on instinct. His only thought was to get Thor away from his family.

Thor choked and gagged but offered no resistance as Dad pulled him toward the cellar door.

He'd lost his head and he knew it. He was *in fact* the awful thing Dad was calling him over and over again.

Bad Dog.

Dad opened the cellar door with his free hand and swung Thor through the doorway, literally throwing him down the stairs.

"Bad Dog!" Dad shouted, and slammed the cellar door.

Thor couldn't believe what he'd done. He'd known, even as he'd opened his mouth to bite Teddy, that it was wrong, it was Bad.

He slinked into the darkest corner of the cellar and lay on the dusty cement floor, staring straight ahead at nothing, feeling the awful weight of his Badness press down on him. If the cellar door were to open, he would retreat deeper into the corner. He needed to be alone in his moment of shame. He couldn't bear to face the Pack.

He'd picked up a half dozen painful bruises on the way

down the stairs, but was only marginally aware of the pain. His mind was overwhelmed with the wordless question:
What have I done?

He ran the incident through his mind again and again, trying to find where he went wrong, where he might have done something else. He only knew that in trying to do what was right, he'd done wrong. He'd done the worst thing he could possibly do: He'd used violence against a Pack member.

It didn't matter that it was the kind of safe, symbolic violence that would be permissible in a wolf pack—it was not permissible in *his* Pack, and he knew it. But what else *could* he have done?

Uncle Ted was a threat. He'd approached the Pack. Thor had to be there. He couldn't leave the Pack unguarded with a threat in its midst.

Teddy had blocked his way. He had to get past Teddy, he *had* to. What else could he have done? He *had* to get into the kitchen.

But biting Teddy was wrong, and nothing could ever make it right. It was the worst thing he'd ever done.

He could hear the Pack talking about his Badness, and he heard no kind words or forgiving tones. He became convinced that the door at the top of the stairs would never open again. He would never again be welcomed into the Pack, never again feel the warmth of the Pack's love.

He felt a terrible emptiness inside, and his chest felt tight, as if something were squeezing it, keeping him from taking a full breath. His body trembled uncontrollably, though he didn't feel cold. He felt like he was shrinking inside. Somehow, he was getting smaller and smaller inside his own body.

How long could this go on? Could he feel this horrible forever? Anything would be better than this enormous, oppressive aloneness that didn't let him breathe.

There was only one hope: forgiveness from the Pack Leader. The die had been cast, and his fate was in Dad's hands.

If Dad didn't forgive him, he could never be part of the Pack again.

Time seemed to stand still while he lay in the shadows, trapped in the limbo of the unloved and unlovable.

Upstairs, the discussion wasn't nearly as one-sided as Thor imagined.

Dad examined Teddy's wrist. Two rows of deep indentations crossed his arm where Thor's teeth had caught it, but there was no break in the skin, no blood. Dad understood that Thor had bitten Teddy exactly as hard as he'd intended, as a warning and not to do serious harm, but he was still angry and worried. There was no reason for Thor's strange behavior, and his behavior was getting more erratic and irrational every day.

Why was Thor following Uncle Ted in the first place? He'd never seen Thor do anything like that before. What was going on? If only he could ask him. . . .

But he couldn't, and Thor's behavior put a genuine scare into him. Was the dog sick?

And more important, was he becoming a danger to the family?

Dad didn't want to consider that last possibility, but once it entered his mind it wouldn't go away.

Nonetheless, he was not willing to believe it on the basis of what he'd seen. If it was true, if Thor was a threat to the family, there was only one thing to do, and he wasn't ready to do that yet, not by a long shot.

Besides, he told himself, it was a stupid mistake to tell Teddy to block the dog's way. He'd seen the way Teddy and Thor had fallen out lately, and he'd lectured Teddy more than once in the last month about not teasing the dog. Stupid, really stupid.

But Thor's reaction . . .

Once before, when Thor was a pup, he'd bitten Teddy the same way—tooth marks, but no blood—after Teddy had teased him too much. Dad had disciplined Thor and Teddy and the incident was never repeated—until today.

But Thor was a pup then, not a powerful brute capable of injuring or killing. If Thor were to go bonkers, he could conceivably kill the whole family.

It was Thor's love for the family and his deep sense of responsibility that made him safe to live with. Could those qualities be slipping?

It was too scary to think about. And too awful. *Of course* Thor could be trusted. Strange behavior or not, Thor loved the family, Dad was sure.

What to do?

Thor spent just over two hours in the cellar. What little sunlight filtered through the small, dusty windows was beginning to fade. He felt thankful for the deepening shadows that engulfed him.

Suddenly the latch on the cellar door clicked and the door swung open, and a shaft of electric light pierced the darkness, jolting Thor out of his meditation of despair.

"Thor!"

Dad's voice was stern but not outraged. Was that a trace of forgiveness in his voice? Thor haltingly lifted himself off the floor on trembling legs.

"Thor! Come up here!"

He ran up the stairs, a bundle of mixed emotions. He knew forgiveness was a possibility, but amends had to be made first. And even if he was forgiven, he would have to prove all over again that he was worthy to live with the Pack.

All he wanted was the chance to prove it.

He slowed down as he neared the top of the stairs. Dad was standing there with a rolled-up newspaper in his hand. Thor held his head and body close to the stairs, his ears flat, and his tail tucked between his legs. His tail felt no urge to wag, even involuntarily. It was much too soon for that.

"Come up here," Dad said, his voice still stern and formal.

Thor crawled through the doorway with his body low, his eyes nervously scanning the floor. He didn't even dare to look at Dad's shoes.

Teddy stood in the dining room with his sleeve rolled up to expose his wrist; Uncle Ted was nowhere in sight. Dad grabbed a handful of loose skin on the back of Thor's neck (not his collar—a *very* good sign), dragged him away from the doorway, and closed the cellar door (another good sign). Thor's tail thumped the floor in fits and jerks, embarrassing him.

"Are you going to be a Good Dog?" Dad asked.

Thor didn't move, but his tail beat a rapid tattoo.

"Are you?" Dad demanded, slapping his own thigh impatiently with the newspaper.

YES, YES, YES, YES, YES!

"Come over here."

Dad walked into the dining room where Teddy waited.

Oh, no.

"Get over here!" Thor thought he heard an unspoken "Bad Dog" on the end of Dad's sentence. He almost wished he was back in the cellar, but he obeyed. He dragged himself into the dining room like a soldier crawling under barbed wire.

"Teddy, hold your arm out," Dad said.

Dad cupped Thor's chin in his hand and lifted his nose up to Teddy's wrist. Thor was too ashamed to look directly at the boy's arm; he got the message.

"You see that?" Dad demanded.

"NO!" he said, punctuating the awful word with a newspaper-swat on Thor's snout. The newspaper hardly hurt; its real function was to make a loud *smack* as it hit him. The punishment was psychological; that Dad would want to hit him at all hurt more than any physical pain. He trembled violently as he braced himself for the blows.

"NO!"

Swat!

"NO!"

Swat!
"NO!"
Swat!
"NO!"
Swat!
"Understand?"
YES, YES, YES, YES, YES! his tail answered.

"All right." Dad released Thor's head and tossed the newspaper aside.

"Are you going to be a Good Dog?" Dad asked again. Thor answered by wagging his tail and frantically licking Dad's hands.

"Don't tell me, tell Teddy," Dad said sternly, pointing to his son. Thor wheeled around and licked Teddy's hands twice, then came back to Dad, showering his hands with desperate kisses.

"You tell *Teddy* you're sorry," Dad repeated, and pushed him toward Teddy. Again, Thor kissed Teddy's hands briefly and came back to Dad.

He could apologize to Teddy forever, but Teddy couldn't forgive him. Only Dad could do that.

"Okay," Dad said, giving in at last. "But you better be Good from now on." Thor involuntarily leaped up and planted a kiss on Dad's mouth.

"Stop it!" Dad said sharply, but without real anger.

The session was over. Thor felt as if he were climbing out of his own grave, into sunshine he'd never expected to see again. He was forgiven, but he would have to be extra careful from now on. He still had to prove he was a Good Dog.

Dad walked to the back door and opened it.

"Out you go," he said. Thor nearly leaped from the dining room to the back door in one bound.

Tom watched him run into the backyard, torn by self doubts. He wasn't at all sure he'd made the right decision.

Maybe it had been a mistake to get a German shepherd in

the first place. He'd often heard German shepherds can be "overprotective."

And aside from the breed being too protective, Thor himself was acting strange. He'd always loved Ted, but ever since Ted came to stay with them Thor had treated him like a total stranger.

Tom didn't want to think he might be endangering his family by giving Thor a second chance. He tried to block it out, but it was there, unspoken, in the back of his mind.

CHAPTER

12

THOR was relieved to be outside, where he could better protect the Pack. He could already feel the Bad Thing coming again. The sky was darkening fast, but the moon would soon rise, bringing its cold brilliance to the night. He started across the yard to the garage, when something startled him.

A brilliant white spot shot across the grass from behind the garage, then darted back again. Kitty was practicing pouncing on some imaginary prey. Thor worried for her safety. He trotted over and tried to nuzzle her in the direction of the house, but the kitten resisted, playfully taking a swing at his nose. He barked once, quickly remembered the trouble he'd gotten into for barking lately, and whined and mewled at her instead. Misunderstanding him completely, she leaped at his face, but he dodged the attack and she hit the ground and rolled a few feet.

It was no use. He'd tried once before to herd the kitten into the house, and all he got for his efforts was a row of painful scratches across his nose. The kitten would not be herded.

But the Bad Thing was coming. Thor wasn't sure how to handle the situation, but at least he knew where the Bad Thing would come from.

He walked to the foot of the garage stairs and waited. He could hear Uncle Ted moving around inside. He felt an urge to run up the stairs and bark at him, to order him to stay inside, but he didn't dare. Following his urges had gotten him in big trouble lately. Holding his urges in check was absolutely essential.

So he sat on the grass and waited as the sky darkened.

He didn't have to wait long. Uncle Ted opened the door and stepped onto the landing in a brand-new sweatsuit. He took one step, saw Thor, and stopped short. A worried look crossed his face and he turned and went back inside, closing the door behind him. A few seconds later he pulled a drape away from a window and checked the landing at the top of the stairs, obviously expecting to see Thor there.

But Thor was still on the grass. Uncle Ted closed the drape.

Thor looked back at the house, hoping to see Dad in the kitchen doorway. If only he could tell Dad the Bad Thing was coming, or at least make Dad aware of Uncle Ted's Badness. But Dad was nowhere in sight.

A curtain moved slightly in an upstairs window of the house, but Thor didn't see it. Peeking through the smallest possible opening in his bedroom window curtains, Brett watched the showdown between Thor and Uncle Ted.

Thor made himself comfortable on the grass, settling in for what he assumed would be a long wait. When Uncle Ted came out, Thor would follow him until the Bad Thing showed up, and then he would deal with the Bad Thing. If Uncle Ted managed to chain the Bad Thing to a tree, he would stand guard over it. If the Bad Thing tried to approach the house, he would attack. That was his plan. By Thor's standards, it was pretty elaborate.

Uncle Ted looked out the window again and finally came

out onto the landing. He stood there staring at Thor for a moment, then looked over his shoulder at the blackening eastern horizon, where the moon would rise in a matter of minutes. With a look of resignation on his face, he tentatively started down the stairs, pausing briefly on each step to watch Thor's reaction.

Thor sat in place, watching him.

The trip down the stairs seemed to take forever, but Uncle Ted eventually set foot on the pavement, less than three feet from Thor, who sat motionless the whole time.

Slightly emboldened and growing more desperate by the second, Uncle Ted cautiously began walking toward the woods. Thor immediately got up and followed him, maintaining a constant distance of about ten feet between them.

Uncle Ted turned on him angrily with his arm held out straight, pointing to the house.

"Go home!" he snapped.

Bluffing.

Thor ignored him. Uncle Ted might be part of the Pack, but he hadn't established any clear rank, let alone dominance over Thor. Thor felt no obligation to obey him.

Uncle Ted was beginning to look as nervous as a cornered animal. He stepped toward Thor and slowly, tentatively, reached for his collar. Before his hand came within two feet of Thor's face, Thor's upper lip curled, showing his fangs, and a low growl rumbled from deep in his throat.

Uncle Ted wisely withdrew his hand, as slowly as he'd extended it. He was running out of time.

He had to do something, and fast; the sky was completely dark, and he thought he saw the edge of the moon peeking over the horizon. Where was Tom? Why did he leave the dog out? He took a nervous step toward the house, but Thor quietly snarled an ultimatum: The only way he was entering the house was over Thor's dead body.

Uncle Ted bit his lip and rubbed his chin nervously, then slowly turned and walked back to the garage, trying not to run. If he ran, Thor would chase him. If Thor chased him, he would catch him. He didn't want to think about what would happen after that.

But things were going to start happening soon, whether he moved or not. The top of the moon was just visible on the horizon.

Thor followed him to the garage stairs and let him walk up the stairs by himself.

Something odd was happening. Uncle Ted's scent was changing, and he was glancing at his hands and touching his face every few seconds. He reached the apartment door and was about to go inside when the kitchen door opened and Dad stepped onto the back stoop.

"Thor!" Dad called. "C'mon in! Bedtime!"

Thor looked at Dad, then at Uncle Ted. He stood frozen, torn between obedience and instinct.

"THOR!" Dad repeated sternly. His tone of voice broke the deadlock.

Thor's sense of Duty told him to disobey, but in a rare flash of insight, he realized disobedience would land him in the cellar again, totally unable to protect the Pack. He *mewled* loudly, pitifully, and walked to the house, glancing over his shoulder at the Bad Dog the whole way.

He came within a few feet of the back steps and stopped. Looking straight at Dad, he barked three or four times in an attempt to convey the seriousness of his mission, but Dad showed no sign of understanding.

"Come *on!*" Dad snapped. More strange behavior from the dog. More cause for concern. He took a deep breath and said, as patiently as possible, "Get in here." He wanted to give the mutt every chance to redeem himself.

Thor knew he was dangerously close to the edge. Whining his dissent, he climbed the stairs into the kitchen and sat down with a disgusted grunt. He looked directly at Dad with accusing eyes. He couldn't see the garage from his position, but he knew what was happening outside.

Dad looked at him oddly and slowly shook his head.

"What's *with* you?" he said, wishing the dog could answer. He closed the kitchen door with his back to the yard, facing Thor. If he had looked over his shoulder at that moment, he would have seen Uncle Ted running for the woods as if the devil himself were on his tail.

Dad squatted down and scratched the thick fur on the back of Thor's neck. Thor's eyes involuntarily closed from the pleasure of Dad's touch, but he forced them open to look pleadingly at Dad.

"You be a Good Dog, all right?" Dad said as he petted Thor gently. Thor whined at him for a second, then gave up. It was hopeless and he knew it.

Satisfied, Dad got up and went to bed. It was way past his bedtime, and Mom was waiting for him.

Thor sat in the kitchen until Dad was out of sight, then ran to the back door, stood up against it with his paws on the windowsill, and scanned the yard outside.

Uncle Ted was gone and the Bad Thing had arrived. He could feel it. It was out there somewhere, and the Pack was in danger.

His instincts told him he should be with the Pack, but he was at a distinct disadvantage as long as he was inside the house. The Bad Thing was bigger and possibly stronger than himself, and he would need complete freedom of movement to fight it. The house made him vulnerable, and worse yet, its doors separated him from the Pack members. The best way to protect the Pack was to keep the Bad Thing from getting in, and the best way to keep it from getting in was to kill it outside.

But he could only get outside if someone opened the door, and he dared not bark to be let out. He knew what would happen if he barked, and he couldn't afford it. It was an impossible situation, and it was his fault. He'd mishandled the problem from the start, and now it was completely out of his control.

The sense of the Bad Thing's presence was growing stronger; the Bad Thing was coming. It was already closer to the Pack than it had ever been before. Thor darted from window to window, whining and mewling involuntarily, unable to contain his apprehension. He kept his mouth shut, but the sound came through his nose, high-pitched and fluctuating. It sounded like someone torturing a violin.

And the Bad Thing kept coming closer.

A stair creaked in the living room. A short, involuntary *woof* escaped Thor's mouth as he dashed to the stairs, then relief washed over him; it was Brett.

But the Bad Thing was coming. It was dangerous here, and getting more dangerous by the second. Brett should be upstairs, preferably in Dad's room. The whole Pack should be in Dad's room. Thor tried to block his path with his body and push him back up the stairs with his nose, but Brett refused to be herded; he grabbed the banister with both hands and pulled himself down.

"What's wrong, boy?" he asked as he fought his way to the living room. "What's the matter?" Brett had watched too many *Lassie* reruns on cable, and thought dogs could answer general questions with their actions.

Brett made it to the floor and started toward the kitchen, toward the approaching Bad Thing. Thor couldn't block him on the open floor, and short of barking or threatening him, there was nothing he could do.

Desperate, he ran ahead to the kitchen door, stood on his hind feet with his forepaws on the window, and mewled frantically to warn Brett of the approaching danger, but Brett misunderstood.

"You wanna go OUT?" he said, approaching the door.

The word OUT hit Thor like ice water. He forgot about herding Brett to safety and jumped off the kitchen door, whining and fidgeting uncontrollably while he waited for Brett to open it. Brett's hand seemed to move in slow motion as he reached for the doorknob. His fingers closed around it and twisted the knob. He began to pull the door open, and as soon as an inch of space appeared, Thor jammed his snout into it, wedged it open, and shot out, pushing the door into Brett so hard that it almost knocked him over. Before Brett had regained his balance, Thor had crossed the yard and disappeared into the woods.

Brett had never seen Thor move so fast in his life.

The Bad Thing wasn't far. Thor sensed its presence, but only his nose could lead him to it. Uncle Ted's scent trail was fading fast, replaced by the ever-growing scent of the Bad Thing, just like last night—except that last night, Uncle Ted's scent didn't fade out until he was deep in the forest. Tonight, the Bad Thing's scent appeared almost as soon as Uncle Ted's trail left the backyard. The urgency of the situation goaded Thor into running faster than his nose could follow the trail, and he had to stop and double back after overshooting points where the Bad Thing had changed direction. Fortunately the trail was leading deeper into the woods, away from the house.

A few hundred feet inside the forest, a glint of moonlight on the ground caught Thor's eye. He stopped to check it out, and found Uncle Ted's handcuffs lying on the ground. A few feet down the path lay his sweatpants and shirt. The shirt was ripped to shreds, and the pants were torn apart at the waistband. They smelled of Uncle Ted, but mostly they bore the powerful scent of the Bad Thing. Another yard, and Thor found first one running shoe, then the other. From that point on, no trace of Uncle Ted's scent remained. Only the full-bodied, canine smell of the Bad Thing. It seemed to radiate malice.

The Bad Thing's trail tended to follow the main jogging paths, but occasionally took side trips through the bushes, as if the Bad Thing had spotted an animal and given chase. The bushes were fairly tall; the Bad Thing had forced its way through by breaking the branches in its path. Thor dropped his head between his shoulders and flattened his ears against his head, and ran through the underbrush much faster than the Bad Thing. He knew he could catch up with the Bad Thing in the underbrush, but when the trail returned to the open paths, Thor had to slow down to avoid outrunning his nose. On the open paths, the Bad Thing's lead widened.

The moon was above the horizon but still low in the sky, and its slanted beams didn't do much to light the forest. If the Bad Thing were waiting in ambush, Thor might not see it until too late. But he pushed on nonetheless. His Duty was more important than his own safety.

Without realizing it, he kept ongoing mental notes on the moon's position in the sky, which told him where he was and where he was heading. The Bad Thing's trail led him deep into the woods, where the scents of small animals were abundant. The Bad Thing was hunting.

He plunged deeper into the forest, running when he could, slowing only momentarily when he lost the trail. About half a mile in he found the remains of a raccoon, torn to pieces, but not eaten. Its body had been ripped apart and scattered all over the area.

The Bad Thing was hunting, but it wasn't hungry. It was mad.

Suddenly Thor realized with a shock that the Bad Thing's trail had been gradually changing direction, until it was now heading back toward the house.

That meant the Bad Thing was closer to the Pack than Thor. *The Pack was unguarded.*

Still another mistake.

His first thought was to abandon the Bad Thing's trail and run for the house, but he wasn't sure where the house was. He knew it was in the general direction of the moon, but if he just ran toward the moon, he could come out of the forest a block or more away from the house. He had to catch up with the Bad Thing.

Luck smiled on him; the Bad thing's trail left the paths again. As long as the Bad Thing stayed off the main trails, Thor stood a good chance of catching up with it before it reached the house. He hurtled through the underbrush with the force of panic.

He knew the Bad Thing was going after the Pack—he didn't know *how* he knew, but he knew. Could the Bad Thing have picked up the Pack's scent from out here? Was that why it left the paths? It didn't seem possible. *Thor* couldn't find the Pack's scent out here, and it was the most familiar scent in his world. When he'd seen the Bad Thing last night, the first thing he'd noticed was its puny, undoglike nose, no bigger than a human's. And humans never seemed to smell anything. How did the Bad Thing know where to find the Pack?

Worse yet, the Bad Thing seemed to have deliberately waited until Thor was deep in the woods before doubling back—a very humanlike thing to do. How intelligent *was* the Bad Thing? Had it outsmarted him, deliberately luring him away from his Duty?

The troubling thoughts quickly faded from his mind, replaced by the urgent need to get home.

The Bad thing's trail suddenly rejoined a jogging path. Thor's eyes had finally adjusted to the deep shadows of the undergrowth, and when he emerged onto the open path, the moonlight seemed as bright as day. He recognized the path immediately: He was about a quarter mile from the house. Knowing where all the tree roots and other obstacles lay, he charged down the path at full speed. Just as he hit his stride, a high-pitched screech pierced the night.

Fear cut through him like an icicle and a new surge of adrenalin pushed his legs still faster. He'd instantly recognized that awful shriek of pain and terror; it was Kitty. And Kitty never crossed the creek behind the house. If the Bad Thing got her, it was already in the Pack's territory.

Thor felt like he was in a bad dream. He'd made nothing but mistakes, day after day, and now he'd been maneuvered away from the Pack, away from his Duty. The only way to correct his errors was through sheer muscle. If he didn't reach the house before the Bad Thing got in, all was lost. He was only seconds away, but the Bad Thing was already there.

The forest flew past him in a dark blur.

Kitty shrieked again, a horrible cry that sent a stab of guilt and shame through him—*he should have been there to protect her.* But he also felt a shameful sense of relief—if the Bad Thing was still attacking Kitty, then it wasn't in the house yet.

The trees thinned out as he ran, exposing more and more of the bright moon between their branches. Voices up ahead called his name. He was almost out of the woods, almost there.

He could see the end of the path, and beyond it, the house. His breathing was hoarse and ragged and his legs ached, but he willed them to push still harder and run still faster.

He cleared the woods and leaped the brook between forest and yard in one bound. The yard shone bright under the full moon, and the upstairs windows of the house were ablaze with lights.

He didn't waste time scanning the landscape for the Bad Thing; he went straight for the house, frantically examining it for signs of entry as he ran. A smeared white blotch flashed by in his peripheral vision as he passed the garage.

A dark furry figure was approaching the back door. Thor barked at full volume to alert the Pack and hopefully frighten the Bad Thing. But instead of running, the Bad Thing turned to face Thor. Thor locked his eyes on the Bad Thing's throat and leaped, but the Bad Thing's foot swept up with lightning speed and struck Thor in the ribs, slamming him sideways into Mom's car. Before he could regain his balance the Bad Thing kicked again, catching him with an uppercut to the jaw that made Thor's vision blur and his legs wobble underneath him. Everything seemed to happen in slow motion.

A part of Thor's mind told him the next blow would be fatal if he didn't regain control, but the next blow didn't come; instead, bright lights burst from the Pack's house, and the Bad Thing looked over its shoulder at them. A window opened noisily. Voices were calling Thor's name. Thor shook himself, trying to clear his head. Another light went on in the house next door, suddenly bathing the Bad Thing's face in its glare. Thor saw the glisten of Kitty's blood on its mouth.

The sudden flood of light seemed to startle the Bad Thing. It turned, dashed to the fence and began to climb through the rails to the sheltering shadows of the neighbors' yard, just as Thor's mind came into focus.

Thor charged, targeting the Bad Thing's trailing ankle. He calculated that the Bad Thing would be through the fence by the time he got there, and aimed himself at the space between the rails.

His calculations were dead on: As the Bad Thing pulled through, Thor's head shot through the rails, jaws open and snapping viciously at the retreating ankle. His fangs sliced through the Bad Thing's flesh and the smell of blood filled his nostrils, but his teeth caught only skin—not muscles and tendons, as he'd hoped.

Even so, it was the first thing he'd done right all day.

An open wound is a beacon. As long as the Bad Thing was bleeding, Thor could follow it over any distance and for any amount of time—as long as it took. There was no place on earth where the Bad Thing could hide from him. It was classic wolf hunting technique, honed and perfected over hundreds of thousands of years.

The Bad Thing let out a subdued *yelp* that only Thor heard. It twisted around and swung a clawed hand at Thor's nose and glanced hatefully at Thor for the briefest instant before dashing across the neighbors' yard and into the deep shadows of the hedges.

Another light came on in the neighbors' house as the Bad Thing vanished into the hedges.

All the bedroom windows in the Pack's house faced the backyard, with no view of the driveway. Thor's encounter with the Bad Thing had almost gone unseen. He ran to the back of the house to check the faces in the windows, trying to tell if everyone was there and if they were all right.

As far as he could see, they looked unhurt. But one was missing.

In the lone bathroom window on the side of the house, Brett quietly retreated into the shadows, afraid the monster might see him. Then he ran to his bedroom to see what Thor was doing in the backyard.

With an overwhelming sense of relief, Thor saw Brett's face appear next to Teddy's in their bedroom window, just as Dad's face disappeared from his window. The Pack was whole—except for Kitty.

Thor turned to look for the Bad Thing in the neighbors' yard, just as the kitchen lights went on and the back door opened, sending a near-blinding beam of light across the backyard.

Dad stood in the doorway in Mom's bathrobe and slippers, with a flashlight in one hand. Thor was glad to see him, but worried for his safety. He didn't see or hear anything in the neighbors' yard, which could mean the Bad Thing had left, or that it was sneaking back from another direction. Thor had no idea what to do next, but he knew he couldn't afford to be lured away again. He should never have left the Pack alone in the first place—he should have stayed put and waited for the Bad Thing. He turned to Dad and barked a warning, but as always, Dad didn't understand.

"What the hell is going on here?" Dad grumbled, obviously still half asleep.

Upstairs, Debbie and Mom looked out from Mom and Dad's bedroom window. Debbie was crying, and Thor caught Kitty's name between her sobs.

Dad stepped off the back stoop and walked straight toward the garage.

The Bad thing could be back there!

Thor barked at him and dashed ahead to see if anything was hiding behind the garage, glancing over his shoulder at the driveway as he ran around the garage in a wide circle to avoid an ambush.

The Bad Thing wasn't there. But Dad was halfway across the yard and the kitchen door was wide open.

Thor barked frantically at Dad—what else could he do? He couldn't let Dad prowl around in the dark by himself and he couldn't let the Bad Thing get into the house, *especially* with Dad outside. He tried to block Dad's path and barked furiously. Surely Dad must understand.

But Dad didn't even slow down. He just acted annoyed.

Thor did what he could. He barked at Dad from the back door to call him back, then ran in front of Dad and barked to warn him off, his shepherding instincts in full command. But his barking only seemed to annoy Dad further.

Thor had no way of knowing that in Dad's eyes, he was acting like a Bad Dog trying to keep his master from seeing what he'd done.

Dad played his flashlight over the ground around the garage and gasped as the beam found Kitty's headless corpse. If her fur hadn't been so white, he wouldn't have known what he was looking at. The tiny torso had been opened from neck to tail, and only a few tufts of white fur peeked out from under the blood that sheathed it.

"Oh, my God!" he said under his breath. Thor was still running back and forth across the backyard, barking at him.

"Did you do this?" he demanded, pointing at the mangled carcass. He didn't expect an answer, but he was relieved to see no trace of guilt in Thor's bearing. Thor had never in his life successfully faked innocence.

But if Thor didn't do it, who—or what—did?

Dad looked at the open kitchen door, and thought what Thor had been thinking the whole time.

Thor was overwhelmed with relief to see Dad going back inside with the Pack, where he belonged. He gratefully escorted him back to the house. If Dad had stayed behind the garage, Thor would have been forced to abandon him, in favor of protecting Mom and Debbie. He was glad he didn't have to make that awful choice.

Meanwhile, Mom had come down the stairs with Debbie at her chest, and was standing in the kitchen door.

"Did you find the k-i-t-t-e-n?" Mom asked quietly.

"No," Dad lied. "I'll talk to you later. Right now we'd better get inside." He spoke calmly, but his choice of words scared Mom. She backed away from the doorway, her eyes silently questioning him.

Dad stepped into the kitchen and turned to look at Thor.

Thor stood at the foot of the steps, unsure of what to do. Defending the Pack from outside hadn't worked very well, but going inside would limit his ability to fight.

Dad looked at him and thought about the kitten, and about Thor's recent erratic behavior. The hair on Thor's back was still high, but there was no malice in his face.

"Get inside," he said at last. Thor leaped up the stairs in one bound, happy to leave the decision making to his Leader.

Dad closed the door, locked it, checked the front door, and finally started up the stairs with Mom. Thor rudely pushed past them to check on Brett and Teddy.

Teddy was standing in his bedroom door, waiting for his parents. Thor ran past him and into the dark room, where Brett was in bed with the covers pulled up to his chin.

Brett whispered, "Hi, Thor," and reached out to pat his head.

Thor was satisfied. He turned and left the room, barged past Mom and Dad at the top of the stairs, and went down to take his position at the front line of defense.

"Dad?" Teddy said nervously, "Brett wants to talk to you."

"I do not!" Brett shouted from inside the bedroom.

Tom looked at Janet and rolled his eyes. *Now what?*

"Maybe you and I should talk," he said to Teddy. "Step into

my office for a moment." He turned toward the bathroom and motioned Teddy to follow him. Teddy shrugged and followed him in. Tom closed the door behind them and sat on the toilet with his hands on his knees. His dead-tired mind wondered idly if he would ever find his way back to bed.

"Okay, what's up?" he asked.

"Well . . . Brett saw something in the yard," Teddy said. "He says it was a . . . " He looked at the floor, embarrassed. " . . . a werewolf."

Tom broke into a wide grin despite himself. He didn't want to humiliate his son.

"Well, did you tell him there aren't any werewolves?"

"He knows that. That's why he didn't want to tell you. But he's really scared, Dad. I mean, *really* scared."

"Okay. I'll talk to him. C'mon, let's get out of here."

They walked together to Brett and Teddy's room. Brett lay in the dark, with his face to the wall, silent and motionless, pretending to be asleep—and perfectly aware that he wasn't fooling anyone.

Tom turned on a lamp and draped a T-shirt over the lamp shade to subdue the light. He sat on the edge of Brett's bed and gently shook him, playing along with the sleep charade.

"Hey, guy," he said softly. "I heard you saw something outside. Wanna tell me about it?" In his mind, Tom saw himself as Hugh Beaumont, the father in *Leave It to Beaver*. A little patience and a little understanding would work everything out.

Brett turned around, and Tom was stunned by his expression. He wasn't frightened, he was *terrified*. Hugh Beaumont was immediately forgotten.

"Brett?" he said as calmly as possible. "What's wrong?"

Brett just looked at him.

"C'mon, Brett," Tom urged. "Talk to me."

"I saw it," Brett said, barely able to hold back tears, "and . . . I think it saw me!" As he spoke, Brett gradually pulled the covers tighter around his chin. Tom noticed Brett's breathing was rapid and shallow.

"Saw what, Brett?" Tom asked. He wasn't sure what to say, but he knew better than to let any trace of disbelief sneak into his voice.

"It . . . it was hairy all over, and it had long teeth. But it . . . it looked like a man."

"You're sure you weren't having a bad dream?"

"No!" both boys shouted in unison. Tom threw Teddy a questioning look, then Brett continued.

"I went to the bathroom and I heard Kitty and I looked out the window and the werewolf came toward the house and then Thor came and fought with him and chased him away." Tom suppressed a smile. It sounded like a dream all right. He turned to Teddy.

"What do you know about this?" he asked.

"Nothing," Teddy said. "But I wasn't in the bathroom. Brett wasn't dreaming, Dad. We were awake the whole time."

What the hell? Tom thought.

"Are you sure this werewolf wasn't Thor?" he asked Brett, hoping the answer would be no. There were no other big dogs in the immediate neighborhood, and no other plausible explanations.

"No, Dad! Thor was in the woods! He came back after the werewolf killed Kitty! He chased him through the neighbors' fence!"

Tom was at a total loss. Whatever was going on, it wasn't going to be resolved tonight, that much was sure. And he was dying to get back to bed.

"Well, look," he offered, "as long as Thor chased him away, we're safe, right? And Thor is in the house now, so I'm sure if there *is* a werewolf out there, he won't try anything. We can figure this out tomorrow, okay?" He tousled Brett's hair and hoped his attempt to trivialize the night's events had some effect.

Brett went through the motions of being reassured. At least

Dad *knew,* even if he didn't believe. And now that Brett had unloaded his story, he started feeling tired. He even began to doubt what he'd seen. Werewolves were possible when you were hiding under the covers in the dark, but with a light on and Dad sitting here, they were just movie actors with hair glued on their faces. He relaxed his grip on the covers, and Dad turned off the light, walked to the door, and went to close it.

"Dad?" Brett said.

"Yeah, Brett?"

"Could you leave the door open a crack?"

"Sure," Tom said, thinking Brett wanted the hall light to illuminate his room. In fact, Brett wanted Thor to be able to get in.

Tom left the door open about an inch. "That okay?" he said from the hall.

"Thanks, Dad," Brett said. "Good night."

"Good night, Dad," Teddy said.

"Good night, guys."

Thor waited to hear Mom and Dad's bedroom door close before going upstairs for one last check on the kids. He sniffed Debbie's door and pushed it with his nose; it was shut tight, as it should be. But Teddy and Brett's door was ajar. He wedged it open with his nose and walked over to Teddy's bed. It was clear from the rhythm of Teddy's breathing that the boy was quickly sinking into sleep. He crossed the room and laid his head on Brett's bed and sniffed Brett's fingers. Brett reached out and petted him. A slight tremble in Brett's hand confirmed Thor's interpretation of his breathing: Brett was scared.

"You know, don't you, Thor?" Brett whispered.

His words were meaningless, but the fear in his voice was disturbing. Thor hopped onto the bed, putting his body between Brett and the open door, and pretended to settle down for the night.

He lay there for almost a half hour, until Brett's breathing said he was asleep. Then he carefully crept off the bed and out of the room. He checked Debbie's door one last time and, ignoring the muted conversation behind Mom and Dad's door, went downstairs to continue his vigil.

An hour later the house was calm and everyone but Thor was asleep. He lay on the easy chair near the stairs, watching the living room windows and listening to the silence.

The Bad Thing was out there, and when it returned, Thor would be waiting for it. He would not be tricked into leaving the Pack again. And he would not let the Bad Thing near the Pack. Not under any circumstances, not for any reason.

The Bad Thing had killed Kitty. And while Thor's feelings toward her weren't as deep as his feelings toward the rest of the Pack, she was still Pack, and guarding her had been his responsibility. Her death was his fault.

He'd failed in his Duty. His gut felt like an inner tube that had been tied in a knot and stretched tight.

He would not sleep tonight.

CHAPTER

13

As dawn approached, the Bad Thing's presence faded out completely. The Bad Thing was gone again, to wherever it went when it wasn't around. But it would come back. And Uncle Ted would come back, too.

Thor knew Uncle Ted wasn't in his apartment, and never would be when the Bad Thing was around. Thor didn't understand the connection between them, but he knew they were connected.

About a half hour before dawn, the sound of twigs snapping in the woods announced Uncle Ted's arrival. Thor ran to the kitchen and stood up against the door. He growled quietly to himself as he watched Uncle Ted step naked from the woods wearing only his running shoes. He walked hunched over, clutching his bloodied ankle with one hand.

The sight of the wounded ankle sent a shock of recognition through Thor. Suddenly everything fell into place.

Uncle Ted was *the Bad Thing*.

Thor needed no further explanation.

Unlike humans, Thor's reality was based on observations, not explanations. He had no explanation for birds or butterflies or cars or rain, but that didn't cause him to doubt their reality.

He watched Uncle Ted with growing hostility as the naked man hopped up the stairs to his garage apartment. The apartment door quietly closed behind him, and Thor lay down on the floor. The Pack was safe for a while.

The morning sky lightened, and Thor relaxed.

His head settled onto his crossed forepaws, he sighed deeply, and his eyes fluttered closed.

They opened an hour after sunrise, when his biological clock told him Mom was overdue for her morning jog.

The house was completely still. He rushed up the stairs and poked the bedroom doors. Mom and Dad's door was shut tight, and there was no fresh scent of her in the upstairs hall. Mom hadn't left without waking him (which was just about impossible, anyway). She was still in bed.

Brett and Teddy's door was open, and the boys were asleep in their beds. Debbie's door was closed, and like Mom and Dad's, it bore no recent scent trail. She was in bed, too.

Thor went downstairs and was on his way back to the kitchen, wondering why Mom wasn't up, when he realized it was Saturday. For the first time in his memory, a weekend had arrived without his anticipating it. And for the first time, he didn't care. He was in no mood for fun. He was too busy with the problem of protecting the Pack.

He'd made a lot of mistakes, and each one had increased the danger to the Pack. He'd respected the Pack's rules and allowed Uncle Ted free run of the Pack's territory, and now Kitty was dead. And it was Thor's fault. He'd failed to protect her.

The enemy was in their midst, but Thor was torn between his instinct to protect the Pack at all costs and his instinctual prohibition of violence within the Pack. For whatever else Uncle Ted might be, Thor *felt* he was a Pack member. And in the end, it was feelings—and *only* feelings—that held the Pack together.

Why didn't Dad resolve this problem? How could Thor deal with such complex issues, issues he couldn't begin to understand, issues any human could (he was sure) breeze through without effort? Why did they burden him with unsolvable problems?

And yet they did. They acted as if nothing was wrong.

How could they fail to see the danger in their midst?

But they *did* fail to see it. Only Thor saw.

And his solution to the problem was Bad. It required actions only a Bad Dog could take. Actions only a Bad Dog could even contemplate.

It wasn't fair. It wasn't right.

But Thor's Duty wouldn't go away, and Uncle Ted wouldn't go away, and Dad wouldn't intervene. It was Thor's problem, and no one else's.

He could not allow Uncle Ted to get to the Pack again, not under any circumstances, not for any reason.

If Thor had to be a Bad Dog to save the Pack, then he had to be a Bad Dog. There was no other option.

Mom and Dad eventually came down to the kitchen together. Thor immediately noticed that Dad was quietly keeping an eye on him.

Unsure of his position with Dad, Thor lay on the kitchen floor and wagged his tail instead of getting up to greet him.

"Hi, Thor," Dad said, but the cheerfulness in his voice was false. He reached down to pet him, but he watched Thor warily, as if he might have to withdraw his hand at a moment's notice.

Thor could see that Dad was afraid of him; the realization pierced his heart like a knife.

He was already a Bad Dog just for *thinking* about protecting them from Uncle Ted.

Dad touched Thor without much feeling, but with increasing confidence. It made Thor feel a little better, but it didn't make him feel good.

Nothing would ever make him feel good again. He was going to commit Badness on a monumental scale today. Badness for which there could be no redemption or forgiveness.

Today was the last day he would ever see the Pack.

Tom was worried. Thor was acting strange, secretive, possibly guilty, he couldn't be sure. Had Thor killed the cat? Had Tom endangered the family by letting him back in the house last night? Thor hadn't looked guilty then, but he sure did now. Thor hadn't shown any sign of sickness, no fever or foaming at the mouth. But then again, he hadn't been eating much lately. What if Thor had some strange disorder that was causing personality changes? That would explain Brett's "werewolf." Maybe he should take a closer look at Kitty's remains, and Thor's reaction to them.

Maybe he should get the dog out of the house—now.

"C'mon out," Dad said with a false geniality that Thor heard clearly. Dad opened the back door and watched Thor trot out to the garage stairs, where he sat down and tried to look casual.

He walked across the yard and called for Thor to follow him to the back of the garage. Thor glanced up at Uncle Ted's door and followed Dad. He didn't have to be at the base of the stairs to hear the door if it should open.

They rounded the garage and Dad scanned the ground.

Kitty's body was gone.

Tom studied Thor for some clue as to what the hell was going on. He saw nothing. The dog's expression seemed to mirror his own feelings: tension, confusion, and nothing else.

Tom walked back to the house as Thor resumed his watch at the foot of the garage stairs. He wasn't planning on letting Thor back in the house, not until he had some idea what was happening. He wasn't worried about Thor bothering Uncle

Ted. Ted had been sleeping in later and later in the last few days. Before he'd come to live with the family, Ted had made it clear that he sometimes stayed up all night, and he wanted to be left alone on those occasions.

But he'd apparently slept through the events of last night and the night before, Tom remembered suddenly. The lights had been on in the apartment both times, but Uncle Ted had never once stuck his head out the door, or even looked out a window to see what the commotion was. What *was* he doing all night? Tom wished he could think of a subtle way to ask Ted about it. Maybe later.

He'd completely forgotten the question that was on his mind when he woke up: How did Thor get out last night?

Tom stood on the kitchen steps and took a last look at the strange tableau in the backyard. Whatever this obsession with Uncle Ted was all about, things looked placid enough for the moment. And Ted wouldn't be up for hours. Tom went inside, closing the kitchen door behind him. He had an important football game to watch.

Deep in the fourth quarter Tom had no idea why he was still watching. His team would have to make three touchdowns and two field goals just to tie up the score, and in the meantime the opposing team had possession and was well on its way to another TD.

So when the front doorbell rang, it was a relief instead of a nuisance to be pulled away from the slaughter.

The man on the porch looked vaguely nervous but determined. Tom instantly recognized the posture of the process-server. Immediately his heart started thumping in his chest.

The man cleared his throat and began:

"Are you . . . ?" he said, and recited Tom's full name, middle name and all.

Tom's mouth felt suddenly dry and he found himself unable to swallow. He nodded in response to the man's inquiry. The process-server took it in stride. He'd obviously seen this before.

The situation seemed somehow unreal to Tom, even though he'd half expected this for some time now—ever since Flopsy failed to show up at his office.

I probably shouldn't have humiliated him, he thought, *even if he didn't have a case. So now I'm getting sued. Great. After all the suits I've threatened, filed, deflected, and defended for other people, it's finally happening to me.* He felt almost as if he were in a state of shock.

Then a strange question popped incongruously into his head.

What's wrong with this picture?

The man on the porch seemed to deflate a little as it became obvious that there would be no shouting, screaming, threats, or violence. He was almost apologetic as he handed Tom the papers.

What's wrong with this picture? the tiny voice in Tom's mind repeated as he tried to keep his mind on the business at hand. *What's missing?*

Tom watched the man turn to go as another idiotic thought entered his mind: *Do you tip process-servers?*

He closed the door and scanned the papers nervously as he walked to the kitchen, noticing that his hands were shaking slightly. The details of the suit were sketchy, as he'd expected. There was no mention of physical injury, which was good. If Flopsy had been pissed enough, he might have gone and gotten another dog to bite him, then sworn it was Thor. But then, if he could get another dog to bite him, why waste it—why not sue *that* dog's owner too? No, Flopsy wasn't attempting any large-scale deception. The suit was primarily for the "traumatizing effect" of Thor's "unprovoked attack."

He flipped through the papers impatiently and found what he was looking for. A motion to have the dog destroyed. Of course. Flopsy didn't stand a chance in hell of winning the suit, but he had a very good shot at having Thor killed. Tom sat down at the kitchen table with the papers in hand, wondering exactly what he was going to do about this, when suddenly he realized what had been missing during the encounter with the process-server.

Thor.

He hadn't come to the door. He was in the backyard when Tom last saw him, so it wasn't surprising that he hadn't heard the man approach the front door, but even from the backyard he should have heard the doorbell and come running, the way he always did.

What the hell?

Tom went to the kitchen window and pushed the little curtain aside. Thor was still lying at the foot of the garage stairs, apparently asleep.

Then, as Tom watched, the apartment door at the top of the stairs opened.

The click of the latch at the top of the stairs snapped Thor awake instantly. Uncle Ted stepped onto the landing fully dressed, his wound concealed. He looked at Thor and took a tentative step down the stairs. Thor showed no animosity.

Inside the house, Tom dropped the curtain and dashed through the back door and onto the steps. Then, fearing that he might startle Thor into action, he stopped himself and tried to act calm.

"Hi, Ted!" he said nervously.

Thor heard the apprehension in Dad's voice and thought Dad finally understood that Uncle Ted was a threat. But he did his best to pretend nothing was up while he waited for the last piece of evidence: the one that would confirm or deny everything.

"Good morning," Uncle Ted said. His voice and posture overwhelmingly proclaimed his guilt, but Thor still waited.

Uncle Ted continued down the stairs, trying not to be too

obvious about watching Thor. Dad came up quietly behind Thor and reached down to pet him.

There was something artificial in Dad's touch, but Thor kept his attention focused on Uncle Ted. Uncle Ted stepped onto the cement walk and Dad slipped his index finger into the loop on Thor's choker. Thor noticed but pretended not to. He knew if he betrayed his intentions prematurely he would never get another chance.

He'd only succeeded in doing one thing right since the trouble started: He'd drawn blood from the Bad Thing's ankle. He couldn't afford to make another mistake. He sat perfectly still and tried to look normal.

Uncle Ted walked up to Dad and Thor, as guilty as any Bad Dog Thor had ever seen. Thor was certain Dad could see it—he'd always seen Thor's guilt.

Uncle Ted came into range, and Thor nonchalantly sniffed the bottom of his pants leg.

Underneath Uncle Ted's pants was a clean cotton bandage, the potent odor of disinfectant, and dried blood. Thor had no difficulty matching dried blood with fresh, but the unexpected disinfectant smell confused him for a second. He took a few deep breaths to numb his nose to the disinfectant. The blood scent came through, clear and strong.

It was the Bad Thing's blood. There was no doubt.

Smelling is knowing.

Thor glanced up at Uncle Ted for an instant to see exactly where his throat was. Then he leaped.

Tom felt his hand suddenly rise up into the air. It was halfway to Uncle Ted's neck before he realized what was happening and pulled back hard.

The chain closed painfully around Thor's neck and he felt his flight cut short as Uncle Ted brought an arm up to shield himself.

Thor snapped at Uncle Ted's forearm and his fangs sank into flesh, but Dad yanked him backward before he could clamp down and do any real damage. Uncle Ted stumbled back, stunned, as Dad slipped on the grass and fell backward, pulling Thor with him.

Thor found his balance, dug his claws into the ground, and pulled violently to get at Uncle Ted, snapping his head from side to side and choking himself in the process. Blood spread onto Uncle Ted's torn sleeve as Thor lurched at him with jaws open and fangs bared. Dad lay flat on his back, his index finger nearly dislocated but still in the choker, which he held on to desperately with both hands. The collar closed around Thor's neck and he gagged horribly as his teeth snapped uselessly on air.

Uncle Ted stumbled backward onto the stairs as blood ran down his arm, soaking his shirt sleeve and coating his hands. He squeezed his forearm to slow the bleeding as he chanted, "Oh shit! Oh shit!" over and over again. He ripped away the sleeve with his teeth and looked at the bite. It was only a flesh wound, just deep enough to bleed like hell. He was okay. Still, he felt his blood pressure drop and he sat down on the stairs and started to put his head between his knees.

"Get upstairs!" Dad shouted, *"Quick! I don't know how long I can hold him!"* Uncle Ted stumbled up the stairs in a daze, leaving bright splashes of blood in his wake.

Thor growled and snarled and snapped at him from the end of Dad's arm, but the attack was over and he knew it.

And once again, he had failed.

Dad struggled to his feet and pulled the choker with both hands. His index finger hurt like a bitch, but he dragged Thor back to the house with his front feet off the ground, retching and gagging all the way. Dad hated choking him like that, but he didn't dare let Thor's feet touch the ground. Thor was much too heavy and powerful; it was a miracle that Dad had managed to hang on to him this long.

Mom stood in the kitchen door with her hands over her mouth, panic-stricken. She quickly stepped aside as Dad hustled Thor through the kitchen to the cellar door. Thor struggled as hard as he could without attacking Dad, but once his hind feet touched the slippery kitchen floor, he gave up. He offered no resistance as Dad opened the cellar door and pushed him through. He tumbled down a few steps before his feet found the stairs, then continued down on his own. He headed straight for the darkest corner and dropped to the dirty cement floor.

He felt only guilt.

There was no question of the Badness of what he'd done. The attack, as necessary as it might have been, not only violated Dad's Law, but Natural Law as well. Any violence within the Pack was anarchy, a threat to the very existence of packs.

And Thor hadn't committed just any violence: He'd tried to *kill* within his Pack.

He was a pariah, a disease, unfit to live in a pack.

His guilt was total. He felt the tightness around his chest, and the feeling of shrinking inside himself returned. He would not feel better. He was permanently and irrevocably alone, and he knew in his gut that he wouldn't live long without his Pack.

He had no wish to go upstairs and seek forgiveness. He couldn't face the Pack. He didn't deserve their love, their companionship, their food, or their home. He was a menace to Natural Order.

Sounds from upstairs reached his ears, but he heard nothing. Even his sense of smell seemed to fade away. He stared without seeing, and thought only about the terrible thing he'd done.

He remembered biting Teddy, he remembered Kitty, whom he'd shamefully failed to protect, he remembered his disobedience, culminating with the way he'd fought with Dad only moments ago.

But worst of all, he remembered how he'd *enjoyed* the taste of Uncle Ted's blood—the final proof of his Badness. Only a Bad Dog could enjoy the taste of a pack member's blood. Only a Bad Dog could know what it tasted like.

He expected to die in the cellar, and hoped death would

come soon. In the meantime, there was nothing to do but wait.

All sense of time faded out, along with the details of the cellar around him. He felt nothing but emptiness and Badness. He felt ugly and misshapen and was glad no one could see him.

He didn't hear the frantic conversations and scurrying around upstairs; they were none of his business. The Pack was no longer his concern—he no longer had concerns. He was totally alone, totally separate from the Pack. He would never go home again. He had no home to go to.

Janet held Uncle Ted's arm over the kitchen sink as cold water washed over the gash.

"You'll need to see a doctor," Tom said.

"No I won't," Ted said. "It's just a flesh wound. No veins or arteries or tendons cut, nothing I can't handle."

"You're going to need a tetanus shot," Tom said.

"I'll give myself a tetanus shot," Uncle Ted insisted. "You think I can go into an Amazon rain forest for six months with a first-aid kit? I have sutures, I have local anesthetic, I have disinfectant, and I have penicillin. I have everything I need and I've had plenty of practice using it. This won't be the first tetanus shot I've given myself." He paused for a moment and added quietly, almost ruefully, "Besides, I don't like doctors. Believe me, it's no big deal."

"Okay," Tom said. There was something terribly disturbing about Uncle Ted's comments—or was it his attitude? Tom couldn't put his finger on what it was.

There was nothing else for Tom to do but make the phone call, the one he dreaded making. The one to the pound. He wished someone else could do it, but there wasn't anyone else. He picked up the phone book and looked up the number.

He felt like shit.

CHAPTER

14

TIME stood still in the cellar. Hours went by unnoticed as Thor waited for nothing, his pain punctuated by darting, uncontrolled, random memories of times spent with the Pack. Already, he missed the Pack desperately.

His depression was so deep that he didn't react when the cellar door finally opened. Ordinarily, he would have been thrilled. Ordinarily, it would have meant a chance for redemption. But those days were gone forever.

He hoped no one would come down into the cellar. He didn't want to be seen in his current state. He was a Bad Dog. Why didn't they leave him alone?

He recognized Dad's footsteps on the stairs—the worst of all possibilities.

Did Dad want to tell Thor what a Bad Dog he was? Why? Thor knew.

Unfamiliar footsteps followed Dad halfway down the stairs, and Thor experienced an odd sensation of understanding.

Dad found him in his Bad Dog corner and approached him cautiously.

Seeing Dad's fear made him feel even worse. He'd done what he'd done to protect the Pack, but his Badness was so profound that the Pack not only rejected him, they *feared* him. Was there no limit to his Badness?

Dad held a knot of leather in his hand. Thor watched impassively as Dad cautiously, nervously knelt next to him and slipped the thing over his snout and fastened it in place with metal couplers. At least Dad didn't look at Thor's eyes while he did it. Dad acted almost as ashamed as Thor, though Thor didn't notice it. He was just glad to be spared another confrontation. As soon as the muzzle was in place, Dad hooked a leash to it and stood back to make way for the two men who waited on the stairs.

They wore white suits with an emblem on their shirt pockets. Thor couldn't remember having seen them before, but there was an awful familiarity about them that terrified him.

One of them tugged gently on the leash, then tugged again a little harder after Thor failed to move.

"C'mon, Thor," the stranger said. Something told Thor his suffering would end faster if he went with them. He listlessly got to his feet on trembling legs, and followed the tugging leash without looking around at his former Pack Leader.

Dad stayed in the cellar as they took Thor upstairs. That figured. Thor was no longer Dad's dog, no longer *anyone's* dog. Why should anyone follow him?

The man with the leash led Thor through the kitchen and out the back door. His partner followed, carrying a shotgun.

There was no one in the kitchen, and no sounds in the house. The Pack was gone, except for Dad. The Pack's car was gone, too. In its place was a small white truck with no windows on the back.

The man with the leash opened the back of the truck and led Thor inside with surprising gentleness. Thor made no attempt to sniff either of the men, but their scents reached his nose nonetheless. They were totally unfamiliar.

And yet he felt he knew them and where they were going.

He got into the empty truck. The man put the free end of his leash through a slot in the door, so he could grab it from outside before opening the door again. The inside of the truck was all metal, with no padding or upholstery. Thor lay down as soon as he was inside, and waited to leave.

In the cellar, Dad sat in the dark with his face in his hands, his body shaking with silent, bitter sobs.

Thor couldn't escape the feeling that he knew where the truck was going; it filled him with a mixture of relief and unspeakable dread.

As the truck bumped and swerved its way through the streets, Thor became restless. Something in the distance worried him. Something he thought he heard over the sound of the truck's engine.

After a short drive, the truck slowed to a stop and Thor began to tremble. The moment the engine died, he heard what had bothered him. It was the distant, muffled howling of a hundred dogs and cats.

One of the white-suited attendants opened the back door, and the living music of despair filled Thor's ears. He trembled horribly as they dragged him out of the van. Ahead lay an ugly, squat, cinder-block building. Animals wailed from inside.

A horrible déjà vu came over him: He *knew* this place.

He knew what he would see and hear and smell inside the blocky, featureless building. He struggled to get away and yet . . . he felt a strange attraction for the building, almost as if it were . . .

????

They pulled him to the front door, opened it, and dragged him into a small lobby. Then one of them opened a second door, and they took him into the holding area.

He caught a whiff of the interior and fear swallowed him whole. His legs felt like they would give way, the blood drained out of his face, and the tightness in his chest threatened to suffocate him on the spot.

He *had* known what the place would smell like, and sound like, and look like.

He'd seen the wire cages before, hundreds of them, covering the walls, stacked up to the ceiling, each one occupied by an animal waiting to die. He'd heard the voices of the condemned animals rise in a symphony of despair. He'd smelled the acrid soup of urine and feces, dirty dogs and cats, and above all and beneath all, the smell of death.

This was the House of Death.

This was the place where the Angel of Death walked, taking animals from their cages every day. And every day, the voices of fear and misery were silenced. And every day, new voices of fear and misery replaced them. And the smell of death was always strong and fresh.

Thor whimpered and clawed at the smooth concrete floor, trying to get a grip, trying to find some way out. But there was no way out. The men pulled him steadily to his cage to await the Angel of Death. His bladder emptied on the floor, humiliating him further, though he was almost too deep in shock to notice what he'd done.

And yet it wasn't death that he feared. It was knowledge. Some unthinkable memory that had been locked away forever was getting out. He wanted to run from it, but there was no escape.

He knew this place because he was born here. This was his true home.

His original Pack, his *real* Pack, had all been pups. He'd cried and wailed with them in their tiny cage, and the Angel of Death had answered their cries. One by one, the Angel of Death took them from the cage and into another room, where their cries were stilled and they joined the other Bad Dogs in silence. One by one they left, until only Thor remained—nameless, unloved, alone, and terrified. His time was coming—the Angel of Death was on his way—but something happened, someone intervened.

A pack of humans visited the House of Death, and all the Bad Dogs somehow knew the visitors could save them. All the Bad Dogs howled and yelped at the visitors to get their attention, to tell them of their sadness and loneliness, to beg forgiveness for their Badness, and to beg to be taken away from the House of Death.

The visitors were Mom and Dad and Teddy and Brett.

Janet hated the pound from the moment she set foot inside. She looked without seeing, stunned by the misery around her, the hopelessness of the animals, and worst of all, the animals' apparent understanding of their situation. *These creatures knew they were doomed.*

She'd thought it would be like a trip to a pet shop. It was more like a tour of a concentration camp.

While Janet tried to shut herself off from the reality around her, Tom carefully examined the dogs. He didn't like the pound either, but he didn't want to waste the trip, and he didn't want to have to come back. His eyes met Thor's for an instant, then passed on to the next cage. Thor whimpered to him, but he didn't look back. Janet followed Tom blindly down the row of cramped cages. They stopped about five feet from Thor's cage and turned to face each other.

Janet told Tom she wanted to leave. She didn't like being here for even a short visit, and she didn't like the kids being here, either. She wanted out, and right away.

But while Janet and Tom talked, Teddy pressed his face to Thor's cage, looked in, and said, "Bitchin'!"

Thor looked up and their eyes met, and Teddy saw the loneliness there and looked away, but he'd already made up his mind.

"Let's get this one!" Teddy cried, startling his parents.

Brett ran to see what his big brother had found. Teddy was eight and Brett four. Teddy was Brett's God. Anything Teddy wanted, Brett wanted. As soon as Brett was sure he knew which dog Teddy meant, he yelled, "Yeah! Me too! Let's get this one!"

Janet and Tom came back to Thor's cage and looked again.

"I don't want a German shepherd," Tom said. "They're overprotective. Besides, Teddy, look at the size of his feet! And those ears! He's going to be a giant! I don't think we can afford such a big dog."

Teddy looked like he might start crying at any second.

"You said we could get any dog we wanted!" he said accusingly.

"I meant 'we, the family,' not you."

"And me!" Brett insisted defensively.

"Okay, that's two votes," Tom said diplomatically, "but Mom and I get to vote, too, and we don't want him." He looked to Janet for solidarity. She shrugged, which he took as tacit approval. He was wrong. Before he could suggest another dog, Janet spoke.

"Tom, I want to get out of here, *now*. And I want the kids out of here, too."

Teddy knew an advantage when he saw it.

"You *promised!*" he screamed, almost as loud as the hopeless wailing around him. "First you said we could get any dog we wanted, now we can't even get a dog!" Brett looked shocked by this announcement; his eyes welled with tears. Teddy pressed the attack home without mercy. "And we can't come back for him tomorrow, 'cause if we come back tomorrow, he'll be *dead!*"

Brett's eyes opened wide with horror. Tom was furious. Brett hadn't known that the dogs were condemned, and Tom had hoped they could get in and out without his younger son finding out. Now Teddy had gone and spilled the beans. Terrific. Bringing the kids here had to be the dumbest idea he'd ever had in his life. Brett looked to his father, his face almost as desperate as the furry faces in the cages, and said just one word.

"No!" He began to bawl uncontrollably.

"It's true!" Teddy shouted, for Brett's benefit, before Tom could say a thing. "Isn't it?" he challenged.

Tom thought, *Thank God I'll never have to face him in court.* He looked at the shepherd puppy, then at Janet. Her expression hadn't changed. She wanted out. There was only one way out.

"You win," he said to Teddy.

They called the attendant.

Thor was confused and terrified. He'd thought he had understood the emotional currents that were battling in front of him, thought there was hope in the human pups' triumph, but instead, the Angel of Death came for him. He backed into the farthest corner of the cramped cage, trembling and wetting himself as the Angel's huge gloved hands reached in. But when the Angel lifted him out, he handed him over to Teddy.

And in that moment, Thor's life changed utterly.

The humans took him out of the House of Death and into their pack. At first even the warmth of their caresses frightened him; their affection was a completely unfamiliar experience. He shivered as they filled out papers in the lobby, and he shivered all the way home in the car.

But eventually (and not after very long at that), he discovered love—both the human Pack's love for him, and his love for his Pack. And he discovered that loving the Pack enriched his life as much as being loved by them.

The Pack had saved him. They'd taken him from the House of Death and into light, into warmth, into life itself.

And he'd failed them.

He was a Bad Dog. He'd always been a Bad Dog. He was *born* a Bad Dog, and his Badness had finally come out. They'd been wrong to take him from the House of Death, and he'd finally shown them their error. And they'd finally corrected it.

They'd sent him back where he belonged.

The uniformed men led Thor to a wire cage on the floor—he was too big to lift into a higher cage—and pushed him inside. It was too small for him to stand up, but he didn't care. He had no desire to stand up. He was just able to turn around and silently watch them lock the cage.

He quickly lost awareness of the constant din around him. He was alone in the world, and the presence of other animals did nothing to change that. He felt only his Badness. Only the Angel of Death could quiet the turmoil inside him.

When the Angel finally came for him, Thor would gratefully kiss his gloved hands.

CHAPTER

15

Tom sat at the kitchen table in the shadows, sipping a cup of coffee and watching the garage. He'd been sitting there for over an hour, watching the room darken with the sky, but he never made a move to turn on a light. It was past his bedtime, but he was fully dressed in a dark brown shirt (the darkest he owned), new blue jeans (also his darkest), and hiking boots.

He'd left Janet upstairs, watching TV in the bedroom.

He'd told her he needed to be alone, probably wouldn't be able to sleep tonight, might take a long walk later on.

It was a lie. What he needed was to spy on her brother.

An early riser and early sleeper by nature, he never drank coffee after six P.M., said it kept him up all night. It was just past nine, and he was on his second cup.

The door of the garage apartment opened, and Tom instinctively withdrew another inch from the kitchen window. There was no reason to; he was six feet away from it and completely enshrouded in shadow.

He fingered the flashlight in his lap nervously as he

watched Ted creep down the stairs in a brand-new sweatsuit. Carefully, silently, Tom pushed his chair away from the kitchen table. Ted couldn't possibly hear it, but Janet might.

He had no idea what his surveillance might reveal, but he had a gut feeling that Janet would rather not know about it.

Something metallic glinted in Ted's hand—could it be the *handcuffs?* What for?

Out of nowhere, Tom realized what he had found so disturbing about the conversation he'd had with Ted after Thor attacked him: It was Ted's acceptance of the situation. He'd never once wondered *why* Thor had attacked him. If anything, he'd seemed to take it for granted.

Things had been getting progressively stranger from the day Ted arrived, and the time had come to find out why. The idea of spying on him had seemed childish at first, but it sure looked like a stroke of genius now.

Ted reached the bottom of the stairs, crossed the yard to the creek, jumped across, and disappeared into the trees.

Tom rushed to the back door, silently opened it, and sprinted across the yard. He waited a moment at the garage to give Ted time to clear the immediate area, then peeked around. He couldn't see a thing in the dense woods, but it was easy enough to hear Ted. He was on a jogging path, heading into the depths of the forest. And he was making damn good time for a man without a flashlight. If Tom didn't move fast, he would lose him for sure.

He hopped over the creek and stepped into the woods. His ears were trained on Ted's movements while his eyes strained to see the twigs and leaves on the path. He couldn't afford to step on a single one.

He took a few steps into the woods and stopped dead. As soon as he left the ambient light from Ted's apartment windows, the ground in front of him became as featureless as black velvet. The moon was just beginning to peek over the eastern horizon, but if he waited for it to light the way, Ted would be long gone. He cupped his hand over the flashlight lens, so only a tiny beam of light played over the ground. Hopefully, Ted wouldn't see it if he turned around.

About a quarter mile into the woods, Tom was having an increasingly hard time keeping up with Ted. A full moon had begun to peek over the horizon behind him, but what little light reached through the trees didn't do much to illuminate the path. And Ted was going much farther into the woods than Tom anticipated. And he was picking up speed, too.

Where the hell is he going, Tom wondered, *and what's his hurry?*

Wherever it was, Tom wasn't going to see it if he didn't get a move on. The gap between them was widening, and the only way to close it was to take more chances. He could see *most* of the sticks and leaves in the path, and after all, Ted wasn't being quiet—if Tom made just one or two little noises, he probably wouldn't notice.

He picked up his pace as Ted led him deeper into the woods, far from the familiar jogging routes. They followed a small ravine into the foothills, on a narrow path that must have been used exclusively by kids; it ran over large roots and under branches that Tom had to duck. Sometimes the path (if that's what it really was) cut across the small creek that cut the gully. Whoever used the path didn't care about getting their feet wet.

Finally the path led onto flat ground again, and the trees thinned out somewhat, but Ted was nowhere in sight. Tom stopped and listened and heard nothing. Instead, he *felt* something, something powerful and vicious in the shadows. He shook himself, told himself to grow up, and headed west, the general direction Ted had been taking. He noticed that he hardly needed the flashlight anymore. The moon was almost off the horizon and beginning to light the landscape.

He scanned the ground and found a path. He took a few cautious steps forward and heard a burst of rustling sounds in the distance. He'd heard it before, on outings with Thor. It was the sound of small animals being flushed from their nests, fleeing an intruder in their midst.

He peered through the silvery landscape and was just able to make out a human silhouette in the middle of a large clearing. Ted was looking at the moon and examining the trunk of a lone tree in the clearing.

Again Tom's gut told him to stay away, go home, do anything but meet the figure in the shadows. And again he shrugged off the sensation, marveling at how easily his imagination ran away with him.

He crept to within about a hundred feet of the clearing when his foot came down on a dry branch. It snapped like a firecracker in the stillness of the forest.

Ted spun around and spotted Tom immediately. Something like a deep laugh came out his throat, something that also sounded like a growl.

"Ahhhh," Ted said, "Company! Company! Just what I came here to *get away from!* Who is it—Tom? Is that you?"

Tom stepped forward and raised his flashlight to his face. "Yeah, it's me," he said, trying to sound nonchalant. "What's up, Ted?"

Again that strange, growl-like laugh.

"So! Playing James Bond, are we, Tom?" Ted said. His voice sounded unnaturally gruff, as if he were a lifelong chainsmoker. Not at all the way he'd sounded just two hours ago. "Well," he said, "you've caught me at an awkward moment, Tom. I was just about to . . . " again the awful growl " . . . about to . . . *restrain* myself. . . . "

He looked down at the handcuffs in his hands and slowly shook his head. "But now that you're here, that might be . . . somewhat pointless."

"What are you talking about?" Tom asked, unwisely taking a step closer. He shined the flashlight on Ted's face and was startled to see a beard—the man looked like Richard Nixon with a two-day growth. But he was clean-shaven at dinner tonight! What the hell?

"I'm talking about . . ." Ted said, then stopped and thought hard, as if he'd forgotten what he was about to say. "I'm talking about . . ." Then he remembered.

"Lust! Yes, yes, *lust! That's* what I'm talking about! 'The moon is a harsh mistress.' Ever heard that before, Tom?"

"Yes."

"Well, you don't know *shit!* You don't know what a harsh mistress *is!* You *can't know,* because *you don't know lust!* I know lust, you son of a bitch! I know the lust of the moon, what it does, and what it demands! And I *serve* those lusts, motherfucker! I am the moon's servant!"

He threw his head back and a ragged laugh came out of him that chilled Tom to the bone. "I'm her indentured servant, asshole! Get it? In*dent*ured servant!" He laughed again, and went through some kind of inner struggle. He calmed himself and said, "I feel sorry afterward you know, when the moon is gone and the sun is out . . . I really *do,* Tom, and it's important to me that you believe that . . ."

His mood shifted again, hardened.

"But when the moon calls, as she's calling now, I *answer!*" He gazed at the growing white sphere on the horizon. A thought suddenly entered his mind and he patted himself down, looking for something.

"Handcuffs . . ." he said, and shook his head in disbelief. "Handcuffs!" He found them and held them up in the moonlight. "I was going to use these—on *myself!* Can you believe that?" His face reflected another inner struggle, and his whole body convulsed suddenly, as if he were about to throw up. Then he straightened up and smiled horribly.

"But not now. They were supposed to keep people from finding out about my . . . private affair with my mistress. But you already *know,* don't you? Yes, you do. Handcuffs won't keep my little secret anymore.

"Come closer, Tom. Take a good look at my secret. You came this far, come a little closer."

Tom stayed put. There was no longer any doubt in his mind: Ted was dangerously insane.

"Wha's a matter?" Ted taunted. "You don' wanna know my little secret after all? Got cold feet, *shithead?*" His voice was deepening by the second, and his speech was deteriorating with every sentence. He looked at the handcuffs in his hands one last time, snorted, and tossed them contemptuously over his shoulder.

" 'Handcuffs?' " he said, " 'We don' *need* no stinking handcuffs!' " He laughed maniacally at his own joke.

Am I losing my mind? Tom thought. *Did his beard just grow while he was talking?* He played the light over Ted's face, and felt something like an electric shock. Ted needed a shave on his forehead! And his cheekbones! And his hands!

Tom backed up a step.

"Oh, don' go 'way, Tom! Things're just gettin' started! Look! Moon's not even up alla way yet!" Tom glanced over his shoulder; the moon was three-quarters visible. Something told him he'd better not be here when it cleared the horizon.

Tom backed up slowly with his eyes locked on Ted, until he felt a shoulder-high mass of branches and leaves against his back. He blindly groped behind himself for an opening, not daring to turn his back on his brother-in-law.

Ted let out an ear-piercing shriek and flew at him with his arms outstretched, plowing through the underbrush faster than Tom thought possible. Tom stumbled backward in panic, sidestepped the attack at the last possible moment, and fell through the bushes on his ass.

The thing that Ted had become lunged into a wall of bushes that nearly poked an eye out. Infuriated, the creature savaged the branches in mindless rage, then spun around to find his quarry was gone.

Tom looked around and realized he'd backed into a space between bushes; the foliage had opened up, let him through, and closed behind him like a swinging door. A path led off to his right, through a low, tunnel-like cover of arched branches. It wasn't much of an escape route, but there weren't any other choices. He scrambled under the branches, hunched down like a sprinter at the starting line.

The werewolf looked down at the sweatshirt and pants it wore as if noticing them for the first time. It flew into a frenzy, tearing the clothes with its claws and teeth.

When its fury was spent, it wore only a small chain around its neck, with the handcuff key and a key to the garage apartment. It was completely unaware of the chain. It looked around, trying to remember what it had been doing before it shredded the despised clothes.

It tore into the bushes where the man had vanished, finally breaking through into a small clearing. The human was nowhere in sight.

The creature stood still and listened. A scuffling sound in the underbrush revealed Tom's location. The prey had made good use of his time; he was many yards away and increasing his lead with every second. The werewolf's mouth curled in a twisted, vicious smile.

What had looked like a simple kill had become a hunt. It was going to be fun.

The werewolf drew a deep breath, savoring the smell of the night air. But something was wrong—its instincts told it to track the prey with its nose, but its nose wasn't giving it the clear, distinct information it expected. And the prey was getting away.

Confused by the inadequacy of its sense of smell, the werewolf followed the sounds in the distance. It would have to track the prey with its ears, but that was all right. Head start or not, the prey was slow on his feet, and ill-equipped to defend himself. The werewolf would catch the prey before the night was over. And it would taste the prey's blood, and eat the prey's heart.

* * *

Tom ran through the woods in blind panic. He still had the flashlight, thank God, but he had no idea which way he was going. Not that he cared. All that mattered was getting away from the hideous monster Ted had become.

He'd gotten a good head start while the creature was fighting with the foliage, and it looked like he would get away.

He wasn't even sure the thing was following him. He stopped, turned off the flashlight, and listened for a moment. The moon was off the horizon now, but it was behind him. That meant Tom had run deeper into the woods, away from home. It also meant that when he looked behind him, the landscape was shrouded in shadows.

Something moved in the darkness a hundred yards back.

Tom looked around frantically for a weapon. There was nothing he could see on the ground, but he was just a few yards from the ravine he'd followed on the way in. There were rocks down there, smooth and round from erosion but heavy and hard, and a hell of a lot better than nothing. He scrambled into the gully and gathered as many baseball-size stones as he could stuff in his pockets, then emerged with one in his right hand and the flashlight in his left. If the thing caught him, at least he'd go down fighting.

There was a sudden burst of rustling sounds in the distance, then another one, about a hundred feet closer. The werewolf was closing in.

Tom scanned his surroundings, surprised by the brightness of the moonlight. There was a hill to his right that didn't have a path but wasn't covered with bushes, either. He scrambled up as fast as he could, wondering if the rocks in his pockets were really such a good idea after all.

The werewolf charged out of the shadows and tore through the foliage, determined not to let Tom out of its sight. It leaped the stream and started up the hill, looking like a giant insect in the moonlight. At the speed it was climbing, it would be on him in seconds.

Tom hurled a rock with all the strength his fear could muster. The stone struck the werewolf's shoulder with a sharp *crack* and almost broke its collarbone.

The force of the blow stunned the werewolf and it lost its footing for a moment and staggered backward. It threw back its head and let out a deafening howl, venting its pain and announcing its rage.

Tom almost panicked but his will to survive triumphed, and in the midst of his terror, a small quiet part of his mind took control. As the werewolf reared back as if to pound its chest like a gorilla, Tom quickly dug another rock out of his jacket pocket and whipped it at the beast's head.

The rock smashed into the werewolf's pointed ear, crushing the thin flesh and tearing open a painful-looking gash. The werewolf shrieked and started up the hill when another, smaller rock whistled down and struck its right cheekbone just below the eye. The creature's hands flew to its face, wailing in pain as its claws made contact with the fractured cheekbone. Another rock flew past, and the beast took cover.

As soon as he saw the werewolf duck behind a tree, Tom turned and scrambled over the top of the hill, emerging onto a level area of woods. He glanced over his shoulder and saw the werewolf coming up. He threw two more rocks at it and missed both times.

He only had two rocks left. Better save them. He turned and ran toward the thinnest-looking underbrush on the plateau— he'd long since forgotten about finding paths.

He wanted desperately to believe it was all a dream, that any moment he would would wake up, frightened but safe in his bedroom. But the pain in his lungs, the ground hitting his feet, the branches that whipped his face and cut his hands were all undeniably real, regardless of the grotesque impossibility that was chasing him.

He wished he could stop and hide for a second, just to catch his breath and see if it was still chasing him, but the insanity of the idea only deepened his terror.

Don't look back, it might be gaining on you.

He ran as only a man in fear for his life can run; ceaselessly, mindless of the fire in his lungs and legs. His hands burned from the scratches they took pushing branches out of the way. His legs felt warm, then hot, then almost weightless, creating the eerie sensation that he was floating through the forest without touching the ground. It occurred to him that the shadows no longer stretched out in front of him. Had he somehow turned around?

But no—the moon was almost directly overhead.

How long had he been running?

He slowed down just a little, trying to hear if there was anything behind him. What if the monster had given up and gone back to the house instead?

It was impossible to listen while he ran—all he could hear was his own breathing. He chanced a quick look over his shoulder and saw nothing. He couldn't keep running forever. He had to find out if the werewolf was still back there.

He picked out a large tree up ahead, just next to the path, and decided to duck behind it. By the time he made his decision he was almost there.

The tree came up the path at him and he scooted behind it and pressed his body against the trunk. He tried to hold his breath, but it was impossible; his chest refused to stop heaving—his blood was screaming for oxygen. He took five deep breaths and clamped his hand over his nose and mouth.

In the stillness that followed, a series of rapid footsteps suddenly came to a halt twenty or thirty yards back. The werewolf had been behind him all along, gradually closing the distance between them without revealing its presence. And Tom had stopped and let him catch up even more. He was lost.

His only chance was to keep perfectly still and hope the thing didn't find him. His lungs heaved and his body rocked as he held his nose against the urgent demand for air. If he let go and gasped, the werewolf would be on him in seconds. But he couldn't hold his breath forever.

He unbuttoned his shirt with his free hand and pulled it over his mouth and nose. He pressed the fabric into his mouth and willed himself to take a shallow breath, but his will was no match for his lungs.

He sucked in air like a drowning man, wheezing and gasping so loud that he couldn't hear anything else. Then he regained control and heard the footsteps dashing in his direction.

Desperate, he looked up the tree; there was a single branch, about eight feet off the ground. He leaped for it and, to his astonishment, snagged it on the first try. He heard the werewolf's footsteps racing toward him as he gripped the limb with both hands and hauled himself up. In the midst of his panic, he heard a perfectly calm voice in his head say, *It's amazing what you can do when your life depends on it.*

The werewolf rushed the tree just in time to see Tom's feet swing up and out of his reach.

The werewolf regarded him with hungry eyes that showed no trace of recognition. Moonlight gleamed on its sharp canine fangs and saliva ran down its chin.

The werewolf leaped and grabbed the limb. As its short, stubby fingers closed around the branch, Tom swung the flashlight down hard on the creature's knuckles. The werewolf howled and jerked its hand back, then grabbed the tree with both hands, bit it, and shook it with tremendous force. Tom held on for his life.

"Please God please God Jesus please don't let it get me please God Jesus please please please," he chanted, only dimly aware that he was speaking out loud. The werewolf let go of the tree, leaped suddenly, and caught hold of the branch with both misshapen hands. Tom swung down in panic, but the werewolf was ready for him. It reached up and grabbed the flashlight and threw it into bushes about twenty feet from the tree.

The werewolf began to haul itself up and Tom kicked its fingers and ground his heel into its knuckles. Again the werewolf howled and tried to pull away, but its hand was pinned to the branch by Tom's boot. Tom dug a rock out of his pocket and hurled it straight down into the werewolf's face. It struck the monster across the bridge of its nose, and Tom was sure he heard the sharp *click* of breaking bone.

The creature yanked its hand out from under Tom's foot and he almost fell out of the tree.

The werewolf shrieked and licked its damaged fingers and touched its puffing face tenderly. It stared up at Tom with boundless hatred, hissing and showing its fangs.

Tom unconsciously pulled himself up another inch or two, transfixed by the living nightmare below.

One of the werewolf's eyes had swollen shut and a thin line of blood trickled from it to the creature's mouth. The werewolf glared at Tom with its good eye, as if wondering how to get him out of the tree.

Then its face brightened suddenly. As if remembering something important, it took one last look at Tom, grinned hideously, and ran off.

Tom breathed a sigh of relief as he watched the creature disappear into the forest.

Toward the moon. East.

Toward the house.

Oh my God! Tom thought. *Janet! The kids!*

CHAPTER 16

THOR lay in the cramped cage, listening to his heartbeat in the darkness. The Angel of Death had left for the day, and with no humans to hear them, only a few die-hard animals still howled and cried. Perhaps Thor's turn would come tomorrow. He hoped he wouldn't have to wait long.

A scraping noise at the front door startled him out of his gloom. Maybe the Angel of Death had come back for him.

A piercing screech of metal against metal shocked the animals into silence, followed by a series of loud *bangs,* the high-pitched scream of glass shattering, and the squeaky crunch of feet grinding glass into cement. Someone had broken into the outer lobby.

Muffled voices in the lobby sounded strangely familiar. A crowbar scraped against the metal frame of the inner door for a moment, then stopped. The voices argued for a second, then the glass pane of the inner door exploded with a terrific crash, scattering bits of broken glass across the floor. A crowbar swung around the opening, knocked a few of the larger pieces of glass out of the door frame, and Teddy and Brett stepped into the House of Death.

"Jeez," Teddy said. "If we let him out now, he'll cut his feet. You look for his cage while I find a broom." He handed the crowbar to Brett and tried the doorway to Death. It was unlocked. Thor panicked as he watched Teddy step into the Death room. But seconds later, he emerged, still alive, with a broom in his hands. Brett found Thor's cage and attacked it with the crowbar while Teddy swept the broken glass away from the cages.

Teddy looked up from sweeping and saw Brett struggling with the crowbar and getting nowhere.

"Here, gimme that," he said.

Brett had wedged the curved end of the crowbar into the door, but he wasn't strong enough to pry it open. Teddy grabbed the long end with both hands and put one foot against the cage, and together they wrenched the door out of its frame, with its tiny padlock still locked. Teddy peered into the cage.

"C'mon, Thor! You're free!"

Thor looked back at Teddy with oddly mixed feelings. There was something undeniably pleasant about seeing him, but what was he doing here? Thor was no longer part of the Pack. And even if his crime was forgivable, which it wasn't, only Dad could forgive him—not the Pack's pups. Not those he outranked.

"Come *on!*" Teddy ordered, pulling on the muzzle Thor still wore. He tried to sound authoritative, as he had so often recently, but he possessed no authority, not until he was mature, and Thor would be dead by then.

But Thor heard something else in Teddy's voice besides the false authority—desperation.

Thor could ignore Teddy's bluster forever, but he could not ignore his needs—that would only make Thor feel even more guilty, and he didn't think he could bear that.

Just when the pain had begun to fade and he'd started to feel nothing, these two had to come along.

"Thor, come *on,*" Brett added, and there was a hitch in his voice—he would start crying any moment. Brett crawled into the mouth of the cage and unfastened the muzzle.

What was this all about? Thor looked closely at the boys for the first time, and for a moment forgot his Badness and saw only their terror.

They needed him. Desperately. And it was his fault.

The Bad Thing wasn't dead. On top of all Thor's Badness, all his mistakes, he had failed to do his Duty, failed to kill the Bad Thing. Maybe that's why the Angel of Death passed him by and took other animals instead.

The kids were scared, more scared than he'd ever seen them before.

Pack member or not, he still loved them. He couldn't turn his back on them.

He shakily got to his feet and crawled out of the tiny cage. Brett took his collar to guide him through the glass to the front door.

"I got an idea!" Teddy said. "You take him out and wait for me in the woods. I'm gonna let the other animals out. That way, they won't know who did it." Brett wasn't sure about Teddy's plan, but there was no time to argue. The pound was a good block away from the nearest house, almost completely surrounded by forest, but breaking through the doors had been unbelievably loud. Brett was sure a sheriff's deputy would arrive at any second.

He led Thor to the back of the building and into the woods, where they waited for Teddy. They hid in a thicket behind the building, where Brett could see the gravel road that led through the trees to the town.

Dogs and cats suddenly darted out the front door. Some limped from cuts on their feet, and some limped from being locked in tiny cages with no room to stand or walk, but all were glad to be free. Brett counted seven dogs and ten cats before the flashing red and blue lights appeared at the far end of the road.

"Teddyyyyyyyyyyy!"

One last dog came out and ran directly toward the patrol car, which skidded to a halt. Teddy shot through the door holding the crowbar and circled to the back of the building, and the three of them took off into the woods as fast as their feet would carry them.

The patrol car pulled up to the building with its searchlight focused on the shattered front door, and the officer radioed headquarters before getting out. He'd seen the kid run around the building, but made no attempt to chase him. There was no point trying to find a kid in the woods at night, even with a full moon. He got out and walked around the building to see if there were any more kids around, then went inside to assess the damage and look for clues to the punk's identity.

Teddy and Brett knew this part of the woods better than any adult; they were on a path that would eventually take them straight to their house.

After a few hundred yards, Thor recognized the path, too. He'd taken it once, coming the other way, but had never followed it to the end. He'd heard the animals crying faintly in the distance and turned back, disturbed and frightened and not sure why.

Now he wished he could go back to the place where the animals cried, but he couldn't, not yet. He had work to do.

Janet couldn't believe her eyes. The local TV station was signing off for the night. After Letterman, she'd watched Bob Costas with the sound low and the lights out and no idea what she was watching. And now it was over, and she was still awake. She decided to get up and make herself a cup of decaf and see how Tom was doing. Hell, she wasn't going to get any sleep tonight, either. She was beyond kidding herself that she might.

Fact was, she loved that damned dog almost as much as Tom did, and that was all she could think about. Watching TV had been nothing but a lame attempt to shut out the trauma of the day's events, and it hadn't worked.

She dragged herself out of bed, put on a robe and slippers, and turned off the set. Tom would no doubt be glad to see her after all these hours by himself. She'd expected him to come to bed a long time ago.

On the way to the stairs, she stopped to check on the kids.

She gently opened Debbie's door and crept in. Debbie was sound asleep, clutching a tiny stuffed elephant.

She checked the boys' room. The door was open a crack and she could see them asleep in bed, but she went inside for a closer look; they always looked so angelic when they were sleeping. But Brett's head was completely under the covers, and it was an awfully warm night for all those blankets. She gently pulled the covers away and found a pillow underneath. Startled, she snatched the blanket off. There was a pile of clothes and blankets and nothing else.

She checked Teddy's bed and found the same: wadded covers and clothes, but no son.

They must be downstairs with Tom.

She hurried to the hall and started down the stairs. No light filtered up from the kitchen, and no sound, either. She wasn't even halfway down when she realized there was no one else in the house. She could feel it.

The whole first floor was dark. Where was Tom? She turned on the kitchen light, expecting to see a note on the kitchen table, explaining everything. Nothing.

She felt the cold touch of fear run from the base of her neck down to her toes.

Then she noticed the lights in Ted's apartment—that must be where they are!

She marched across the backyard, mentally composing the tongue-lashing she was about to give her husband. She climbed the stairs, trying to ignore her growing awareness that the apartment was as silent as the house.

She paused on the landing to listen before knocking. There was nothing, not a sound. Anger gave way to fear as she lightly tapped the glass pane with her knuckles.

"Ted?" she said. "Are you in there?" She knocked again, not expecting an answer, then banged the door loud enough to wake the neighbors.

Still nothing.

She saw an image in her mind of her family lying dead on the apartment floor, asphyxiated by a gas leak. Then she remembered there was no gas in the apartment.

She twisted the doorknob and rattled the door, but it refused to open. She thought for a second and gathered up a handful of robe and wrapped it around her fist. She turned her face away and squinted, punched a hole in the window, reached in, and opened the door.

A single lamp burned on the nightstand. There was no other sign that anyone had been in the apartment all night. The bed was made with the covers pulled back, untouched, ready to be used. Everything else was in its place, as tidy as could be. The scene made her think of the *Marie Celeste*.

What the hell is going on here?

She checked the driveway from the landing. All the cars were there, parked and waiting, like Ted's bed.

"Teddy! Brett! Tom!" she shouted into the night. No answer.

She hurried back to the house to call the sheriff, but once in the kitchen she wasn't sure.

There was no sign of foul play. The kids obviously left of their own free will if they stopped to stuff their beds first. And no one could have sneaked into the house and taken them all with her in the bedroom. She told herself to be rational, get a grip: No doubt the boys couldn't sleep, so they went downstairs to talk to Tom. Then Ted came in, and they all decided to go for a walk.

Sure. A walk in the middle of the night. Just the four of them.

Why didn't Tom leave a note? It wasn't like him. It didn't add up.

She turned on the lights in the kitchen and looked for a clue to their whereabouts. Nothing. She went back upstairs and examined the boys' room more carefully, but still found nothing. Finally she went back down and stood on the front porch, calling their names at the top of her lungs, then did the same at the back door.

She was standing on the back steps, just about ready to get her car keys and start looking for them, when she heard something coming from the woods and breathed a sigh of relief.

"What are you *doing* out there, dammit?" she shouted, unable to see who it was in the dark. Then the creature stepped out of the woods and into the moonlight.

It was tall, as tall as a man, but covered with hair and grotesquely hunched over and twisted-looking. Its face seemed to be all teeth. Janet gasped and took a single step backward into the kitchen, slamming and locking the door behind her.

The thing in the gully wasted no time. It dashed across the backyard and onto the back steps, slamming its fist through the glass pane and bloodying its clawed hand in the process. But it didn't seem to know enough to reach in and unlock the door. Instead it pounded and kicked, trying to make the window opening big enough to pass through. Janet jerked a flatware drawer open, sending spoons and forks clattering onto the floor. She grabbed the biggest knife in the drawer and she ran for the stairs. She had to protect Debbie.

The werewolf gave the door a final vicious kick and it split down the middle.

Thor and the kids were almost within sight of the house when they heard Mom's calls and the crashing sounds that followed.

Thor had been following the boys disinterestedly, but at the sound of Mom's distress he forgot his problems and his gut took over. He broke into a full run toward the house, leaving the kids behind as if they were standing still. He leaped the gully and dashed across the yard toward the broken kitchen door.

"Hurry up!" Teddy yelled at Brett.

"I'm scared," Brett confessed tearfully, standing in the path and holding his crotch.

"You wanna miss the *action?*" Teddy asked, incredulous. He had no doubt of Thor's ability to defend them.

Brett hesitated and Teddy lost patience. "You do what you want. I'm goin'!" And he ran for the house, hoping he wouldn't miss the fight between Thor and the monster.

Brett watched his brother cross the yard, thought for a second, then took off after him. No way he was going to stay in the dark woods alone.

Thor burst into the kitchen, ready for trouble. He could feel the danger in the air.

The Bad Thing's scent was everywhere, mingled with the scent of Mom's fear. He ran straight for the stairs without checking the living room or dining room. He knew where Mom would be.

He was halfway up when he heard her scream from Debbie's room. He sprang onto the landing, his claws uselessly skidding on the hardwood floor as he pulled a tight U-turn around the banister. The Bad Thing was hurling itself against Debbie's bedroom door, and the door was cracking. Mom's screams filled the house.

He barked savagely as he charged at the Bad Thing, hoping to distract it, but the Bad Thing ignored him. It threw itself against the door and it popped open, sending the creature tumbling into the room and onto the floor.

Thor leaped onto the Bad Thing's back, snapping at its neck. The Bad Thing howled and stood up, hurling Thor off.

Before Thor could regain his balance, the Bad Thing dove at him, sinking its fangs deep into Thor's thigh.

Thor whipped his head around and snapped at the werewolf's face, catching its nose with his fangs and tearing one nostril open. The werewolf pulled away with its teeth still in Thor's flesh, opening a long gash in his leg. Thor scrambled to his feet and leaped at the werewolf's face, ready to bite any part of the beast that came within reach.

The werewolf was tall and powerful but not fast. It tried to bite Thor but got its own face bitten instead. It tried to swipe him with its claws, but Thor caught its hand in his teeth and nearly severed a finger.

The creature backed into a corner and Thor lunged for its ankles, but the werewolf managed to land a wild kick in Thor's rib cage, knocking him off his feet.

But instead of closing in for the kill, the werewolf turned and leaped at Mom, who was still crouching in a corner with a huge knife in her hand and Debbie cowering behind her.

Mom screamed and thrust the knife forward and the blade sliced cleanly into the Bad Thing's forearm and lodged in bone. The werewolf howled and flailed its arm, sending the knife flying across the room.

Thor got to his feet as the knife clattered to the floor. He lunged at the monster.

With the werewolf's back turned to him, he went for the only available target: its leg. His teeth sank into the Bad Thing's calf and he jerked his head violently, trying to pull the Bad thing's foot out from under it. The Bad Thing wailed and stumbled backward, and for the first time there was a note of fear and desperation in its howls.

Thor pulled free, taking a chunk of skin and muscle with him as the Bad Thing tripped over Debbie's dollhouse and fell onto its back. Thor leaped on its chest and the Bad Thing brought its arms up to protect its throat. Thor snapped at its hands, but the Bad Thing rolled over sideways, tossing him off and sending him sliding across the floor.

The Bad Thing made a dash for the door, but Thor snagged its ankle. It spun around and kicked him in his ribs, following up with a sharp kick to Thor's head.

Thor staggered for a split second, then his front legs folded underneath him, and he fell to the floor, barely conscious.

The Bad Thing bent over Thor's stunned form, about to tear the dog to shreds when white-hot pain suddenly exploded in its back as Mom plunged the knife into it again and again.

It swung its arms around and blindly struck Mom's face. She staggered backward as the werewolf dashed for the open door.

Thor pulled himself to his feet just in time to see the Bad Thing dart out of the room, closing the door behind itself like a human.

Thor barked maniacally at the door, but it did no good. He was trapped unless Mom let him out, and Mom was huddling in a corner with Debbie. She had no intention of opening the door.

Brett and Teddy had reached the top of the stairs just as Mom was stabbing the werewolf's arm. Petrified with fear and completely unaware of his actions, Brett backed toward Mom and Dad's bedroom as he watched, tugging on Teddy's jacket the whole time. Teddy unconsciously allowed himself to be pulled backward, clutching the crowbar in both hands like a baseball bat.

There was a terrific scuffle in Debbie's room and the werewolf suddenly broke free and burst into the hall, slamming the bedroom door behind itself. Teddy and Brett both screamed as Brett pulled Teddy through the doorway and slammed the door behind them. Luck had led them to the right room; Mom and Dad had a lock on their bedroom door. Brett snapped it shut and he and Teddy leaned against the door in panic. But the werewolf wasn't interested in them; it ran past the door and down the stairs.

Teddy opened the door as soon as he heard the creature's

footfalls on the stairs. He ran to Debbie's room and opened the door, terrified of what he might find, and was immediately knocked off his feet as Thor rushed after the Bad thing.

Thor flew down the stairs and caught up with the beast in the kitchen, but the Bad Thing heard him coming, and turned the kitchen table over in Thor's path.

Thor's head struck the tabletop and his field of vision burst into fuzzy whiteness that faded quickly into black.

The Bad Thing hesitated for a moment, then heard Teddy's footsteps coming down the stairs. It was in no shape to confront more attackers. It ran through the open doorway to the forest, where it could lick its many wounds.

Tom cleared the last few feet of forest and leaped the gully into the backyard, carrying a heavy branch for a club. He'd run home as fast as he could, his feet and legs and lungs burning the whole way. All that mattered was seeing Janet and the kids safe and unharmed.

He huffed up the yard toward the house just as the werewolf emerged through the split kitchen door, limping and snarling and shiny with its own blood. Tom had no way of knowing whose blood it was; in his mind he saw his family torn and bleeding, and savage hatred engulfed him.

He ran straight for the monster, swinging the club in a circle over his head and screaming in rage.

The injured werewolf dodged and tried to duck as their paths crossed. Tom swung at its head, missed, and brought the club around again. The next swing came low and struck the werewolf's back as it ran for the woods.

The beast's bloodlust was completely forgotten. Bleeding and battered as never before, it thought only of escape and survival. It limped past Tom faster than most humans can run, and disappeared into the sheltering darkness of the trees.

The moon was already approaching the western horizon.

* * *

Neighbors on both sides of the house peered through lighted windows, trying to see what was happening. Mrs. Truud next door got a clear look at the werewolf and called the sheriff to report that she'd just seen Bigfoot. The deputy on duty was unconvinced, but agreed to send a patrol car. Mr. Truud believed her, though, and stood guard at his back door with a shotgun until the law arrived.

Thor felt like he was under water. Bright light assaulted his eyes; his gaze moved lethargically from one strange face to another as they gradually became familiar. Mom. Brett. Teddy. Debbie. Dad.

Dad was talking to Mr. Truud, who had come over to lend Dad his shotgun for the night.

The kitchen came into focus, and Thor realized he was home. Then he remembered it wasn't his home anymore.

He crawled into a corner, and when Brett went over to pet him, he got up and crawled into the alcove with the washing machine and his dish.

Dad watched Thor flee the family and swallowed hard. He'd never felt so ashamed of himself.

Flashing, spinning lights filled the living room as the squad car pulled up in front of the house. Dad thanked Mr. Truud, stashed the shotgun in the cupboard, and he and Mom went into the living room to talk to the deputy.

Teddy saw the flashing lights from the patrol car and assumed it was for himself and Brett and Thor. He waited until Mom and Dad were at the front door, whispered to Brett, and quietly walked to the back door and opened it. Brett had been tugging on Thor's collar without results, but as soon as Thor heard the door open he slinked out of the kitchen and through the door like a blob of mercury.

* * *

Thor felt a tremendous sense of relief once he was out of the house and away from the Pack. He ran straight into the woods, ignoring the pain in his thigh and the dull throbbing in his head. The warm weight of exhaustion urged him to rest, and he smelled his own blood trickling from the wound the Bad Thing had inflicted on him. Instinct told him to lie down and tend the wound and allow it to heal, but there was no time. The moon was in the western sky and dropping fast; its light would soon be gone. And Thor's loss of blood was sapping his strength. He had to catch the Bad Thing before he grew too weak.

At least he would have no trouble finding the Bad Thing. It had left two trails to follow: the fear-laced body scent that told where the creature had been, and the powerful blood scent that told where it was now. The two trails coincided perfectly, which meant the Bad Thing was making the worst mistake a hunted animal can make: It was running directly into the wind.

Thor pressed forward, noting with pleasure that the blood scent was gradually getting stronger, which meant he was closing the gap between them. He'd gone a fair distance when he noticed the Bad Thing's body scent was beginning to fade, and yet strong traces of it remained. Then he realized that the unchanged scent was from hairs left behind. The Bad Thing was molting, losing its fur. The fur scent grew stronger until suddenly Thor felt a fiery itch inside his nose. He stopped in his tracks and sneezed uncontrollably.

He'd sucked one of the Bad Thing's hairs into his nostril. It took multiple sneezes to blow it out and as soon as he sniffed again, he sneezed again. The air was thick with drifting hairs. The Bad Thing had lost almost its entire coat in this one spot. Thor stopped and sneezed helplessly for minutes before he finally held his breath and plunged through the cloud of hairs.

When he'd gone a few yards, he took a tentative breath; the air was clear and the blood scent was still strong, but the Bad Thing's body scent was gone. In its place was Uncle Ted's.

The sudden smell of Uncle Ted brought with it a fresh stab of guilt, but Thor pushed the feeling aside. Guilt or innocence didn't matter anymore. Nothing mattered anymore, except for the one thing he still had to do.

Eliminate the Threat.

The blood scent on the wind abruptly got stronger, much stronger. That could only mean Uncle Ted was doubling back. Thor looked around to orient himself and was satisfied that he was deep enough in the woods to enjoy complete privacy. He focused his ears in the direction of the house and stood perfectly still, scanning and listening intently for any sounds of pursuing humans.

Nothing.

Perfect.

The sky began to lighten as he pressed forward, taking his time to conserve his strength, now that he knew the prey was coming to him. He hadn't gone far before he heard the first telltale sounds of twigs snapping and leaves rustling in the distance. Instinctively, he lowered himself into a semicrouch as he crept forward silently.

The sounds of Uncle Ted's clumsy approach came closer and closer. Thor's fatigue seemed to fade away as a new surge of adrenalin flooded his bloodstream. He heard a sudden burst of stumbling footsteps that abruptly stopped, then the sound of Uncle Ted's heavy, ragged breathing, and then the man came into view. He stood just a few yards away, clutching a tree for support, a dark figure looming against the sky. The smell of blood radiated from him and his posture announced pain and weakness. As the forest gradually lightened, Thor saw the wounds on Uncle Ted's face and arm and leg. They were open and still bleeding from the exertion of his flight, like Thor's. Uncle Ted looked like he was ready to die on the spot.

Thor crept toward him as slowly and silently as a cat, with his eyes locked on the man's throat. The hair on his shoulders stood at attention.

Uncle Ted looked up from his injuries at the faint but growing light on the horizon. He seemed confused, unsure of his whereabouts. And unaware of Thor's presence.

Thor inched closer, trying to stay in the shadows. He got to within fifteen feet when Uncle Ted finally saw him.

"Thor!" he said as if he were greeting an old friend. "Well, well, well, if it isn't Thor! I thought you were gone, old buddy."

Thor stopped and regarded the shadowy form.

"So. I guess I've been a Bad Dog, huh? Is that why you're here?" He snorted. "Unless I miss my guess, the game's up. Isn't that right, Thor?

"So what's it gonna be? You gonna stand there all night, or are you gonna resolve this fucking mess once and for all? There's only one way this can end, you know. And you're the one with the answer. I'm counting on you. Why don't you get it—"

Thor leaped, turning his head sideways to accommodate Uncle Ted's neck.

Uncle Ted almost fell backward as Thor's fangs slammed into the flesh on either side of his Adam's apple, penetrating the skin as if it were tissue paper and clamping his trachea shut, but his grip on the tree tightened involuntarily, as if holding on could somehow save him. For the briefest instant, Thor dangled in the air, his body suspended by the man's windpipe. Then he jerked his head violently to one side, and a section of Uncle Ted's trachea tore loose in his mouth, dropping him to the ground.

Uncle Ted staggered backward and fell on his back, unconscious. He was physically able to breathe, but when Thor's fangs entered his neck, they severed his carotid arteries. By the time he hit the ground, millions of Uncle Ted's brain cells had already died of oxygen starvation. Only seconds remained of his life.

The smell of blood was overwhelming, almost suffocating, a sure sign that the Bad Thing was mortally wounded. But he had to be sure. He pulled himself to his feet, saw that Uncle Ted wasn't moving, and collapsed.

He'd done his Duty. He'd killed Mom's brother.

He didn't have to go back to the House of Death; the Angel was coming to him. Thor could feel the gentle fingers stroking his head, relaxing the tension in his face. Already his pains, physical and emotional, were beginning to fade under the Angel's touch.

The Angel delicately stroked his eyes shut and Thor slipped away from consciousness, away from pain, away from Badness and aloneness, and into oblivion.

CHAPTER

17

"FIVE thousand is ridiculous," Tom said into the phone. "You don't have a case and you know it." He gazed out his office window and wished he could bluff a little more convincingly, but his heart wasn't in it.

"Look, counselor," the lawyer on the other end said, "I'll be straight with you: The suit may not fly, but the Animal Control people are a little easier to convince than a jury. Now five thousand is a lot for a dog, it's true. But I have to tell you, my client would be just as happy to see your dog die. I don't know what went on between you two, but I've never seen him like this before. It's not business as usual this time. I've been specifically instructed not to bargain on this, and the only reason I am bargaining is so you won't lose your dog."

And so you won't lose your commission, Tom thought. *Who do you think you're fooling, you pathetic little sleazeball?*

"All right," Tom said. "Five thousand." He idly flipped through his desk calendar and said, "Today is Thursday. . . . a week from tomorrow is the first chance I'll have to take care of this. Can you be in my office then?"

The man on the other end pretended to consult his own calendar, then said, "Sure. How's three o'clock?"

Tom's secretary stuck her head in the office and said, "Sheriff Jensen is here to see you."

Tom cupped his hand over the mouthpiece and said, "Just a minute." To the phone he said, "Fine. You have Flop . . . your client here ready to sign the waivers, and I'll have the five thousand." *Unless Thor's already dead by then, in which case you can both go straight to hell.*

He finished the call and gently put the receiver on the cradle, watching his hand to see if he could detect any shakiness. *Oh, what the hell?* he thought. *I'm nervous and I'm going to stay nervous until this is over. No point trying to bullshit Art about that.* He took a deep breath and unconsciously ran his hand over his hair, a gesture usually reserved for crucial board meetings and expensive consultations.

"Well," he muttered to himself, "can't put it off any longer." He got up and walked to the door of his office, opened it, and said with slightly forced bonhomie, "Hi Art! C'mon in!"

Sheriff Jensen wore a tight smile that spoke eloquently of his discomfort with the situation. He and Tom had been friends for more than a few years, and he didn't relish this confrontation. He folded the tabloid newspaper he'd been reading, wedged it into his back pants pocket, and, looking more like the accused than the accuser, walked resignedly into Tom's office and made himself as comfortable as possible in the overstuffed chair that faced Tom's desk.

"No interruptions while Sheriff Jensen is here," Tom said to his secretary as he closed the door.

He sat down behind his desk and the two of them looked at each other for a moment. Finally Tom said, "Ball's in your court, Art. What can I do for you?"

"Not gonna make it easy for me, are you?" Sheriff Jensen said with the same rueful smile. "Okay, first of all, this isn't an official visit. This is strictly between you and me. Badge comes off right now." He removed his badge and slipped it into his pocket, then tossed the tabloid on the desk with the front page facing Tom. The headline screamed, EXPERTS CONFIRM! SASQUATCH ATTACKS OREGON FAMILY, KILLS FAMOUS NATURE PHOTOGRAPHER!!!

"They're really behind the curve," Art said. "The *National Evening Star* has already made the connection with the murdered girl outside Ted's cabin. They also found out about Ted's girlfriend disappearing in Tibet. So now 'experts' have confirmed that Bigfoot and the yeti are one and the same. I tell you, it's bad enough to get evidence from newspapers, but these fucking rags aren't even real papers, and they *still* know more than I do. I'm supposed to go before the grand jury tomorrow—you did get your subpoena, didn't you? Good. Well, there you go. I'd like to know what you're going to tell them, Tom, but more important, I'd like to know what *I'm* going to tell them. Can you fill in any of the blanks here?"

"What is it you want to know?"

"You really *aren't* going to make it easy for me, are you? Can't you just tell me what happened?"

"I told your deputy what I know, Art," Tom said. "I really can't say any more. I'll answer any questions I can, but it has to be this way. What do you want to know?"

Sheriff Jensen sighed and said, "Okay. Who killed Ted?"

"I don't know."

"Who do you *think* killed Ted?"

Now it was Tom's turn to sigh. "Okay. I think, in the final analysis, the creature that attacked my family killed him."

" 'In the final analysis,' " Sheriff Jensen said, weighing the meaning of the phrase. "How about in the immediate analysis? His wounds don't bear any resemblance to the wounds on that girl—except for one—the fatal throat wound. The other wounds are particularly disturbing. He was stabbed repeatedly with a knife. His blood is all over your daughter's bedroom, in fact, it's all over your house and property. It would appear that our 'sasquatch' was your brother-in-law in a monkey suit."

"If you say so," Tom said.

"Dammit, can't you help me at all?"

"Art, I know this sounds like bullshit, but if I told you what I knew, not only would you not believe me, you'd think I'm crazy."

"Maybe so, but you're not holding back to maintain my high opinion of you. You're protecting someone."

Tom pressed his lips together tightly for a moment and said, "I'm sorry, Art."

"What was he doing out in the woods at night, three miles from the house?"

"I don't know."

"Why was he naked?"

"I don't know."

"Why did you follow him into the woods on the night of the attack?"

"I saw him leave the garage after dark and go into the woods. I wanted to know what was going on."

"What did you find out?"

"Nothing. He lost me in the woods, and then that . . . *thing* came after me. I ended up in a tree. I never saw Ted again until the next morning."

"Uh-huh," Sheriff Jensen said, pulling a small notebook from his shirt pocket. Reading as he spoke, he said, "You apparently waited until the officer left that morning, then went back into the woods with a shotgun. An hour or two later, you called my office to report you found Ted's body about three miles from your house. How did you know where to look?"

"Is this really off the record? 'Cause if it is, I don't know why you're asking me questions you already know the answers to. I told your deputy, I followed a trail of blood. And I waited for the sun to come up, not for your deputy to leave. As I recall, your deputies weren't exactly eager to search in the dark."

"Yes, but my deputies didn't know Ted was out there, and you didn't volunteer that information."

227

"I didn't know either. Like I told you, Ted lost me out there. How was I to know he didn't come home while that creature had me treed?"

"But why didn't you mention it to anyone?"

"I had other things on my mind. My family had been attacked, almost killed. I'd forgotten all about Ted."

"You understand, Tom, I'm just asking what the grand jury is going to ask."

"Thanks, Art, but don't forget that you're also responsible for finding out what happened, and the jury's going to ask you one or two questions, too."

"Dammit, Tom, I resent that! I came here to help you, I'm putting my ass on the line just by being here! Now I'm being straight with you, and I'd appreciate it if you could try being just a little straight with me! There's no stenographer here, this is your office, I'm not taking notes, and as a lawyer you know damn well that just the fact that I told you this is off the record means I can't use a thing you tell me as evidence! But if it makes you happy, I'll pull out my pen and take notes while I ask you one question *on* the record. Okay?"

"Shoot."

"Did *you* kill Ted?"

Tom laughed out loud.

"You've got to be joking! You want to know if I ripped his throat out with my teeth? You want to check my mouth? Maybe I didn't floss all of his trachea out from between my incisors, huh? Jesus Christ, you *must* be desperate."

"Tell me what you know, Tom."

"Tell me what *you* know first."

"You know I can't do that."

"Why not? I'm your only suspect, right? So press charges; I'll file under discovery, and you'll *have* to tell me everything you know. So what do you have to lose?"

Sheriff Jensen thought for a long moment. Finally, he said, "If I tell you what I know, will you tell me what you know?"

"I'll tell you what I can."

"Christ, you're really being an asshole about this."

"I'm sorry, Art, I really am, but it has to be this way."

Sheriff Jensen stared at him for a moment and said, "Okay. But I never told you any of this. I came here officially, just asking questions, and you didn't answer any of them, and that's all that happened."

"That's all that happened," Tom agreed.

The sheriff consulted his notebook.

"Whatever happened in Nepal was a major turning point in Ted's life, but when I tried to look into it I ran into a stone wall. I called the Nepalese constable who interrogated him; he insisted on knowing Ted's condition before he'd tell me anything, and when I told him Ted was dead, he just said, 'Then the matter is settled,' and clammed up. He seemed awfully relieved to hear about Ted's demise, and obviously didn't give a damn about helping me with my problems.

"In any case, as soon as Ted got back to the 'States, he put his Seattle home up for sale and moved into his summer cabin permanently—or at least until the hiker's body turned up. But the most revealing change was in his phone bills.

"Before Nepal, all his long-distance calls were either to your house or business-related: magazine editors, foreign embassies, ticket agents, that kind of thing. After Nepal, all the business calls stopped, but his long-distance bills went up. For the first two months, he called libraries and bookstores almost every day. He started with the biggies: the New York Public Library, the Library of Congress, and big bookstore chains. By the third week, he'd worked his way down to obscure dealers of out-of-print books, and occult bookstores. Seems he was only interested in the history—not fiction—of werewolves, but none of the books he found satisfied him. Apparently, the folklore says werewolves were witches, warlocks, that kind of thing, and they changed themselves deliberately with potions and spells. He wanted to know about people turning into werewolves after being bitten by one, and there's nothing like that in the literature.

"Eventually his research changed direction. Just curious . . . did Ted ever mention Robert Harris while he was living with you?"

"The guy they executed in California?" Tom asked.

"No, that's Robert *Alton* Harris, a completely different guy. This Robert Harris was a Hollywood screenwriter in the thirties. I never heard of him myself until I started calling people on Ted's phone bills. It seems Ted became obsessed with this guy Harris, who's been dead for some time, by the way. Ted spent about three solid weeks calling friends, relatives and acquaintances of Harris, starting in Hollywood and going back to the East coast. He wanted to know anything he could find out about Harris' private life. I finally did a little research of my own, and . . . well, it's really kind of stupid, but in 1935, Harris wrote the first Hollywood werewolf movie. A mostly forgotten little effort called *The Werewolf of London,* in which an Englishman turns into a werewolf after being bitten by one— in Nepal."

"So what are you saying?" Tom asked. "You think Ted was a werewolf?"

The sheriff laughed. "Give me a break, Tom. I've met some pretty superstitious people in my time—and I don't mean good-luck charms and astrology, I mean people who believe in witchcraft and ghosts and demonic possession—and even *they* don't believe in werewolves. No, I'm afraid I'm not ready to make that leap."

I am, Tom thought.

"On the other hand," Art continued, "Ted had obviously made a few leaps of his own. Maybe he killed Marjorie and couldn't handle the guilt, and ended up in some sort of delusional state where he convinced himself he really was a werewolf. And maybe, in order to maintain the delusion, he kept on killing.

"Everything points to your late brother-in-law as a psychopathic killer. The hiker who died outside his cabin wasn't killed by an animal; it looked more like a ritual murder. The killer tore her throat out just the way a wolf might, tore her body open with wolflike claw and tooth marks, and even left wolf hairs on the scene. But wolves don't remove people's hearts and leave everything else. Only humans do things that irrational."

"Jesus," Tom said quietly. He hadn't known about the woman's heart.

"And not a word about that to anyone. That's the one thing we've managed to keep quiet. Now, as far as your brother-in-law's death, the tooth marks on his neck don't match the ones on that girl, and there was no 'surgery' performed on his corpse; no torn torso, no missing organs. Although we did find a lot of hairs around the body."

"And?"

"They match the hairs found on the hiker."

"So?"

"So they're from his monkey suit. He put it on, attacked your family, then ran into the woods, where he took it off. Probably buried it, or we would've found it by now. He was on his way back when . . . someone . . . stopped him."

"Someone?"

"Your dog also followed him into the woods, but he didn't wait till sunup. When you went looking for Ted, or whoever, you found the dog, too," Sheriff Jensen said. "But the dog was only a few hundred yards from your house, nowhere near Ted's body."

"He was weak; he'd lost a lot of blood."

"He'd lost something else, too. All the blood that should have been on his face from his fight with our hairy friend." He consulted his notebook again. "Says here he was found in the creek bed, behind a neighbor's house. His face was wet, as if someone had washed it with creek water, and his body was conveniently lying on a slope with his head low and his wounded leg high, as if someone had placed him in that position to minimize blood loss and keep his brain supplied with blood."

231

"Is that how it looks?"

"We do know that Thor attacked Ted the day before he died."

"So what do you think?"

"I think someone found Thor somewhere else, somewhere that would have gotten him in trouble—like next to Ted's body. And that someone carried him far away from the body and left him for one of my deputies to find."

"Sounds awfully complicated," Tom said. "Why not just take him home?"

"Because that someone couldn't afford to answer questions about where he found the dog. Because that someone was a lawyer, and he knew what would happen if he were caught lying to a law-enforcement officer."

"Do you have any evidence to back up that theory?"

"I'm not looking for any," Art said quietly. Tom turned to face him with an expression that said "thank you" and "I'm sorry" all at once.

"So anyway," the sheriff continued, "after Thor attacked Ted—the first time, the time we know about—you called Animal Control and had him taken away. He was scheduled to take a long nap the next day." Tom bit his lip hard, as Jensen had expected.

"Now things get strange again. A kid shows up at Animal Control after midnight, breaks in and releases a large number of dogs and cats. Of all the animals released, though, only one belonged to a family with a twelve-year-old boy: Thor. A deputy arrives on the scene and catches a glimpse of the kid. His description, while sketchy, matches your son. And yet you and your wife swear your kids were home the whole night."

"They were," Tom said, looking out the window as he spoke. It was getting difficult to look Art in the eye.

"And now I find that you called Animal Control the next day and told them the whole thing was a mistake, and you were keeping Thor after all."

"I can do that," Tom said. "There was never any determination by Animal Control that Thor was dangerous; they took him because I asked them to. I filed the complaint, and I withdrew it."

"I see. Tell me, how does Janet feel about Thor?"

Tom looked at him sharply, and said between clenched teeth, "Thor saved her life. He saved the whole family. She appreciates that."

"Yeah. I guess she would. By the way, no one has seen your dog since that night. Where is he?"

"In my basement."

"What's he doing there?"

"He appears to be sick," Tom said, still staring out the window.

"Doc Warner, the vet who treated him, doesn't think he's sick. He says he's just suffering from blood loss, complicated by a refusal to eat. At least, Warner couldn't get him to eat. How about you?" Even from an angle, Jensen could see Tom's eyes glistening.

"No luck," he whispered, and added, "I think he's dying."

"I'm sorry," Sheriff Jensen said.

"Yeah. Well. Any more questions?"

"I hope you know what you're doing, Tom."

"Thanks."

CHAPTER 18

THOR ignored the sound of Dad's car in the driveway and lay in the cellar, staring at nothing, waiting for the end. He'd been in the cellar for three days, and had hardly moved the whole time. He hardly had any strength left anyway; he hadn't eaten or felt a whisper of hunger since the day he bit Uncle Ted's arm. He knew if he just stayed in one place and did nothing, his suffering would eventually end. He'd been lying in one spot for three days now, and could feel himself getting weaker and weaker, though he'd felt this way right after killing Uncle Ted, and he hadn't died then.

Instead he'd awakened on a stainless steel table in a bright room filled with a powerful smell of disinfectant. And behind the disinfectant smell, the scents of dogs and cats—and fear. A familiar man in a white smock loomed over him, pulled a needle from his leg, and painfully shined a light into his eye.

"Is he going to be all right?"

Thor was startled to hear Dad's voice.

"He's lost quite a bit of blood, and he'll favor that leg until it's healed, but he'll be okay. Be sure you feed him plenty of red meat to replenish his blood. I've given him an I.V. to bring up his blood sugar, but he'll have to replace his own blood. There aren't any blood banks for dogs, you know." Thor recognized the veterinarian's voice. He'd been here before, though he'd never understood why. The place scared him, and yet he knew Doctor Warner was a good man.

He kept his eyes on the ceiling or the blank tile walls, unable to look at either man. He'd killed Uncle Ted. Not the Bad Thing, but Uncle Ted—Mom's brother. Guilt lay on him like a lead blanket.

No longer a part of any pack, he ignored the men's conversation, though he wasn't quite able to ignore the sadness he heard in Dad's voice. Dad left the room and talked to Doctor Warner's phone, calling it "Janet." Every time Dad said it, Thor thought his heart would break. He lay on the table and waited to die.

Some minutes later he heard the familiar deep rumble of Mom's car as it pulled to a stop outside. Dad came back into the room and startled Thor by gently lifting him off the table and setting him on the floor on his feet.

Dad's touch sent shivers of revulsion through him. He was unfit to be touched. Dad should know better. Dad should leave him alone, let him die in what little peace he could find. He fled from Dad's touch, crawled into a corner, and stared at the wall.

But Dad wouldn't leave him alone. He opened a door so Thor could see Mom's car, with Mom sitting behind the wheel. He walked out to the car and called Thor to hop in. Thor ignored him.

Exasperated, Dad came back in and put a leash on Thor and dragged him to the car. Thor offered only passive resistance. He didn't want to go with Dad, but he wasn't about to growl or snap or show his teeth. He didn't need any more guilt. He had more than enough already.

Dad pulled Thor to the car and lifted him onto the back seat.

As Dad was getting into the front seat with Mom, Thor leaped out the window and slinked off toward the bushes that flanked Dr. Warner's office. Mom closed the car windows while Dad followed him into the bushes and dragged him out. Back in the car with no escape, Thor lay on the floor behind the front seat, hiding from Mom and Dad, but especially from Mom.

Mom started the car and drove off, but they didn't go to the House of Death, as Thor had hoped, but home, as he'd dreaded. He just hoped he could go where no humans could see his Badness.

Dad got out and walked around the car to the passenger side. He opened the back door and called Thor out. Thor stayed put. Dad muttered, "Dammit," and dragged him out by his leash and into the house.

The cellar door opened and Dad came bounding down the stairs with his arms filled with Thor's favorite canned dog foods, dog biscuits, a rawhide bone, a tennis ball, a Frisbee, a pound of precut stew beef, and Thor's dish.

Thor figured the reason he was still alive was fairly obvious: The unthinkable Badness of killing Mom's brother required further punishment. He accepted his fate, and waited for Dad to punish him.

But Dad didn't punish him. He acted as if they were still fellow members of the Pack. Dad waved a brand-new Frisbee in his face (as if Thor were in any mood to play, let alone being fit for human companionship). When Thor didn't respond, he bounced a brand-new tennis ball in front of his nose (which Thor had turned toward the wall). What could Dad be thinking?

Dad rummaged through the grocery bags and pulled something out (Thor didn't see what, since his face was turned to the wall). He came back with an inch-thick cube of red beef and waved it in front of Thor's nose. The smell made Thor's stomach turn, and he pulled his face away, stood up, and started to retch.

Dad was stunned. He'd had no idea how profound Thor's guilt was. He knew the dog hadn't eaten in days, but now he suspected Thor was deliberately starving himself.

Dad threw the offending stew meat in the direction of the grocery bags, and sat on the floor next to Thor.

"Hey, hey," he said gently, "it's okay, Thor." He tried to pet him, but Thor's flesh twitched and crawled under his touch and the dog looked around desperately for an escape.

He withdrew his hand, looked at Thor for a moment, took a deep breath, then stood up and walked across the room to a dirty, overstuffed chair, and sat down hard. He watched Thor's heaves subside—they'd brought up nothing—and was unable to hold back his tears. He trembled and began to sob silently, only his staccato breathing revealing his pain. Then the dam broke, and he wept openly, holding his face in his hands and shaking violently.

The sound caught Thor's attention as nothing else had. He wondered if he was to blame for Dad's sorrow, too. But something inside him shifted slightly. Instead of feeling guilty for making Dad cry, he felt guilty for not trying to cheer him up.

But he stayed put.

The worst was the day Mom had come down to the cellar. Thor had hidden in the darkest corner he could find, but Mom found him. She knelt beside him and he smelled her scent, so like the scent of her dead brother. His guilt swelled until he thought he would explode. He trembled violently and whimpered out of control. Mom leaned over and put her arms around his neck. For a moment he thought she was going to kill him, but she didn't. She just hugged him tight, suffocating him with her scent, suffocating him with guilt. He started hyperventilating and she recoiled in horror at his reaction. As soon as she let go of his neck, he slithered away from her, trembling so hard that it looked like he might be having some kind of seizure, and leaving a trail of urine in his wake. Devastated, Mom quietly retreated to the stairs and didn't come back.

After that, only Dad visited him in the cellar. Every evening he came down, and sometimes during the day. For a while he took Thor on forced walks through the woods, throwing the ball and the Frisbee, uselessly pointing out small animals Thor might want to chase. But Thor only wanted to go back to the cellar and lie with his nose in a corner.

All attempts to cheer him up, to make him see that no one was angry with him, failed. Dad took to putting stew meat in Thor's bowl with his dog food in case he felt like eating in the dark (where no one could see him).

Each day was the same, only worse. Each day Thor was a little thinner and a little weaker. He looked awful. His ribs were already beginning to stand out through his fur, which told Dad he was on a short schedule. If he didn't get Thor to eat soon, there'd be no point in prolonging his agony. He would take him back to Dr. Warner and have him put to sleep.

And now it was another day and Dad was coming down the stairs again. Thor was weak and light-headed. Dad was desperate. Thor could feel his desperation.

Dad sat down on a dusty old cot without turning on the light, and sighed heavily. He'd had a drink before coming home, and another in the kitchen before coming downstairs. He looked at Thor and almost started crying. He'd tried everything he could think of to pull Thor back into the world, but nothing had worked, and he was running out of time. Thor looked so bad that he didn't want the kids to see him. He'd just had a talk with Mom, and as little as either of them liked the idea, they'd agreed to take Thor to Dr. Warner and have him put to sleep if Dad couldn't get him to eat. It wasn't fair to let the dog starve like this.

"C'mere boy," he tried for the umpteenth time. Thor didn't move.

He couldn't bear the thought of killing Thor. Why? Because he saved the family. Was that some kind of crime?

The thought made him angry.

"Goddammit, Thor, get over here!"

Thor twitched, which wasn't much, but it was a reaction. For a brief instant, it almost looked as if he was going to get up and come over.

Dad tried again, gently.

"C'mere, Thor." He lowered himself onto the floor and patted the cement at his side, inviting Thor over. Thor lay on the floor, eyes averted, but he didn't crawl away and hide.

"Come here, Thor." A little firmer.

Thor couldn't obey. He knew Dad wanted to love him, but Dad was confused. Thor didn't deserve love. He was a Bad Dog.

Dad knelt beside him and stroked his head gently. Thor turned away from the inappropriate caresses, deeply ashamed of his reaction to the petting.

But he'd enjoyed it. Dad's touch had felt good.

Dad sat down on the cot and pointed to the open space at his side.

"Get up here," he said sternly. An order, not a request.

Thor didn't move. How could Dad give him orders? Thor wasn't part of the Pack anymore. Dad had no authority over him.

And yet he *felt* Dad's authority. And he felt an urge, almost a *necessity* to obey. He resisted his feelings.

"Get up here!" Dad commanded.

Thor looked up at him.

Why do you do this to me?

"Get up here!" Dad shouted, enraged. Thor's shame took another turn for the worse. Dad had given him a direct command, and now Thor was Bad for still another reason. Disobedience.

"Get up here!"

Thor struggled to refuse. Didn't Dad understand *anything?* He was a *Bad Dog.* Why call a Bad Dog?

"I said, get up here, dammit, now *get up here!"*

Against his will, Thor felt his legs move, felt his tail tremble. He crawled toward the bed without lifting his body off the floor.

"Come on! Get up here! *Now!"* Thor reached the edge of the bed and couldn't crawl any farther. He looked at the welcoming darkness underneath, but didn't try to hide. Instead, he slithered onto the bed like a snake, turning his face away from Dad's gaze. As soon as he was on the cot he stopped and shook all over.

The two of them sat at opposite sides of the cot with about three feet between them.

"Come here," Dad said more calmly, patting the open space at his side. Thor looked around desperately at the opposite side of the room, as if there might be something there to save him.

"Come on," Dad insisted.

Shaking uncontrollably, he inched toward his Pack Leader, whose word somehow still had the power of Law.

"That's it," Dad encouraged as he came closer. Dad slid over to meet him halfway and put his hand on Thor's neck affectionately. Thor moved to pull away.

"STAY!"

Thor froze. He wanted to get away, he wanted to die, but he dared not disobey. He couldn't bear to add to his Badness. Dad put his hand on his neck again and stroked it gently. Thor's shaking got worse, but he didn't move away. Dad leaned down and put his face close to Thor's.

"That's a Good Dog," he said. Thor couldn't believe his ears. His shaking continued as Dad continued to pet him.

"That's a Good Dog," Dad repeated. "Good Thor. Good Dog."

Was Dad mad? Why did he taunt him, telling him he was

a Good Dog? The words stung him, and yet—somewhere deep inside, they felt good.

Thor knew Dad was wrong, *must* be wrong, but his hand felt so good, and his voice was so soothing. He felt awful for enjoying the affection he didn't deserve.

But Dad would not give in.

"Good Thor," he said, again and again. "Good Doggie. Good Thor."

In spite of Thor's will, his tail began to wag, which only encouraged Dad's behavior.

"Good Dog, Good Thor."

Could Dad be wrong? Dad was never wrong, *never*. Could he be wrong now? Thor had violated the First Law of Nature, but Dad's Law had always superseded Natural Law, hadn't it?

Dad reached behind himself with one hand while he petted Thor with the other. He picked up something next to the bed, and when his hand came back, there was a small cube of raw beef in it. The smell hit Thor's nostrils with the force of a rolled-up newspaper. It was overwhelming, the first time food had smelled good—or smelled like *anything*—in days.

"Good Thor. Good, Good Thor." Thor's shaking couldn't possibly get worse, but it did.

He inched a little closer to Dad. His tongue lapped Dad's hand as Dad offered him the meat. His tail wagged jerkily, out of control. His body shook, and he realized with a start that Dad was shaking too.

And he realized with a start that Dad *needed* him, just as Brett and Teddy had needed him when they came for him at the House of Death. He'd never thought Dad had ever needed anything from him, not protection, not even love.

But he'd been wrong. He understood for the first time that Dad needed his love, just as he needed Dad's.

His Duty was more than protecting the Pack; it demanded that he love them as well.

Good Dog or Bad, he had to do his Duty. Fearfully, he

raised his head and kissed the corners of Dad's mouth, and tasted salt.

"Good Dog," Dad said quietly, strangely.

Afraid he might be making a terrible mistake, Thor gently took the cube of meat from Dad's hand and swallowed it without chewing. His stomach lurched for an instant at the sudden appearance of food after so many days empty, but it settled down quickly, and he felt ravenous hunger.

But he couldn't ask Dad for more food yet. Not until he'd done what he could to help his Pack Leader feel better. He gently kissed Dad's hand, and nervously, tentatively, kissed his chin and mouth.

Dad held Thor tighter than he'd ever held him before.

"Good Dog," he whispered hoarsely, as Thor licked the tears from his face.

"Good Dog."